STROKE OF FIRE

THE FIRESTORM DRAGON CHRONICLES

KIRA NYTE

xoxo Kira Nyte

STROKE OF FIRE
The Firestorm Dragon Chronicles

Copyright © 2019 by Kira Nyte

Edited by: Raina Toomey
Cover Design by: Daqri at Covers by Combs
Interior Formatting by: Author E.M.S.

Published by: Dark Illusion Publishing
ISBN: 978-1-947077-03-4

Published in the United States of America.

Books by Kira Nyte

Nocturne Falls Universe

A Dragon Speaks Her Name

A Dragon Gambles for His Girl

Merry & Bright, A Christmas Anthology
A Dragon's Christmas Mayhem (novella)

The Princess Protects Her Huntsman

Touched by Her Elven Magic

Touched by His Vampire Charm

Winter Wonderland, A Christmas Quartet
Touched by His Christmas Magic (novella)

Science Fiction/Fantasy Romance

The Gala Lover

Dear Readers,

If this is your first journey into the world of the Firestorm dragons and their lifemates, welcome! I hope you find their world and ways as fascinating as I have. If you wish to start from the beginning, be sure to read A Dragon Speaks Her Name and A Dragon Gambles for His Girl, both of which are part of Nocturne Falls Universe.

Happy reading!
Kira Nyte

Website for Kira Nyte: www.kiranyte.com

Find Kira Nyte on Facebook:
www.facebook.com/kiranyte

Contact Kira Nyte at mailto:
kiranyteauthor@gmail.com

Stroke of Fire

At almost thirty, Briella Everett is finally getting the chance to spread her wings away from her overprotective parents and pursue the life of an artist in New Orleans. She has fun new friends, an apartment she loves and the promise of a showing of her paintings at a small art gallery. The fact she can listen in on other people's thoughts and has the occasional, freakily accurate premonition is the little secret that inspires her work.

Syn Terravon is content with his vagabond life. He travels the world and lives as he pleases, never staying in one place too long. It's a good way to forget about the horror that drove Syn and his fellow Firestorm dragons from their homeland three decades ago, separating them from their mortal companions. He's about to leave the Big Easy in search of his next adventure when he spots her. His lifemate. The connection is hot, raw and immediate. On his part.

Briella is more annoyed than afraid when a tall, dark and dangerously attractive man with flames—actual flames—in his eyes accosts her outside her apartment. Yeah, sure he's there to protect her. She's shocked to learn the safe life she enjoys is nothing more than an illusion.

For a woman to whom hard-won independence is sacred, putting her faith in a chivalrous stranger might just be the most dangerous challenge she's ever taken on.

CHAPTER 1

Rain never put a damper on the French Quarter.

In the short time she'd called it home, she'd learned that little subdued the eclectic, vibrant, pulsing enclave beloved by locals and tourists alike.

Briella Everett doused the light in her small studio apartment, pulled the hood of her raincoat over her head, tucked her waterproof portfolio under her arm, and ducked out into the early evening. She was running late for her appointment at Stackwood, thanks to the phone call from her mother, who persisted in her campaign to convince Briella to return to Upstate New York.

She suffered through the same old conversation at least once a week.

Briella's sole slipped in a small puddle. She snagged the nearest light post to keep from falling on her ass. Her dark purple tights and knee-length flared skirt weren't spared a hefty splash of the dirty water.

"Damn it. Gross." Water seeped down her legs into her ankle boots. She scrunched her face. "Real gross."

1

She'd moved to her small apartment off Bourbon Street only three months ago to pursue promising leads with her art. A co-worker back home who had seen her paintings at an art festival insisted she was gallery material and quickly put a call in to a family member who owned an art gallery in New Orleans. After an impromptu weekend trip to Louisiana, Briella found herself without an art show at a large gallery, but directed to approach three smaller galleries. Stackwood was one of the three.

She decided to make the move, temporary as it might be, and follow her dreams. Her parents made sure her bank account was full for any expenses that might occur. She was pretty much set if there was an apocalyptic event. How her parents could afford what they did when neither worked was beyond her. Family finance was always taboo subject, as was questioning their overprotective nature.

Although she was financially set, she'd found a part-time position at a restaurant. It provided her with a sense of independence most people her age had a chance to become intimate with.

On off nights, she found herself with her new friends, who begged for psychic readings. Once they got wind of her "abilities," it turned into the highlight of every gathering.

She wasn't psychic, but she had an advantage they didn't. Her father said it was a gift.

To Briella, it was a gift, a curse, and a nuisance.

As it was proving to be now. Voices plagued her head the closer she came to the hustling throughway of the French Quarter.

She learned at a young age to paint as a form of expression. Her paintings always reflected the inner turmoil of strangers' detached thoughts.

Thoughts she could hear as clearly as her own.

The audible sounds of bar music, raucous laughter, and loud conversations as she approached Bourbon Street did little to muffle the mental onslaught of thoughts that demanded her attention. Briella sighed. She could easily turn off the noise in her head, but she found inspiration for her paintings in the small blurbs of these strangers' lives.

Some might consider you a creep, Brie. A peeping Tom of the mind.

"No guilt," she muttered.

Tugging the belt of the raincoat more tightly around her waist, she crossed Bourbon Street and followed the crossroad to the gallery.

She hesitated outside the heavy wooden door with a medieval-looking iron grate over a small window, blocked further by a black iron plate. Narrow beams of light escaped the shuttered windows to her right. She read the sign that rocked on two chain-link tethers over the door. *Stackwood Gallery of Fine Art.*

"Well, it's a start."

Drawing up her confidence, she tried the door.

Locked.

"Damn." She knocked. After a few minutes of waiting, she knocked again. She could see no doorbell or other means of notifying whoever resided inside that someone waited to be received. She pulled back the cuff of her raincoat and glanced at her watch. Six-ten for her six o'clock appointment. "Thanks, Ma."

She tried knocking one last time before digging into her purse for her phone. When she came up empty-handed, a deflating breath fled her lungs and her shoulders drooped. She must've left her phone on the counter in her rush to leave.

Well, late was late. She'd made her impression, present or not.

Resigned to a failed meeting tonight—she'd call the gallery's director in the morning and try to set up a second meeting—Briella lowered her head and turned back toward Bourbon Street. Nothing a hurricane and a hot bowl of gumbo couldn't cure.

"Ms. Everett?"

Briella spun, too fast. Her soles slipped on the rain-slickened sidewalk. She gasped and reached for the wall to keep from falling. A pair of hands snatched her biceps and steadied her on her feet.

She stared at the middle-aged man as he let go and gave her an apologetic tip of his chin. He had a pleasant face—and, apparently, the soft steps of a cat. She hadn't heard so much as a creak from the wooden door when it opened behind her.

"I'm terribly sorry for startling you. Let's go inside?"

Without waiting for confirmation of her identity, the man ushered her through the ancient-looking door. It closed with a solid thunk behind them.

The interior of the gallery shocked her. She hadn't expected to walk into a space as sleek and modern as it was sensual and alluring. Pushing the hood off her head, she gazed around in awe. The gallery was divided into two main sections to the left and right that stretched to the far back of the building. It looked like each side had several partitions to section off areas where pieces of art hung on display. A virtual maze of beauty with lighting to capture hues and highlights and the unique aspects of each work. In front of her hung a single painting beside a mounted card with the biography of the artist.

"Again, my deepest apologies. I had been caught up in the storage room and didn't hear you knock right away. May I take your coat?"

"Yes. Thank you." Briella leaned her portfolio against her leg and slipped out of the wet coat. The man took it from her. "I'm Briella Everett." She held out her hand.

The man smiled, pushing wire-rimmed glasses onto the bridge of his nose with one finger before taking her hand in a firm shake. "Abraham Harper. Pleasure to meet you." He held her coat a few inches from his body and spread a hand toward the back of the building. "Why don't we head to my office. I'm anxious to see your work. Bruno had wonderful things to say about your pieces."

Heat brushed her cheeks as she picked up her portfolio and followed Mr. Harper through the gallery.

"I hope you find my pieces to your liking," Briella said, falling behind as she looked at the paintings on display. They were dark, foreboding, with a beat of twisted romance. Maybe, just maybe, Mr. Harper would find her work palatable. "Wow, these are pretty incredible."

"Mr. Tawling is quite a fascinating person with an equally fascinating mind. Many galleries steer clear of a brooding tone, fearing it will turn away potential customers. I, on the other hand, find an unseen beauty in the dark and mysterious." Mr. Harper flashed her a friendly smile over his shoulder. "All art deserves a fair eye. I enjoy catering to those who prefer something other than bright flashes of color and scenescapes. These"—he motioned to the displayed canvases—"touch people on a more primitive level. They connect with those deeper aspects of our subconscious and draw us in. Wouldn't you agree, Ms. Everett?"

"I certainly do agree."

At least he won't snub the dark in my art.

They reached Mr. Harper's office a glass-encased room tucked in the back corner behind a wall of displayed canvases. He motioned for Briella to enter the neat space and followed her in, leaving the glass door open.

As Mr. Harper hung her coat on a hook, he said, "You can put the portfolio on the desk. I'm eager to see what Bruno was talking about."

"I'll have to thank him personally for the high accolades." Briella smiled as she rested her portfolio on the uncluttered desk, unzipped the case, and laid it open. Mr. Harper was at her side in a blink, leaning over the two pieces that lay on top. She looked at them with mingled pride and nerves. "These two are my favorites."

"May I?" He asked, hands stretched out toward one.

"Of course."

With respectful care, he lifted free a painting of two people obscured in shades of gray and black. Ghosts in a sea of darkness, lit by a single candle. She recalled hearing the thoughts of a man planning to propose to his girlfriend, and with them all the self-doubt that rambled over and over in his head. Between the two ghostly figures, strokes of gold and red and diamond-like hues of white conveyed the couples' emotions, their love for each other.

Mr. Harper placed the canvas on an easel and played with the lights on a strip at the upper cross-section. At last, he stepped back, hands folded in front of his chest, eyes wide.

"Genius," he murmured.

Briella hated herself in the next moment when she opened her mind to this man's thoughts. She couldn't help it. She wanted to know what he was really thinking. Those raw thoughts that would never come to his lips.

...great potential. A unique vision I can't pass up. My clientele will jump on this...

Pride swelled in her chest. Whatever Mr. Harper did with the lighting brought the eye straight to the promising center of the painting, but somehow managed to add depth to the shadows around the edges of the canvas. It took on new life, new meaning sitting on the easel beneath the masterful lighting.

Minutes slipped by and the silence stretched. Mr. Harper's head tilted one way, another, yet another. His body angled several different ways. He walked past the painting, backed away from it, moved closer. All the while, Briella had to tamp down her desire to tap into his private thoughts again. She stood next to the desk, anxiously awaiting his final verdict on the first of many pieces she had to offer.

Without a single word, Mr. Harper gently removed the canvas from the easel, placed it back in her portfolio, and removed a second. Again, Briella watched quietly as he went through his strange routine, all the while holding her muscles tense and her body stiff to keep from fidgeting. She took several slow, deep breaths and waited in an emotional turmoil like any other aspiring artist who didn't have her supernatural gifts to offer some insight.

Mr. Harper continued to go through the same ritual for each canvas, six in total. When he settled the last one back in the pocket of her portfolio, he quietly closed the case, zipped it up, and rested his hands on his desk.

His eyes met Briella's. She caught the excitement behind those dark irises, stoking her own hope.

"Well, Ms. Everett, I must say Bruno was not exaggerating when he said you had a very unique vision and the talent to back it up." A grin began to tug at the corners of his mouth. "I have an opportunity I would like to extend to you. I've had an artist back out of a showing. It's just two weeks from now. I was going to ask one of my regular artists to fill the spot, but after speaking to Bruno, I decided to wait to see what you might have to offer."

Briella's excitement bubbled up from her belly and into her throat. She wanted to shout and dance, but tangled her fingers behind her back in a tight, almost painful, knot instead.

Mr. Harper rested a palm against her portfolio. "I like your work. In fact, I find it absolutely stunning. I would like to offer you the spot, if you feel you're ready and can provide me with the paintings I require for this type of event. You have brought six exquisite pieces with you tonight. How many do you have in total, and how many do you feel are presentable to paying clientele?"

The breath fled Briella's lungs. Her lips trembled as she smiled. Were those seriously tears in her eyes?

Be professional, Brie. Be professional.

She nodded. "I have dozens of paintings. I can provide you with at least twenty, twenty-five paintings that I feel are worthy of your clientele."

"Can you deliver fifteen to me tomorrow?"

Brielle bounced on her toes before clearing her throat and settling back onto her feet. "Yes. Of course, Mr. Harper."

Mr. Harper's grin melted into a smile. "Wonderful. If you have about a half-hour now, we can discuss the terms of the gallery, showcasing, what I will provide, the promotion I will do, what I expect from you, and what you can expect from me. I usually have a month to put together a showing, and with a new artist I always try to give myself at least six weeks to built interest. Since we don't have the luxury of that time, every minute will count to make this showing successful for you and for me."

"I most certainly have time, Mr. Harper. Thank you. Thank you for this opportunity."

Mr. Harper laughed. "You *can* get excited, Ms. Everett. I don't think I've ever encountered an artist maintain such composure after being offered their first show."

Briella laughed, her body loosening. She clapped her hands together under her chin, arms and legs weak, and blinked back tears. "I think this surreal moment is safest for you and most definitely safest for my pride."

Another laugh echoed through the office as Mr. Harper took the seat behind his desk. "I have a feeling this is going to be the start of a wonderful business relationship."

Briella couldn't get home fast enough to share the incredible news. Her very first exhibit. A debut artist with a lucky break. Mr. Harper wasn't the only one who had to thank Bruno for the recommendation. She would have to call her former co-worker and thank her for the introduction.

She had a bunch of phone calls to make and her friends to meet at one of the local jazz bars, but first she had to change out of her wet clothes and put on a more suitable pair of shoes. At least Mr. Harper offered to hold her paintings to frame for her debut so she didn't have to chance them getting damaged in the rain.

She crossed Bourbon and was two blocks away when a strange tingling sensation crept up along her spine and unleashed goose bumps down her arms. She slowed, opening her mind to any thoughts that might accompany the unsettling feeling.

"...get her when she returns..."

Briella faltered to a stop and licked her lips. Standing in the street, a couple of feet from the sidewalk, she scanned her surroundings. Music and lights and the crazy hustle and bustle of busy Bourbon Street two blocks away lent little comfort.

She was alone, except for a straggler here and there.

Keeping her mind open and her senses tuned into the sodden night, Briella stepped onto the sidewalk. She dug into her purse for her stun gun, a gift from her mother. Pepper spray wouldn't do a damn thing in the rain. She silently cursed her choice of attire, especially her tractionless shoes, and the weather. The combination was a losing pair for her, a winner for an attacker.

The street before her blurred. She came to an abrupt stop, reaching blindly for the wall of the closest building. The vision of a rain-drenched, hooded man covered in shadows filled her head. The dark, hulking figure set off more than a chill that spread to every limb of her body. Fear should have ridden the coattails of the chill, but all she felt was confusion.

It only served to set her more on edge.

In a blink, the vision vanished. She was back on her street, hand braced against the wall, with a faint wave of weakness coasting from head to toe. She almost dropped the stun gun, but grappled for the handle before it escaped her fingers.

"Get her. She'll give it up."

Briella shivered and headed for her apartment at a fast clip. The splash of a disturbed puddle sounded behind her.

She spun, the weight of the stun gun heavy in her hand.

No one.

She observed the buildings and the nooks between brick, wood, and gates. Nothing. No movement. No sensation of a hooded man lurking.

With only a sliver of relief, Briella turned around.

And shrieked.

A strong hand clamped down on her shoulder in the same instant she twisted from his attempt to grab her arm.

"Stop," a gruff voice bit out from a pair of shadowed lips beneath the hood of his jacket.

Briella snorted in disbelief. As if she would. She twisted again, freeing her shoulder, and jumped back when he made another swipe for her. She thrust her arm forward, showing off the stun gun. The attacker paused.

"Put that away," he demanded.

"What do you want?" Briella countered, unwavering. The man took a long-legged step toward her. She shuffled back, well aware of her bad footing with her shoes this evening.

"You need to come with me."

If the situation wasn't dire, she might have laughed. Hard. But the odds of her coming out on top against this particular stranger were not in her favor. In a split-second assessment, she knew if she didn't act fast, his hulking size would overmatch her like a beast against a bunny. At least a head taller and twice her width, she was doomed without an advantage.

He reached for her again. She moved agilely, toward him instead of away, and connected the stun gun to his neck. In the same motion, she pushed the activator.

Electricity sizzled and sparked along his skin.

What the hell?

Every muscle in her body prepared to bolt the short distance to the garden gate that led to her apartment, but the shock of what she beheld in the man's shadowed face held her prisoner. A plume of gray smoke cut through the rain, exhaled from his nose and mouth. The small slices of visible skin on his cheeks turned dark red before changing back to tan. Similar to the dark red that erupted beneath the prongs of her stun gun.

But his eyes... She gasped and darted away as he growled in evident pain, reeling back as he swatted at his neck. She didn't stop, and burst through the waist-high iron gate.

"Don't go in there!" he bellowed at her back.

Yeah, right.

She didn't understand why he wasn't right on her heels, but was grateful for the few seconds the delay gave her. With shaking hands, she dug the key to her door out of her purse. It took three tries and one drop to finally get the key in the lock.

"Stop!" he demanded.

Briella shoved open the door, adrenaline pulsing through every vein in her body. She caught a quick glimpse of the monster as he lunged at the door.

She screamed as she slammed it shut and engaged the bolt lock. There was a crash and the door bulged with the massive weight of the assailant barreling into it. She shuffled back until she hit the wall across from the door, at the base of the stairs that led to her apartment on the second level.

The door shuddered as he banged on it with what she imagined to be a massive fist. "Don't! They may be in there! Please, come out!"

Briella dashed up the stairs to the second-floor studio, threw open the inner door, and flipped on a light.

A gasp fled her mouth before she slapped a hand over it and stared in horror.

Trashed. Her small apartment, trashed. Her paintings, her paints, her easels all lay scattered across the floor. Her dresser drawers had been turned out, her bed stripped, her armoire open and empty. Clothes had been strewn all over the place. A lamp lay in pieces in the area she had designated as her living room. Her kitchenette? Every drawer and cupboard open and empty, contents scattered over the floor.

The adrenaline drained from her veins, leaving her shaking in her boots. The stranger continued to yell and bang on the door below. Keeping her stun gun handy, she snatched up her cell phone from where she'd left it on the counter, and instinctively shuffled toward the nearest corner. She wanted the safety of walls at her back. She couldn't hear any strange thoughts coming from inside her apartment, only a sense of frantic, wild desperation from the stranger below. There was no essence, no energy left by the person or people responsible for this invasion. She was alone.

She tried to steady her fingers and punch in 9-1-1. As the phone rang, she yelled down the stairs, "I'm calling the cops!"

A brisk but soothing voice said, "9-1-1. Please state your emergency."

"My apartment's been broken into and there's a stranger banging on my door trying to get in. Send someone, please." Briella inched along the wall, phone tucked between her shoulder and her ear. She dug out the pepper spray from her purse, keeping the stun gun in her other hand. She nudged a strewn painting with the toe of her boot to keep from stepping on it.

"Is anyone with you now?"

"I don't know, but the guy downstairs is going to break down my door."

She gave the operator her address, and haltingly answered questions she presumed first responders would need to know.

"Stay on the line. I have two units coming to you now."

Oh, she had no problem staying on the line. She'd stay on until she had uniformed officers pulling the phone from her shoulder. She stopped inching along the wall when she could see her entire apartment unobstructed, and keep an eye on the stairway leading down to the pounding lunatic.

Anyone who could produce fire in his eyes had to be a lunatic.

When the hell did this great night tank on me?

CHAPTER 2

"My damn luck."

Syn Terravon slipped away into the rainy night when he saw the flashing lights of the approaching police cruisers. Soaked down to his scales, he had waited over an hour for her to traipse her way home. He had *not* expected her to be feisty to the point of zapping him with a bolt of electricity. It had taken him by surprise, the fierce jolt threatening to unleash the dragon. In those short moments when he battled to control his dragon, she escaped.

Briella Everett ran straight into danger, and he wasn't fast enough to stop her.

Maybe if he had gotten to New Orleans a few days sooner. Maybe if he hadn't taken a call from Cade—the Firestorm *tatsu* clan leader—to aid in thwarting a possible Baroqueth ambush in a nearby town, he would've tracked her sooner.

Cursing his luck, he hung out in a dark alcove a few buildings from Briella's and watched as officers entered the ground-floor entry to her second-story apartment. He had seen the Baroqueth slayer go in, but hadn't seen him leave. That was why he'd been so desperate to stop her.

Right now, eyes on the action behind the illuminated windows over the small courtyard, he wanted nothing more than to march up to that open door and explain himself.

You'll earn yourself a night in jail if you do that.

What had caused her to panic? He hadn't come off as threatening, had he? He certainly didn't want to.

You put your hands on her. You didn't even wait before you touched her.

No. She was spooked before she laid eyes on him. Seeing him sent her into a panic. He felt it when her heart rate skyrocketed and her muscles tensed. Her hand twitched with the weight of that electric gun. Maybe he'd been intense, but he'd worked to keep his voice calm and soothing. She hadn't even given him a chance to lift back the hood of his jacket and explain the situation before she zapped him.

Syn leaned back against the wall, partially sheltered from the rain, and caught another tantalizing sight of the magnificent woman through a window.

Okay, so maybe he'd let his overprotective nature get the best of him, but Briella needed protection. More than she realized. He had no idea what she knew about herself, her gift. Did she know about the Keepers? That she was one?

Did she know about the Firestorm dragons? That she was his lifemate?

Since the attack on Alazar and Ariah in Georgia a few months ago, Syn and Cade had been working tirelessly to track down the remaining Keepers and any family they might have. It was an effort to bring all of them back to The Hollow, the dragon homeland that existed outside the human realm, untouched by mortals. A land of magic and beauty and purity. Two of the eight dragons that survived the last deadly attack by the Baroqueth slayers—their sorcerer enemies—had found their Keepers and their lifemates. It gave the remaining six hope that maybe, just maybe, they would find their own lifemates in hiding somewhere.

Locating the Keepers was their first chore. Determining if the Keepers had daughters—potential lifemates for the dragons—was another. Time was critical, now that the Baroqueth knew there may very well be more untrained female Keepers alive and well in the world.

Syn had been lucky in every facet of the word. He'd only stopped in New Orleans to meet up with one of his dragon kin. By pure chance, he stumbled across Briella at a restaurant in the company of friends. His immediate reaction to her was both visceral and all-consuming. His dragon recognized Briella as his woman, but he chose to be civilized and refrained from approaching her until his business with Taryn Chovetz was concluded. Unfortunately, by the time they were through, Briella was nowhere to be found.

Two days later, he saw her again and refused to let her out of his sight. He tracked her to her small apartment. That had been yesterday. Since then, he'd kept vigil over her, waiting for the perfect opportunity to introduce himself.

"Failed."

The woman with the stunning dark red hair and creamy complexion stood framed in the window. He sensed her distress, her anxiety, the fear and anger that welled up inside her. Her personal space, her private little sanctuary, had been ruthlessly invaded. Her ideas of security ripped out from under her. Her anger resonated deep inside his soul. His dragon yearned to hunt down the Baroqueth responsible for the desecration and destroy him before he went near the woman again.

He wanted nothing more than to comfort her.

"You blew that tonight," he said under his breath. With an aggravated groan, he raked a hand through his hair, pushing the damp strands beneath his hood.

The faint vibration of his phone in his pocket drew his attention from the window. He glanced at the number on the display. With one last look at the apartment, he slinked off, heading away from the activity. For the time being, she was safe. Now, he needed to rethink his plans.

Starting with answering the call.

"Taryn. What's up?"

"Got word our friends are scoping out the area. Doesn't surprise me that they'd eventually come to the Big Easy. Took 'em long enough."

"Friends. I suppose you mean that sarcastically?"

"Man, since when are our 'friends' friends?"

Yeah, okay. His head wasn't into the humor right now. His blood ran an unyielding hot-cold swirl that left his scales itching to come out and his mind spinning with the drive to return to the small apartment.

"Who gave you the word?" Syn asked, banking to the right down a narrow alley, his senses on high alert for anything out of the ordinary.

In New Orleans, that was more than half the city.

He paused and peered up the side of one of the old brick buildings flanking him. Did he really want to leave Briella alone? Could he justify not watching over her until he rectified this shitty night?

"…not even listening to me, are you."

Taryn's grumble snapped Syn from his thoughts. He shook his head and sighed.

"Where the hell are you? What're you doing? Do I need to come meet you somewhere?"

"That might be a good idea." Glancing up and down the alley to ensure he was alone, Syn allowed his talons to extend enough to get a solid grip into the brick. Scaling walls wasn't his preference, but flapping wings would bring unwanted attention. Magic was also out of the question. One of the many reasons he hated this mortal realm. Back home in The Hollow, the Firestorm dragons had full magical capabilities. Power was natural. The land fed them. Crossing the threshold into the mortal world stripped the dragons of almost everything.

There were loopholes, such as what Alazar and his Keeper discovered before the Baroqueth attacked in

Georgia. An ancient Book of Realms that allowed for magic to be transferred from an object taken from The Hollow for the dragon's use.

Syn tucked the phone between his shoulder and ear, protecting the device from the rain as best he could. He dug his talons into the mortar and began climbing to the roof with a small grunt of effort.

"What are you doing? *Please* don't tell me you're riding a woman right now."

"Riding a wall is more like it," Syn muttered, fiercely ignoring the swell of hot hunger that coiled and pooled low in his groin. Taryn's mention of riding a woman brought Briella's potent image to the forefront of his mind. The curse and blessing of lifemates. An instantaneous, overwhelming, and utterly maddening effect, and here he was, no closer to having a decent conversation with her than he was three days ago. "You'll understand when you get here."

"Where's here?"

"Off Bourbon." Syn crested the top of the wall and slithered over the wet, puddle-laden roof until he could lift up into a crouch. Unfortunately, the rooftop didn't provide many options in terms of cover. He gave Taryn the address. "Join me on the rooftop to cloud gaze."

"I'm not a romantic."

"Shame. Hopefully your lifemate can live with that. When you find her."

"You know that's impossible, brother." Taryn sounded resigned. "Zareh and Alazar are lucky bastards. I'm rather tired of the casual romances."

"Maybe you should stop looking for someone in those bars you frequent and search somewhere a little more respectable. Maybe then you'd find a decent woman to hold you over until Cade finishes his search for the surviving Keepers." Syn moved silently over the rooftop, avoiding the puddles as best he could. His jeans were plastered to his legs and the hoodie and T-shirt felt like a soggy double layer of unwanted skin. The phone started to slip from the wet grip between his shoulder and ear. "I'll see you when you get here."

He caught the phone before it hit the roof, ended the call, and shoved the device into his sodden pocket. He wouldn't mind if the damn thing short-circuited. He hated much of the technology in this world.

He made a short drop between two buildings, perched behind a rusted AC unit and peered into the back windows of Briella's apartment. The mess he could see inside fueled his smoldering anger. Beams from high-powered flashlights scoured the small courtyards on either side of her building. Officers and crime scene techs searched the area for any evidence while a detective spoke inside the apartment with a very animated Briella.

What he wouldn't do to hop down onto her narrow balcony for a closer look. From this angle, he could see the deep rose flushing her cheeks, the fear and anger expressed in her face, the shift of body weight as she tapped feet, scuffed boots, and tried to calm herself. Her hands gestured, but shook.

Amusement tugged at the corner of his mouth.

Briella Everett might be small in stature, but the fire that burned inside her delicate frame was larger than life. He could almost taste it on his tongue. It overpowered the subtle essence of Baroqueth that lingered in the enemy's wake and managed to make him harder. Oh, and that hair of hers. He'd love to tangle his hands in its softness, tug her head back, and...

A growl escaped his lips. He rubbed his palms roughly on his thighs, willing away the evidence of his arousal with the harsh motion. The contact only made his hunger grow.

This lifemate business was murder on a man.

Resigning himself to suffering his relentless hard-on, he scanned his surroundings for any sign of an enemy. Whoever ransacked Briella's apartment either found what he was searching for and left, or found nothing of material interest.

Either way, he would be back. Of that, Syn was certain. The Baroqueth would not let the possible lifemate of a Firestorm dragon out of their sights for long.

And neither would he.

"I can't believe this is happening."

Briella mindlessly stirred her tea, ignoring the string tangling around the spoon. The chills continued to spread up and down her body two hours after her ordeal. Chills, and a little something else.

"Brie, doll. I'm sure it was some random act. You said that nothing was stolen and all your paintings were intact. Whoever it was probably got the wrong apartment."

"That *doesn't* make me feel any better."

Briella looked across the table at Emma Nova, one of the friends she'd made since her move. The other woman tended to play the mother, though she was only six years Briella's senior. Briella hated the idea of asking anyone to take her in for a night, but she hadn't wanted to room up at a hotel. If the attacker was after her, he might look at a hotel first. The big man with flames in his eyes had seemed to be more than your run-of-the-mill mugger.

One night. Only one night until the security company installs a system tomorrow. Nothing will happen in one night.

Universal laws had dished out plenty of excitement for one night. One week. Hell, one lifetime. She didn't need any more excitement of the dangerous kind.

Emma slid a plate of beignets closer to Briella. "Café du Monde. I didn't have time to make mine, but these still come in first, in my opinion."

"Thanks." Briella lifted her cheek out of her hand and helped herself to one of the golden pillows dusted with powdered sugar. They were still warm and soft and deliciously sweet. "Sugar is good for the brain after a break-in."

"Any suspects?"

The image of the large guy hidden beneath normal street clothes and a rain-drenched hoodie made a cursed appearance in her mind. She shook her head, dispelling the image, and sighed. "I haven't a clue why anyone would break into my place. I have nothing of value—"

"Um, yeah. Paintings?"

Briella finally pulled the spoon from the mug, unraveled the string on the tea bag, and dropped both on a small plate. Emma caught her hand before she could pull away and held fast until Briella looked up.

"Brie, your paintings are going to go crazy big and you'll be set. Your dreams are coming true. Maybe someone caught wind of your talent and your prospective showing and thought they'd try and get an original."

"Not a single painting was stolen or ruined. They were just…displaced." *Like I am right now.* "My money wasn't taken, just moved. My jewelry, same."

"Well, then, you should rest easy knowing that they didn't find anything they wanted and left. Wrong building. Nothing more."

The rest of the night stuck in her throat, and then shoved back into her chest as she swallowed a bite of beignet. A sliver of guilt tried to creep into her conscience, but she tamped that down as well. She didn't want to bring up the brute attacker whose eyes blazed with literal fire, whose skin took on the strangest of colors, and whose nose and mouth released a plume of smoke that didn't come from a cigarette.

She'd had plenty of time for the initial shock to wear off. She knew what she saw. Maybe she was near crazy to admit it, but whatever that...*thing* was, it was not human. An easy enough concept to wrap her head around, considering the city she lived in, and her own gift. She'd crossed paths with witches and voodoo priestesses, imitation vampires and a few real ones. Ghosts, oh, plenty of those. And two werewolves that had a sniffing fetish they tried to hide behind bouquets of flowers.

She had also encountered darker entities—demons, incubi, succubae and ghouls that made the worst nightmare seem like a fantastical dream.

She stayed clear of the cemeteries after dusk.

She thanked and cursed her gift for the insight into the "other" world.

"Earth to Briella," her friend said in a cajoling tone.

Briella cleared her throat and followed it up with a deep sip of warm tea. She drew her hand back from Emma's and shrugged. "Sorry. Trying to figure things out."

"Sweetie." Emma stood up and rounded the table. She crouched down, one arm around Briella's shoulders, and smiled. "It's getting late. You've had a crazy night. Finish your tea and get some rest. You're safe here. And you'll be safe here as long as you need to stay. Have you called your parents?"

"Oh, hell no. They'd be on the first flight down with wrangling gear to drag me back home. It took me a month of begging to get down here. No way in high hell am I throwing away this opportunity at a gallery showing." Briella shook her head to emphasize her decision. "No stinking way."

Emma released a quiet breath, one Briella knew too well. She should call her parents, but why? So they could worry?

What if Emma was right? It was a random break-in and the person had the wrong apartment. Her parents would rush down here for nothing, and she might lose the chance to see if she could sell her art professionally. The only things she had worth taking were her paintings, and they weren't worth much. Yet.

"Well, I think you should relax. Rest easy in the Big Easy. We'll get Adrienne and Mark together tomorrow to celebrate your amazing offer." Emma pressed a kiss to Briella's temple and straightened up. "I'm sure Mark will be more than happy to spend some time with you."

Briella laughed. Their friend's continued attempts to win her affections wasn't lost on her. "He certainly puts life into the party, I'll give him that."

"Mmm." Emma patted her shoulder. "We'll see."

Briella finished her tea, washed her mug, and headed to the guest room Emma set up for her. After she brushed her teeth and washed her face, she climbed into bed, her mind finally easing.

"Everything will be fine," she reassured herself, folding her hands over her chest. "Everything will be fine."

She shut out the rambling thoughts of the strangers walking by outside. The chills had subsided, leaving her feeling calm. Soothed.

Briella closed her eyes. Seconds turned into minutes as she felt herself drift off to sleep.

"Daddy, how do you know if it's one?" Six-year-old Briella touched the reptilian snout of the statue, one of two her father prized and displayed in his home office. "If it looks like us?"

"My little Belle. Have you forgotten what I've taught you about the secrets the eyes hold?" Her father lifted her onto his lap and pointed to one of the glass orbs that served as the dragon's eyes. "The truth lies here. In the eyes. The fire of their soul and their desire to protect us."

Briella shot upright in bed, eyes wide, cold sweat dotting her hairline and inching between her shoulder blades. She gasped for breath, her father's voice from a near-forgotten memory resounding in her head.

In the eyes. Fire in the eyes.

Her fingers fisted on the edge of the blanket.

"A *dragon*."

CHAPTER 3

In the morning, Briella couldn't shake the insane notion that the man who'd accosted her was a dragon.

A dragon!

She had no problem believing all the paranormal stuff. *She* certainly wasn't completely "normal," and not completely "para" either. She was unpara-abnormal.

But...dragons?

"Yeah, right." She'd been a kid when her father told her stories about dragons. He never went crazy about them, giving just enough details for a child's mind to latch onto and run away with the notion that the magical creatures could exist. Possibly. Maybe.

"Not."

After a quick breakfast, Emma headed off to her part-time job at an antiques store. Briella faced the sunny morning alone and returned to her apartment. The security company would be arriving within the hour, and her fingers itched to paint. Paint the *thing* that had attacked her.

The potent reminder of how his hand felt on her arm shot a whip of warmth up to her shoulder. It wasn't direct skin-to-skin contact, but beneath the fear and panic that consumed her in those few moments, his touch did something unnerving to her. She didn't like it and forced the very reminder into the darkest depths of her mind.

Surprise shook her from her thoughts when she walked through the iron gate into her apartment building's small courtyard to see Mark Heddleman sitting on the single step that led to her private entrance. Lithe, tall, with black hair and dark eyes, he was definitely eye candy. Unfortunately, she lacked the romantic spark he clearly hoped to fan to life.

Her last relationship cost her an opportunity to boost her paintings into the public eye. She wasn't about to let any man stand in her way again.

"Hey, there, Brie. Emma told me you'd be coming home around this time and asked if I'd mind staying with you to make sure you're safe." His dark brow wrinkled over an eye as he greeted her with a kiss on the cheek. Briella had to stamp down the urge to roll her eyes and laugh. Leave it to Mother Emma to use this opportunity to matchmake. Mark asked, "What happened last night?"

"Someone broke into my apartment. I promise, I'm okay. I have a security company installing an alarm system today."

"You managed to get someone out here that fast?"

Briella unlocked the garden door and led Mark up the narrow stairs. "One of the officers that responded to the call has a brother who works for a company. He put in a call for me."

"Making friends with the cops, eh?" Mark chuckled. "It's all about who you know in this town. At least something's being done to protect you today and not next week."

"You know, I do have the means to protect myself." Briella opened the inside door to the apartment and motioned for Mark to enter. She closed and locked it, then dropped her purse on the small side table. Mark started picking up paintings and leaning the canvases against the wall. "I'm pretty self-sufficient."

"I never said otherwise. But your place was broken into. What if you were home and asleep when it happened?"

"I have no problem staying over for a night or two."

Briella laughed despite the heat that touched her cheeks as she picked up his blunt thought. "I don't need a sleeping companion, if that's what you're getting at." She worked on straightening up the paintings across the apartment. "I may be a little country-like girl who's never lived alone, but I'm doing quite well so far."

Mark muttered something under his breath. His thoughts were filled with his desire to do more than keep her company, to win her affections by promising protection. Briella sighed to herself. Her entire life, she'd been cocooned and suffocated. Her mother could have invented the term helicopter parent, while her father schooled her on her strange gifts and to always listen for warnings and threats in the thoughts of the people around her. The stun gun and pepper spray were his suggestions that her mother made a reality. She stopped them at insisting she also carry a dagger and a pistol, but accepted self-defense courses as good sense. Of course, those were held under her father's keen supervision.

At twenty-nine, she was more knowledgeable about how to snap a bone or gouge out an eye than she was about what might be a good deal on a bundle package for cable and phone.

She rested the last painting against a pile of others and rubbed a hand down her braid. Her fingers twitched and her gaze instinctively slid to the clean canvas perched on an easel, waiting for her to create something magnificent.

"So? How did your meeting go last night? Emma refused to dish details."

Briella closed her eyes, reined in her impatience, and forced a smile to her lips. The urge to paint was quickly wearing her down.

"It went well. I'll dish later when we go out for drinks." She turned to face her friend and her determination to get him out of her apartment took a hit when she caught the sparkle in his eyes. She was truly grateful for the friendships she had built in such a short period of time, regardless of certain underlying motives from one new friend in particular. She didn't want to hurt Mark's feelings. "But now? I need to do some work."

"Is there anything I can do to help you? Get paints? Water? Make you a cup of coffee?"

"The only time I drink coffee is when I stay up all night." A huge cup of chicory deliciousness would be wonderful right now, but Mark didn't need to know that. "Painting is a private endeavor. I can't really...work...when someone is around."

Briella refrained from cringing at the directness of her implication. If she knew Mark even a little, Emma probably woke him up out of a dead sleep to send him on a mission to make sure Briella would be okay. As far as she could determine, Mark's natural circadian rhythm was roughly six hours behind that of a normal person. The least she could do was be hospitable for a short time.

A sigh escaped her as Mark's smile faltered.

"You know what?" She waved toward the canvas and managed a grin. "I need to go through my paintings and pick out the fifteen best. Wanna help?"

Mark looked as if she had offered him a million dollars. Or a date. The sparkle in his eyes intensified in the sunshine coming through the window before a sly smile curled his lips.

"You got the gig, didn't you." It wasn't a question. Briella didn't give him an answer until he wrapped his arms around her in a strong hug. "Congratulations! I'm so happy for you, Brie. You've no idea how much I hoped for the good news today. Well, I wouldn't have minded a call last night, but I'll take post-breakfast notification."

"Thanks, Mark."

"Oh, I could hold you like this for a long, long time."

She stiffened as his hug lasted longer than she deemed necessary, and his thoughts trekked down more sensual avenues. Yeah, her nonexistent spark was leaving her feeling a bit awkward.

"Oh, buddy. Wrong woman to be holding like that."

Briella blinked. The strange voice was potent, direct, and unmistakably referred to her current situation. The uncanny warmth that followed the comment confirmed her deduction. So did the awareness that prickled along her neck.

"Okay, well, let's get to work," Briella said, working her way out of Mark's embrace. She tucked the hair that had come free of her braid behind her ears and twisted toward the windows. She scanned the small courtyard below, searching for anyone who might be watching her. Was that monster lurking around her home? Waiting for a perfect opportunity to attack again? What did he want with her?

The voice is different. Not the voice from last night.

The realization didn't make her feel any better. In fact, it made her more uncomfortable. *Two* assailants had an interest in her, and they were roaming around free.

"Let's start with these here," Briella said, tapping the row of paintings closest to the window. "Tell me which ones you think would be good for the exhibit."

"All of them."

Briella rolled her eyes and cast him a humored glance over her shoulder. His attention wasn't even on the paintings, unless she counted herself as a piece of art.

Crazy piece of work is more like it.

"Nice try, smartass. If you're going to help me, you need to be honest. I can only take the fifteen best that I have." She picked up the closest canvas and held it out to Mark, diverting his attention from her to the task she assigned. "What do you think?"

"Okay, okay. Let me go through them and I'll let you know my honest opinion."

"Good. I need to water my plants. I'll be right back."

Briella filled a watering can and stepped onto the narrow balcony outside the small kitchenette. Her mind whirled with the onslaught of voices and thoughts, the acute awareness of being watched, and the residual anxiety of last night's confrontation with the hulking stranger. The French Quarter was alive and well this morning, moving along without a care for her tribulations. The smell of sweet olive trees and roses would normally have soothed her, but her nerves were on high alert. It was more than the voice, more than the sensation of being watched.

Intuition never let her down.

The gift of visions came from her mother's side of the family, while the gift of voices came from her father's. Without her parents' guidance and training on how to control both gifts, she'd be long gone in mental capacity by now. Instead, they'd ensured she was empowered by her gifts.

However, right about now she wanted nothing to do with either gift. She felt antsy, jumpy, and wanted to scratch at her skin until the prickles were scraped off.

The methodical routine of watering her small pot garden of gardenia, daisies, wild flower mix, and ivy helped—until a loud bang cut through her serenity.

Briella shrieked, dropping the watering can on the wrought-iron balcony floor with a clang. Mark popped his head out a second later. Concern etched his brow. She realized the bang had been the sound of someone pounding on her downstairs door.

"Brie?"

"I-I'm okay. Was thinking and…" Briella rubbed a hand over her chilled cheeks. She picked up the watering can and sighed. "Sorry."

"Don't apologize to me." He hitched a thumb over his shoulder. "I think that security guy should apologize to you for the scare."

"I should get that."

"Hey, why don't you go sit down? It's obvious you're still trying to cope with last night. I'll let him in and give him the rundown, okay?" Mark lifted her chin with a single finger until their gazes met. For once, he wasn't thinking about a relationship. He was genuinely worried for her. "I'll handle it. You relax."

Briella followed Mark into the apartment and took a seat at the counter in her kitchenette. The only way she could truly relax was to paint. And to paint, she needed to be alone.

Painting was her escape. Her purge of the bad and bothersome.

The empty canvas beckoned her with unseen force. She knew what would consume the white of the slate. She knew what, in a day or two, she'd find herself staring at.

The image had not left her mind since the night before.

The image of a man with the eyes of a dragon.

CHAPTER 4

Syn gritted his teeth and jammed his fists into the pockets of his leather jacket. He never stopped scanning the crowds that filled Jackson Square, the narrow alleys between streets, and the bustling tourist epicenter. He tried to track the Baroqueth throughout the day, leaving Taryn to guard Briella until she and her friends headed out for the evening.

Now, he wished he hadn't asked the favor of his friend. Taryn's needling personality had slipped his faulty mind.

"I don't know, man," Taryn said. "I think there's something going on between them. She was all comfy and cozy with him."

A tick started at the corner of his mouth. Syn let out a sharp breath, easing up on his jaw before he cracked his teeth. Thankfully, night had fallen and the smoke that curled up from his nostrils was hidden. Not a single person walking past gave him a second glance.

"You know what I've learned in the last thirty-something years?"

"I have a feeling you're going to tell me whether I want to know or not," Syn said.

Taryn snorted. "Exactly. You said yourself that you've been rather reclusive until recently. Women in this realm don't like men who follow them. They find it creepy."

Syn snapped his attention to his friend. Taryn shrugged.

"Trying to make this a little easier for you. First off, if she's Giovani's daughter, then she's wicked strong, both physically and mentally. Matches up with her being wicked sexy."

"Taryn." The warning came on a growl that rumbled from deep in his chest. The fierce protectiveness his dragon exuded startled him when he'd first laid eyes on Briella. Not any longer. It was a natural part of him, now that he'd located his lifemate. "I'm not stalking her."

"Um, yes. You are."

Syn came to a sudden halt and squared off with Taryn, forcing his friend to come up short or barrel into him. Throngs of tourists and residents split around them without missing a step. "How? How am I stalking her? I'm watching out for her."

"Okay. Let me explain something in simple terms. And don't go snapping at my face until I'm done."

Taryn folded his arms over his broad chest, the lightheartedness seeping away from his expression to leave a hard, unyielding man staring Syn down. There was no doubt that living among the humans had loosened his friend up, but when it came right down to it, Taryn was as fierce as every Firestorm dragon.

"What?" Syn finally said, the single word short and sharp.

"You're a creeper. Or at least to any human being you're a creeper. Standing in shadows. Watching from rooftops. Sending me to keep an eye on her all day. You're stalking her. Being close by, but just out of sight. She senses us, and after last night, she's jumpy. I don't know how much she knows or how strong her gift is, but she's aware she's not alone. Before you burn your bridges and lose her trust without ever having the opportunity of gaining it, your best bet is to introduce yourself to her. Face to face." Taryn leaned close to Syn and added in a low voice, "The moment she sees you, you *know* she won't be running away. But you need to do it now."

"And how do you propose I do this? I can't exactly knock on her door."

Taryn rolled his eyes and dropped his arms. "Bro, you seriously need to assimilate with the humans a bit more."

"It's a moot point. Cade wants us back at The Hollow in the next few months. Alazar and Ariah have already relocated. Emery and Gabriel have returned. They leave The Hollow only when they get a lead from Cade on the possible whereabouts of Keepers. Tajan is hunting Baroqueth in hopes of estimating how many there are. There is little reason to learn all the ways of the human world at this stage."

"Well, if you want to win your woman, you should make at least *some* attempt to learn about her world. Starting with an innocent introduction." Taryn grabbed his arm roughly and shoved him toward the river. "I know where she's hanging tonight."

"Where?"

"Wait and see, my friend."

Thursday night, and the Black Duck Bar was filling up. After a satisfying meal and an official celebratory dessert at the Palace Café below, Briella couldn't help but relax into one of the bar's comfortable lounge chairs and sip her fruity martini. Her friends were riled and rambunctious, their chatter hard to follow amidst the noise of other patrons. Didn't matter. For the first time since the attack, Briella felt at ease. Completely and entirely. No potent voices. No chills that warned her of eyes on her.

She did not feel threatened, and she took another satisfying sip of her martini to toast that.

"I still can't believe the gallery owner is putting this whole thing together in two weeks. *Two weeks*. That's crazy!" Mindy, who'd taken the night off to help celebrate Briella's success, squeed, running the toes of her shoes across the floor. Her smile stretched far beyond what Briella was aware possible. She couldn't help but absorb her friend's excitement. For her.

Excitement for Briella's upcoming gallery debut. "And the director is pushing promotion. Holy crap! What about your friend's relative? The guy who owns that other gallery? Is he helping push your debut?"

Briella laughed. Mindy had a knack for putting the tri-state civilian to shame with the rate she spoke. She had to actually replay Mindy's excited questions in her mind to understand what her friend wanted to know. The alcohol in Brie's system didn't help her cognitive case, but it sure helped the rest of her body melt into the chair.

"Mr. Harper has really high hopes for my collection. And Bruno, my friend's uncle, is going to support the promotion through his private venues, as well as his public ones." Briella released a breathy chuckle. She felt like she was floating in clouds. "I still can't believe it's happening. It's so surreal. To think, only a few months ago I was dreaming of this moment and now it's here. Mr. Harper absolutely loved the paintings Mark and I brought to him this afternoon." She nudged Mark's arm with her elbow. "Thanks for helping me choose."

Mark tapped the rim of his tumbler with her martini glass and winked. There was definitely more smoldering affection in those dark eyes than she'd ever seen before.

"Anytime, Brie. You call, I'm there." Mark sipped his drink, his gaze never leaving hers. She had to be careful. Another drink and she might very well give into his charm against her sober-minded better judgment. She silently thanked the impulse that pushed her to shut off the flow of voices in her thoughts. She didn't want to know what he was thinking with that look in his eyes.

Like a hunter.

Emma placed her wine glass on the small table their chairs were arrayed around and rubbed her hands together. "Why don't we see who else has some good fortune coming their way, eh?" She shimmied to the edge of her seat and held out a hand. "Who wants first dibs on a palm read?"

"Oh, this should be funny." Adrienne balked only a second before thrusting her hand into Emma's. "I want to know when the hell I'm going to find Mr. Right. And don't pass that 'when you least expect it' line at me. I get that all the time from those fortunetellers in the Square." She snorted, then started giggling. "My biological clock is tick-tick-ticking away, Em. I'm not getting any younger."

"Girl, you're thirty. That's not old," Mark said. He rested a hand over Briella's. "Ready for another drink?"

Briella glanced at her half-empty martini glass and shook her head. "I need to slow down if I have any intention of making it down those stairs without becoming free entertainment for the diners below."

"I'll help you."

Briella arched her brows and lowered her chin. "Oh, I'm sure you would. All the way home."

She mentally slapped herself for that one. She'd meant the comment to be flip, but it hadn't sounded that way as the words came out her mouth. Mark leaned over the arms of their chairs and whispered against her ear, "Anything you need, sweetheart."

The strangest sensation of heat and chills erupted in the pit of her stomach. By no means was it arousal, but it left her shifting in her seat and hiding a sudden blush that warmed her face.

Keep piling it on, Mark.

"Brie is more qualified for these things than you, Emma. Why don't we see what the master of the universe can pull from her visions?" Mindy suggested. Briella's eyes widened as all four friends turned hungry eyes on her. "What do you say, Brie?"

Shaking her head before Mindy finished the question, she straightened up in her chair and tried to keep from choking on her words. "No. Not…feeling it. Not tonight."

Shutting off her gifts was her plan for the evening, not paying homage to the freakiness of her genetic fabric.

"Aww, come on, Brie. You're always so accurate," Adrienne pleaded. "I need to know if I'll be alone for the rest of my life."

Well, that one was easy. She'd already had a vision of Adrienne bumping into someone in the very near future. At least while her hair remained the rainbow splash of color she preferred now.

"You won't be alone for the rest of your life. I promise." Briella finished her assurance with a deep drink. Looking at the small sip that was left, she contemplated taking Mark up on his offer of another drink. She wasn't driving, so that wasn't a problem, but she never liked it when her mind became fuzzy. It was pretty damn close to happy fuzz right now. "Nothing's jumping out at me, so perhaps Emma's palm reading might be better for tonight."

"Get her another drink. She's dry," Adrienne said, her back straightening and her chest puffing out. Mindy raised her glass.

"Another drink for the lady of the evening!"

"Guys, please," Briella begged. She laughed to cover her embarrassment as other patrons cast them curious glances. "I like that whole under-the-radar thing."

"I'll get the next round," Mark offered, halfway out of his seat. Briella opened her mouth to protest, but managed nothing more than a squeak at his back before he was out of earshot.

Emma put a hand on her arm. "You've been through a lot, Brie. Let go tonight, okay? You're safe. We've got you."

An hour later, after taking Emma's advice, Briella was beyond letting go. She needed to catch herself and put herself back to rights. She resigned herself to indulging her friends with entertainment of the witchy kind, even if the smattering of visions she saw made no sense to her intoxicated mind. Her belly hurt from laughing, her eyes burned with happy tears, and she hadn't even realized she sipped a fresh drink until burning heat of the most unusual kind curled from the base of her spine up to her neck.

Raw, primal arousal. She went from loose and having fun to hyperaware of her body's sensual reaction to the unseen and the unknown. Her heartbeat quickened, a fluttering in her chest that snatched her breath and made her feel lightheaded.

Mark's hand on her knee didn't escalate this new knot of sensations. If anything, she found herself balling her fists to keep from slapping his hand away in a very uncharacteristic motion of impatience.

"Ladies, if you'll excuse me, I must tend to a refreshing," Briella said, the last part of her sentence coming out on a spurt of laughter. Her friends joined in as she stood up. She masked her tipsy sway with a calculated smoothing of her skirt. "Be right back."

One foot in front of the other. Dear heavens, you've got yourself in a mess.

Briella kept her gaze low as she wove through the crowd. The utterly tenuous walk from her seat to the bathroom was almost painful, and the relief that came with arriving without face-planting was extraordinary.

But the heat that lit every nerve and vein in her body on fire...

Her brows furrowed and she swallowed back the urge to moan.

To her surprise, there was no line of waiting women and she quickly took refuge in the privacy of a small stall. She needed to go home, have a coffee, drink a gallon of water, and sleep this off. She was losing control over her mind. Voices and thoughts slipped past her barricades and invaded her muddled head.

She leaned back on the stall door and closed her eyes, acutely aware of her body, from how sensitive her skin felt to the overpowering urge to locate the source of her desire and find satiation in a phantom's arms.

Breaths shallow, she chewed her lower lip. Alcohol hampered her fight for control.

"...protect you..."

The strange, sultry voice filtered through the mayhem of conversations that spun in her head. She latched onto those two words, direct and strong, and prayed for strength.

Briella left the stall, splashed some cool water on her hot cheeks—she'd spent too much time freshening up to remain alone much longer—and returned to the lounge.

The heel of her boot slipped beneath her folding ankle. Her worst fear came to life in a slow-motion image as she lost her balance and began to fall.

Something solid and strong came up under her arms. Her body lifted and she landed on her feet.

"Whoa. You almost took a tumble there."

The fire spreading through her body exploded. A unique scent of spice laced with smoldering campfire wood filled her nostrils and surrounded her in a warm embrace.

Steadying herself on her heels—*Never wearing heels again when I drink. Oh hell, I'm never drinking again*—she swallowed the lump that had formed in her throat and tilted her head back to see who had come to her rescue.

Instantly, she hated herself for being intoxicated and looking like a fool, because the man standing so close behind her stole her breath. She had never seen a man so sinfully handsome. Ever.

Eyes the color of deep chocolate melted into rings of amber around the pupils. A neatly trimmed scruff along his jaw and upper lip enhanced a rugged, sharp-featured face. Dark brows were an erotic addition to the mouthwatering slant of his eyes. He wore his hair, dark and soft-looking, brushed away from his face, but a lock had fallen over his forehead.

A grin tugged the corners of full lips. Lips, she realized after an excruciating minute, she had been staring at as her own slackened and fell apart. Oh geez, had she actually started leaning into him?

"I-I, um…" Briella lowered her head, allowing her hair to hide the fierce burn of her cheeks. "Yeah, guess I did. Thanks for rescuing me from my heels."

The man chuckled. Damn if that sexy gruff sound didn't tickle up the length of her torso until she itched in more ways that she could count, all of them ones she could easily imagine this stranger scratching.

Never, never, never drinking again.

His grip beneath her arms loosened and his hold lowered. He kept a strong hand on her hip as he moved around her body to face her. Boy, he was awfully delectable. The top of her head barely reached his neck, even in her heels, and he was broad-shouldered and narrow-waisted and muscle-armed and…

She could swoon.

She needed an ice bath.

You need a sober-up pill, like, an hour ago.

The gentle touch of his fingers beneath her chin melted what little solidity she maintained. She wobbled. One of those muscled arms slipped around her, keeping her steady. When he brought her gaze to his, the bar around them disappeared outside a bubble that encompassed the two of them.

His attention was more than casual assessment. Maybe if she weren't so tipsy, she'd realize her libido was overheating and anything she read into his gaze was nothing more than wishful thinking on her part. His gaze probed deep, beyond her eyes and her face. He seemed to search for something she could only speculate. She enjoyed his attention.

"Can I get you a water?" the man asked.

"You've had too much to drink. I won't leave you in such a state."

The voice. The same voice she'd heard in the bathroom. The voice she'd heard come from this very man's lips.

You can get me a kiss.

She blinked. Did she really just *think* that? Did his nostrils just flare? And his eyes. Were they growing darker?

His fingertips flexed slightly against her hip, drawing her a little bit closer. And his gaze lowered from her eyes to her mouth.

Oh my God, he's going to kiss me. He's going to kiss—

"There you are."

The bubble burst. Briella tried to swallow, but her throat had gone dry. To her surprise, the stranger didn't move away. Instead, he angled himself in a subtle way that warned the intruder to back off.

The intruder being Mark.

"I was worried something happened. You were gone a long time. Is everything okay, sweetheart?" Mark's attention shifted to the stranger as he spoke the endearment. His expression hardened.

The other man simply observed Mark with a casual reserve that belied the fierceness glowing in his eyes. Only a moment ago, those same eyes were burning her up in an entirely different, more pleasing way.

You're a fool. You almost threw yourself at him. A stranger.

"Everything is fine. Mark, this is..."

"Syn," the stranger answered for her.

She glanced up at him. *Syn.* Can the guy get any more alluring? She suspected he lived up to his name. All the more reason to keep herself together. Falling apart was for the privacy of her own home.

"Syn, this is a dear friend of mine, Mark Heddleman." Briella moistened her lips when Syn's hand lifted from her hip, along her spine, and came to rest between her shoulder blades beneath her hair. Not entirely versed when it came to relationships, she still recognized the motion as one of possession. She couldn't stop herself from leaning slightly into his touch. There was no logical reason for the immense comfort she felt near Syn. "I tripped. Syn happened to catch me before I made a bloody fool of myself in front of everyone."

Mark reached for her hand. The moment they connected, she felt Syn stiffen beside her. A sense of disgruntled jealousy flowed from him and threaded through her mind.

Briella had just become the center of an unspoken standoff between two men. She couldn't believe it.

"Thank you for intervening," Mark said. His gaze fell to her and he smiled. "Everyone's waiting for you. They were threatening to storm the bathroom. It's probably best if we return."

Mark held fast to her hand as he began to tug her back to their table. Briella looked up at Syn before she was forced to separate from his gentle touch. The break resonated through her like a physical tearing of her body.

"Thank you," she murmured, finally turning away from him and following her unyielding friend back to her chair.

CHAPTER 5

Syn tried to ignore the dragon stirring in an agonizing pit of jealousy and desire. He wore that same desire, from the ache in his groin to the tautness of his muscles. Touching Briella Everett unleashed a beast he could barely control. When she looked at him with those blue-gray eyes and those parted pouty lips, he had every intention of giving himself over to her telepathic plea for a kiss.

Then that human interrupted. The same one he'd been keeping a close eye on from the opposite side of the second-story bar and lounge. Oh, there was no doubt the man had a keen eye for Syn's lifemate. He made his point clear when he interrupted Syn's intended kiss. Mark's blatant move to make his position clear also implied the man's insecurity when it came to the redheaded vixen.

And what a vixen. That dark red hair was as silky as he'd imagined. Her petite frame with curves where they belonged and a delicacy that urged him to protect her, explore her, love every inch of her body.

Syn swallowed hard, the image of Briella beneath that cute dress forcing the muscles to constrict around his lungs.

Taryn claimed Syn didn't know how the human world worked. Well, he knew if he gave in to the possessive nature of their bond, one she knew nothing about, Briella would have shot from the bar faster than a bullet from a gun barrel. Letting that guy drag her off was one of the hardest things he'd ever had to do.

"This has turned into a very boring night."

Syn tore his gaze from Briella and her friends long enough to cast Taryn a dour glance. His interest lay in the woman, not his friend's jabbing comments. She sipped her second glass of water, an untouched martini on the table, and appeared detached from the interactions between the three women and the man she'd introduced as Mark. His hopes soared when she looked around the bar as if to search him out, only to plummet when she engaged in a short conversation with a friend. He thought about following her to the bathroom when she made a second trip, but decided Taryn would deem that stalking, and kept his ass planted in the chair.

"Maybe I should've come up with a different plan," Taryn muttered. He threw back the rest of his rum and shook his head. "Whipped already and you've barely said a word to her."

"I introduced myself, as you suggested." Syn eyed the untouched shot of scotch Taryn ordered for him when they first arrived. Three hours of watching Briella from afar was damn near driving him insane.

He didn't want to watch. He wanted to be next to her. The draw to the woman was maddening. The equivalent of forcing two high-powered magnets apart when all they needed was to connect.

He wanted that connection. Craved it as much as he craved the floral scent of her skin in his nostrils and the airy brush of her long hair against his skin. Oh, he craved so much more, but he'd take it slow.

Shifting in his seat, trying to off-load the discomfort in his cock, he pressed his lips together. "Seems I'm going to have competition. Don't know if the reason I don't like the guy is because he's got his eye on her, or if there's something more."

Taryn twisted in his seat to observe the table Syn had barely looked away from. "He's certainly not a slayer, which is good. No indication of magic. He's too lanky." His friend faced Syn and shrugged. "By the look on her face when you caught her, that guy's no competition."

A small relief. There was a time, long ago, when there was absolutely no competition. The thought of it was asinine. The Firestorm dragons were revered in his homeland, as were the Keepers. Each dragon had a Keeper, a companion and friend, a protector and a responsibility. Generations of male Keepers who allowed the dragons to live for centuries.

Female Keepers, the daughters born of a male Keeper's bloodline, were rare. So rare that where Firestorms were considered lore, even in the paranormal circles, female Keepers had become nothing more than fantasy. History had a pattern, though. When the Firestorm numbers were down, a generation of those rare, exquisite female Keepers seemed to come along. Those numbers were slashed from twenty-three to eight a little over thirty years ago when the Baroqueth slayers launched an ambush that nearly wiped out an already endangered breed of dragon and their companions.

In the last few months, two of his brethren had found their lifemates and given them all hope.

Now, it's my turn.

"Are you going to drink that?" Taryn's question pulled him from his thoughts. The bar came back into focus around him. Syn shook his head, pushing the tumbler closer to Taryn, who said, "Shame to watch it go to waste."

"I told you not to bother getting me anything."

"Not like it would've done a thing to you. The least you could've done was enjoy the flavor while you mope. Might keep your teeth from grinding down to the gum." Taryn chuckled and jerked his head back in the direction of Briella's table. "Hey, by the way, if you continue to stare at her like that you're going to burn holes through the humans standing between here and there. You've barely taken your eyes off her."

"Making sure that guy doesn't do anything she doesn't want."

"Bull." Taryn tipped the glass to his lips. "You should be checking for the real threat, not some dandy wanting a go at your girl."

Point made.

Syn rubbed a knuckle against his bottom lip. Reluctantly, he looked away from the beautiful Briella and started a stealthy assessment of each person crowding the bar.

"You don't suspect one of them might traipse into a place like this. It's too public for their agenda." The fight to keep his attention away from Briella was as hard as it was to physically stay away from her. "I never imaged them to be social."

"You're not social, and here you are. The Baroqueth are on the prowl. Any place is on their agenda." Taryn flagged down one of the servers weaving through the crowd and ordered another drink. He leveled a piqued look at Syn. "Should I order two? Just in case I need to wash down my first?"

Syn barely glanced at the attractive server, who wore a sultry grin and watched him with a heavy-lidded gaze. "Scotch. Top shelf. Neat."

"Be right back," she said.

"Love it when you order the best." Taryn snickered. "Man, she's swaying those hips with a little more energy."

"You're used to it," Syn said, unable to hold back a grin. "Maybe you can take her home."

"I think those hips are moving for you, brother."

Syn rolled his eyes and hiked an ankle on his knee. He perched his elbow on the arm of the lounge chair and stroked his chin with his fingertips. "Nice try. I'm off the market."

"Since when were you ever *on* the market?"

Syn remained silent. Taryn knew he wasn't a man to settle down with a woman. None of the dragons were. Not until they found their lifemates. Everything else was temporary.

"In all the years you've been in New Orleans, you've yet to encounter any of our enemies?" Syn asked, looking over each person in the lounge, which was more of a crowd than he felt comfortable around. Especially when women cast him and Taryn hungry looks more times than he could count. What he wouldn't give to leave this place with Briella on his arm. He brought his attention back to Taryn. "I find that hard to believe."

Taryn shrugged. "Believe what you will. It's been me and my partying self, except for drop-ins by the likes of you and the others. Not much to draw attention on behalf of…us. Besides, there is so much paranormal activity in this city that it can overwhelm the senses."

Syn spotted the server talking to some customers— flirting, rather—her tray still empty of their drinks. Without warning, he pushed to his feet. "I'll be right back."

"Oh, man."

Syn ignored Taryn's taunt and wove smoothly through the crowded lounge, pausing beside the server to tell her not to worry about their order, and continued until he reached the bar. He found a break along the bar top and slid between a group of women in business clothes and a cuddling couple.

"He's still here."

The sound of her voice threading through his thoughts made his mouth twitch with satisfaction. He rested his foot on the railing that ran along the bottom of the bar and braced his arms on the counter as a bartender bounded toward him.

"What will it be?"

"A shot of your best rum and a shot of your best scotch. Both neat." Syn pulled out his wallet and tapped the edge against the polished bar top. "And does that party have an open tab?"

Syn made a small motion to the chairs where Briella and her friends sat.

The bartender shook his head. "They've been paying as they go."

"Then just the two drinks."

Syn flicked open his wallet. His skin burned under Briella's perusal. He cast the group a shaded glance, half hidden behind the businesswomen laughing over their martinis and wine. To his dismay, Briella and her friends were gathering their belongings and preparing to leave.

Briella looked like she was in a daze.

"Maybe I should go thank him. Again. No. That's corny."

Syn pushed off the bar and leaned his side against the top instead. Her girlfriends laughed as they led the way down the stairs. Briella followed, her feet dragging, that man's arm around her waist. She looked back, her gaze hitting Syn dead center in the chest with enough force to seize his breath before lifting to his eyes.

"Maybe I should get a water. Another water. Or go to the bathroom. Again."

She turned away and continued down the stairs, her friend Mark rambling on too close to her ear. Her shoulders were stiff as he watched her inch out of the man's hold.

"Chances are, I'll never see that guy again."

"Here you go, sir."

Syn pulled out money for the drinks and handed it, plus a hefty tip, to the bartender. He stayed at the bar as the group descended the stairs.

"You'll see me again," Syn assured her softly through the telepathic link. *"That is a promise."*

Briella stopped at the bottom of the stairs and twisted to look up, finding him once more through the crowd. Her brows furrowed and her lips parted. One of her hands came to rest over her chest, as if to contain the pounding of her heart. He could imagine it, because he felt the same way.

Then, her friends called for her, the man hooked her arm in a guiding hand, and she was gone.

Syn picked up the drinks and started back to Taryn, his desire to leave growing with each second.

He'd barely made it a handful of steps when he caught the glint of something wedged between the seat cushion and the arm of the chair Briella had occupied. Shuffling both glasses to one hand, he tugged a feminine silver clutch from the chair. His first instinct was to chase after his lifemate to return it, but he quickly abandoned that idea. Tucking the clutch under his arm, he returned to his friend and handed him his drink.

Taryn quirked a brow at the clutch, a smug smile creeping over his mouth. "I see you've found a treasure."

Syn tossed back his scotch and lowered the glass to the table. "We'll see."

He had no idea what treasures the little bag contained, but he certainly hoped there would be a proverbial key to Briella's good graces.

CHAPTER 6

The knock against her skull pulled her from a dreamless sleep. She groaned and rolled onto her side. Sunlight cut through the drawn curtains, enough to stab daggers into her head through her eyelids.

"Never again," she groused, her voice scratchy and her mouth dry. Shading her eyes from the brutal sunlight, she squinted one eye open enough to read the small clock on her nightstand. Eleven thirty.

The knock continued, only this time she realized it wasn't coming from inside her head. Tempted to pull a pillow over her face and ignore the summons, she patted her hand over the surface of the nightstand, hoping to find the bottle of over-the-counter pain medication. Anything to get the splitting pain to ease enough for her to think straight.

Her fingers never connected with the bottle, or the glass of water. She could've sworn she'd left it within reach the night before for this very reason.

The doorbell buzzed throughout her apartment.

"Yeah, okay. Okay." Somehow, Briella rolled to her feet. She paused as pain ricocheted through her brain. She pressed a palm against one throbbing eye and tried to breathe through the agonizing ache as she shuffled through the sunny apartment. Sweet God, she was so *not* feeling the cheer today.

With one eye squeezed shut, one open a mere slit so she wouldn't walk into anything, she made her way across the small space to the table next to the door. And stared at the set of keys on it. Keys. Nothing else. No phone. No clutch. Nothing.

"Seriously?"

She needed her phone to see who was knocking at the door. It was one of those fancy smart thingies with a security camera feed she could pull up through an app. One more step of security beyond the normal alarm and monitoring system.

What a way to put your money to good use, Brie. No more drinks. Ever.

Another rap on the door below. Did she have an appointment with someone and she'd forgotten?

"Anything's possible with this hangover."

Each step reverberated up her spine and hammered against her skull. She had no idea how she made it down the stairs, and didn't care. She fumbled with the bolt lock, rattled the doorknob as she tried to grip the twist lock, and pulled open the door.

The front of her small building faced west, so at least the harsh sunlight didn't smack her in the face. The moment her mind registered who stood on her stoop, she wanted nothing more than to rewind time and not look like a walking mess. She was suddenly utterly aware of the skimpy tank top and flannel pants that covered her, as well as her tousled hair.

"I didn't want…to bother you earlier." Syn, the delicious godly man from the bar the night before, stood a few feet in front of her looking every inch as hot as he had last night. It made her hyperaware of her pitiful comparison. His smile of greeting faded. "You don't look well."

"I kind of went over my limit last night. Not a normal occurrence." She fought the pain to open both eyes and drink in the medicinal sight of Syn. *The irony.* "How did you find my apartment?"

"Your license." A half-grin crossed his kissable mouth. He lifted a small, silver object. "You left it on your seat at the bar." He held the clutch out to her. "I didn't mean to bother you. I figured you'd want your belongings back."

Briella managed to tip the corners of her mouth up before a new wave of aching annoyance hit. When she reached for the clutch, her fingers brushed his.

A flood of rapid images pelted her, stealing the sight of Syn from her eyes as she suffered an explosion of sensation from the vision. Shadows, darkness, fire, rain. More fire. Blue electric bolts.

"…get her when she returns…"

Briella gasped, her arms flailing to grab something. Anything.

The solid support that encompassed her both scared and comforted her. She became weightless as the vision receded and her surroundings returned.

"I've got you, Briella. You're safe. Nothing will harm you."

Did that pathetic whimpering sound come from her? Was she gasping for air?

"Are you okay?" Syn's voice was deep and soothing, a rich, accented blanket that wrapped around her as much as the heat coming off his large body. Her muscles involuntarily relaxed, the tremors that followed the vision subsiding. Her mind, on the other hand, tried to work through the hangover haze to figure out the meaning of the vision. The power behind the images had almost knocked her off her feet.

She stilled. Slowly, she looked up at the man who cradled her in his arms just inside the door. She heard his thoughts, or rather, something far more direct than a thought. It was as if Syn *spoke* to her. Telepathically.

His gorgeous eyes watched her, his concern for her almost palpable. Concern. For a stranger.

A wave of weakness hit her and she lowered her head to his chest. She had no idea why this man induced the potent sense of rightness he did, but she was too exhausted and pained to pick at logic.

"Briella, do I need to bring you to a clinic?"

"No, no. No clinic. I need to sleep this off." She winced. His arms tightened around her and lifted in an easy motion. Before she could protest, Syn was climbing the stairs. "I'm sorry. I'm such an—"

"Don't apologize." Syn angled them through the doorway. The sound of the inside door would have set off warning bells if her brain was working properly.

"I'll put you to bed. Do you have something to take for the headache?"

"Somewhere."

"Would you mind if I looked for it? I think it'll help you."

"You don't have to." *I don't need you seeing me like this.* She thanked the severity of the hangover that spared her utter embarrassment, however temporarily. When she woke up sober, that embarrassment would hit her tenfold, as well as the probability that Syn would never want to see her again. "It's my problem."

"Nonsense. I would never leave someone is such a state."

Either he moved as fast as he did gracefully or she was so badly off she couldn't judge the distance they traveled until Syn settled her in her bed. The motion as gentle as it was tender, the man who claimed responsibility for her adjusted her with such care she wondered if he thought he'd break her. In the back of her mind, she knew she shouldn't have allowed him into her private sanctuary. She had no chance to defend herself.

But...

Syn was different. Her intuition whispered that as truth. Her body burned with a potent force despite the headache. Those few moments when she was cradled in his arms she felt as though it were right where she was always supposed to be.

Silly. Foolish. You're not hungover. You're still drunk.

Syn pulled the blanket up to her shoulders and slowly brushed hair from her eyes. "I'll be right back. Stay put so you don't make it worse."

She had no problem with that. The very act of breathing sent spikes through her head. Sleep would be a blessing, even if it meant she'd lose her chance to enjoy Syn's company. Instead, she found herself counting each pulse in her skull, willing them to stop.

A faint scrape at the bedside drew her attention. A warm finger traced her cheek, followed by a hand slipping beneath her head. She opened her eyes.

"Here. Take these."

Syn supported her head as he lifted it off the pillow. She gazed at the two pills in his hand through squinted eyes. Satisfied that they were simple over-the-counter pills and not some other drug, she popped them into her mouth and washed them down with a small sip of hot coffee.

"I need water."

"Drink some of the coffee first. It'll get those pills working faster. I brought a glass of water in for you, too."

She twisted her head enough to see the glass on the nightstand, then took another sip of coffee. Her stomach rebelled against the strong, bitter taste. "It's awful."

"It's black. I expect it would be awful."

Despite herself, she managed a short, quiet laugh, took another sip of the terrible brew, and allowed Syn to lower her head to the pillow.

"Thank you," she murmured.

"No thanks necessary." His thumb rubbed a delightful circle around her temple. The motion, slow, methodical, worked magic that had her drifting off to sleep within minutes.

"My sweet. Sleep and you will feel no pain."

In those seconds before Briella opened the door, he sensed something wrong. It crept over him, sour and dark. His scales prickled along his arms, thankfully covered by his jacket. He couldn't decipher what exactly was wrong until he set eyes on the sexiest bed-ruffled woman he'd seen in his life. It took him a short moment to get his bearings and realize the 'wrong' was her immense hangover. He could see it in her eyes, the pain she suffered.

Syn listened to the soft, even breaths coming from the woman tucked beneath a steel gray comforter. He watched the gentle rise and fall of her chest and the tension released from her muscles as she drifted deeper into sleep. He continued the tender massage at her temples, taking in the smooth features of her creamy skin, her pert nose and full lips. Dark lashes cast shadows over her pale cheeks, long and thick beneath the gentle arch of her dark-red brows.

When he was certain she was asleep, Syn sat back in the chair beside the bed and stared at the beauty. His body burned from carrying her. A pleasant, if not maddening, burn that smoldered beneath his skin. The woman fit too perfectly in his arms, felt too right against his chest, just as she had last night. He hungered to taste her, even if only a chaste kiss.

His relentless dragon didn't help his calm.

Time ticked by. Syn kept vigil over Briella to ensure her sleep was sound and peaceful. Aside from the motions of her breathing, she did not move. He gauged the time by the shadows the sun cast throughout the studio apartment.

One of her paintings caught his attention.

Syn left Briella's bedside, his attention on the canvas perched on one of three easels. He'd been too worried about Briella to take notice of the artwork spread around the room. Dark, shadowy, obscured, and ominous artwork with flickers of hope and happiness.

Syn approached the easel, his eyes narrowing on the image. He'd never realized how many hues of gray were possible, but every brushstroke lent the work a deeper layer, a definitive shape.

That shape?

Is this how you saw me, my sweet? As a threat?

He pressed his lips together, unsure of how to take the blurred image of himself from the other night. There was no doubt the man tucked in shadows with a wet hoodie was him.

Briella had painted his eyes on fire.

She had seen the dragon after she used that damn stun gun on him.

Syn rolled his shoulders as he processed the obstacles that would present. This painting, far from done, was proof that she perceived him as an enemy.

The tone was dark and threatening, filled with an essence of danger.

"I would never hurt you, Briella," he said softly to the painting. "Never."

Syn tore his attention from the disturbing painting and admired her other works. Everything she painted had a gray and obscured feel to it, but each piece was breathtaking and magnificent. His lifemate had true talent, a talent that sucked him into each painting far longer than anything had before. They appeared blurred, like she saw images through a dark, shadowy veil without fine definition or detail. An idea, a suggestion of form and emotion.

She deserved the gallery exhibit she'd been offered. She deserved so much more.

That thought twisted something in the back of his mind. A haunting resonance. Another obstacle.

They dragons and Keepers were returning to The Hollow. And there were no art galleries there.

He longed to return to his home. As he studied Briella's masterpieces, he realized the callousness of thinking she'd come with him without complaint.

He'd be ripping her from the only world she knew, away from her hopes and her dreams.

That's the problem. Any female born outside The Hollow knows nothing beyond this world, this realm. Each of us will be tearing them out of their comfortable lives and forcing them to live in ours.

What a damn mess. It was no one's fault except for the Baroqueth that attacked them all those years ago.

Syn watched the sleeping woman and sighed. He'd found his lifemate. There was no way in hell he was losing her. He'd do whatever it took to make her happy.

Finding Briella was a gift, but it also begged the question of whether his Keeper, Giovani Everett, still lived. And if he did, where was he? Had Saralyn survived the attack? Was Briella the product of their love before death and destruction tore their lives to shreds? He thought so.

Syn recognized Giovani in Briella. Her bright gray eyes with the hint of blue. The arch of her brows. The angle of her nose and the shape of her lips. But the delicacy of her features were a far cry from his Keeper's rougher features. They definitely resembled Saralyn's feminine beauty.

Hope burst to life inside him. The very idea that Giovani and his dear Saralyn survived the attack was nothing shy of a miracle. Most of the Keepers hadn't settled down in committed relationships prior to the ambush. Giovani and Saralyn were an exception.

After another check on Briella and a glance at the time, Syn slipped into the stairwell. He took out his cell phone and dialed Cade.

The *tatsu* leader answered on the first ring with a deep, gruff, "Syn. Where are you?"

"New Orleans. Came here to meet up with Taryn about some questionable activity," Syn answered, his voice low. He pulled the door at the top of the stairs mostly closed, leaving it open a crack so he could hear if his lifemate began to stir.

"What have you found?"

"Oh, there's certainly activity. More than I bargained for." A grin crept over his mouth. "They're snooping around the city, and one particular woman."

Silence answered him for a long moment.

"Another Keeper female?" Cade finally asked.

"Yes." Briella's image scorched through him, leaving him hard and hot. A possessive growl in his voice, he said, "Mine."

"Giovani?"

"I don't know his whereabouts. I made contact with her two nights ago, after a Baroqueth broke into her apartment while she was out. I haven't had a chance to question her."

"Does she have your dragonstone?"

Syn straightened. It hadn't occurred to him the Baroqueth might have ransacked her apartment in search of his dragonstone. It was part of him, and linked him and his Keeper through blood. The magic and power contained in the jewel was highly sought by the Baroqueth.

The dragonstone was a key to life and a promise of death.

"I haven't noticed it. Haven't felt it nearby. I'll ask about it when she wakes," Syn said. The jewel had been dormant since the day before the attack. If he were in close proximity to it, the pull of its magic would have connected with his dragon. "I've been monitoring her, watching her. I'm hoping to open up some doors later today."

"Have the Baroqueth been tracking her since the break-in?"

"I feel their presence, but I haven't seen them again. Taryn's been keeping the area under surveillance as well. As soon as I have more details, I'll let you know."

"I'm going to send Emery and Gabe to you. I don't trust they are in New Orleans without numbers. I suspect there are a few dozen Baroqueth stalking us, and who knows how many humans they've convinced to help in their cause. With their ability to call on magic when we cannot, we need to be diligent."

Syn grunted. Another reason he wanted to return to The Hollow. The human realm stripped dragons of most of their magic and power. Other than their brute strength, keen senses, the diamond shield of their scales, and their fire, they were at a severe disadvantage when it came to facing the Baroqueth.

He couldn't protect Briella the way he needed to in this realm. With the growing threat from their enemies, the chances of the dragons and Keepers surviving another major encounter dwindled.

He heard the bed creak. He eased the door open enough to see Briella's form outlined beneath the blanket. Thank Goddess, because if she was going to walk around in that skimpy little tank top and those breezy pants that teased him with the outline of her legs, he was going to die a death far more brutal than one at the hands of the Baroqueth.

"I'll be checking in on Zareh and Kaylae later this week. I need to convince them to return to The Hollow before she's too far along in her pregnancy to fly safely," Cade said. "In the meantime, we need to locate Giovani, if he's alive. And we need to find your dragonstone."

"Trust me, I'm well aware I need to find it."

"Hey, Syn? Does she know who you are? *What* you are?"

Syn's mind flashed to the incomplete painting. "I don't know, but she's going to find out soon enough. Our time is running out here."

"It is. If you need anything, call. Otherwise, I'll be seeing you soon."

Syn disconnected the call and slipped his phone in his pocket before he returned to the apartment. Keeping quiet, he went to the kitchen and started rifling through the fridge and pantry. Briella was certain to wake up starving. She'd need something hearty to wipe out any residual hangover. Syn couldn't imagine her staying asleep much longer than two hours.

Cooking quietly proved to be a challenge. Pots and pans were haphazardly piled in one cabinet, dishware in another, utensils cluttered in three separate drawers. He chuckled at the disorganization. Briella was as intriguing as she was stunning. Part of her apartment was neat and tidy, part a sheer disaster. Each a compliment to the other.

He managed to whip up a plate of eggs, sausage, hashbrowns, and toast without making too much of a ruckus. The glances he cast Briella assured him he hadn't disturbed her through the process. He covered the plate with another to keep the food warm.

Something sharp poked the nape of his neck. He straightened, keeping his head still, and smiled when the tip of the weapon pressed hard to his skin, right below his skull. Instinctively, his dragon readied a row of scales below the surface of his skin to protect his brain.

"What do you want with me?" Briella asked, her voice icy cold and edged with ruthless warning. "Why have you been following me?"

Syn's brow furrowed. Okay, now he was confused. Maybe she wasn't messing around with him, as he initially thought.

"I made you something to eat," he said, deflecting the questions. "You're going to need —"

He winced when the point of something that felt dangerous dug into his neck. It didn't hurt, but Briella's no-nonsense approach was more than he pegged her for. It was a heady characteristic from the small redhead, and amped up his arousal at an inconvenient time.

"Shut up and answer my question before I silence you for good."

Hot damn. Her fire was alluring.

"What makes you think I've been following you? I found you from your license in the clutch."

She jabbed at his neck.

He hissed. In one sleek motion, he spun around, grabbed the cane-like object, and tugged her into him. The scowl on her lush lips tempted him more than the anger and skepticism in her eyes.

"Now, let's be civil," Syn said. With one sharp twist, he relieved her of the object and cast it into the main room. It clattered across the floor. Not missing a beat, Briella snatched the dirty pan he had used to cook her meal and raised it. Syn groaned, caught her wrist and, once again, twisted the object from her grip. "Briella, enough. Why do you think I've been following you?"

"I heard you," she all but spat. Syn refused to release her wrists from his single-handed bind. He dropped the pan in the sink and raised a brow at her. Her eyes flashed with fury. "Whoever you were talking to, I *heard* you."

"You heard me talk or heard me think?" He relaxed when her mouth fell open and her eyes widened. Lowering her arms, he grinned. "You heard my thoughts because you couldn't have heard me speak. I made certain of it."

"*You* broke into my apartment, didn't you? *You* tried to accost me on the sidewalk." She tugged furiously against his grip. If her accusations didn't stoke his frustration, and he was not certain he wouldn't face another dangerous implement in a fraction of a second, he would have released her. Or maybe not. He rather liked the skin-to-skin connection and the heat that flowed between them. "What were you looking for, you bastard? What do you want?"

"First, I did *not* break into your apartment, nor did I accost you."

She gave her pinned wrists a pointed and peeved look. He growled and released her, watching for any sign she was going to try to attack him again. To his surprise, she merely took a step back, her gaze lancing him with cold steel gray.

"Who. Are. You."

Her demand was spoken in a low and lethal tone. There was nothing weak or vulnerable about Briella Everett. Pride swelled within his chest. He'd always liked strong women, but the strength she exuded was sweeter than ambrosia.

"Syn Terravon."

"That's not what I meant."

He leaned back against the counter and crossed his ankles. Might as well get comfortable. "What do you mean, exactly?"

"I heard you talking about trying to find something here and your time was running out." She absently rubbed her wrists. He hadn't held her tightly enough to hurt her, but the motion made him aware of how she perceived him. The blatant distrust in her expression was a sucker punch to the gut, as was the slight shift of her gaze to the left before returning to him. *She lies.* Well, what more did he expect? "You set this all up."

Syn shook his head. "I had no way of knowing you would leave your belongings at the bar, but it opened up an opportunity to get to know you."

Her eyes narrowed. "Bullshit."

"Actually, no. Not really." He reached over to pick up the covered plate of food. He removed the top plate and set the meal on the small, two-person table against the wall. "Eat. From the shape you were in a short time ago, I'll assume your stomach is feeling quite off."

"What are you talking about? And do you really think I'm going to trust you didn't drug my food?"

"Well"—Syn waved a hand toward the bed—"you certainly weren't quick to refuse a couple of pills from me a little while ago. If I were planning to drug you, Briella, I would've done it when I had the chance. When you were at your most vulnerable. I have no intention of drugging you, accosting you, threatening you, or bringing any harm to you."

Shadows crossed her eyes. The fight drained out of her by degrees. She glanced at the plate of food. Whether she consciously licked her lips or not, the innocent motion damn near ripped his lungs from his chest.

Briella eyed him suspiciously as she slowly moved toward the table.

"I'm *not* going to harm you," Syn said, softening his voice as best he could. He hoped she saw the sincerity in his expression, his eyes. Anything. "You have my word."

"Words mean little."

"Perhaps from those you've encountered to this point, but when I give someone my word, it's binding."

"Chivalric."

He chuckled at her sarcasm. She flashed him another one of those sexy scowls he found utterly tempting and sat down. Never once did the tension flee her shoulders. She sat awkwardly, keeping her body angled in his direction.

For a few minutes, Briella scrutinized him. Syn let her look him over and ponder as long as she wanted.

Her direct attention was fascinating and delightful. Every time her gaze moved, flames raked along the same path, an unseen torture that stirred and stoked both his hunger and his dragon. He tasted the hints of smoke and fire at the back of his throat and swallowed the evidence of his true form down. Now wasn't the time to disclose who he really was.

No, that time would be soon enough.

For now, he'd enjoy not having to share her attention with a to-remain-nameless male.

"Eat before it gets cold," he urged gently.

"Sit and I'll eat," she countered. "No way am I turning my back on you."

"Fair enough." Syn crossed the small space between them and lowered himself into the chair opposite Briella. He had to make an effort not to let his gaze wander over her slender shoulders or that tank-top-clad torso. "I'm sitting."

"*You* are out of line." Briella stabbed a fork into several different items on her plate, her gaze flicking between Syn and the food. Her frustration came out with each and every sharp jab and scrape of metal against ceramic. "You have some balls bossing me around in *my* apartment."

"My apologies if you saw my actions as such." He relaxed in the chair, placing his hands on the tabletop where she could see them. Any and everything he could do to make himself less…intimidating. He was a dragon, after all. Intimidating came with the package. "I think you might have done the same if you were in my position."

Briella's eyes narrowed further. "Why did you stay? Why didn't you leave? What were you looking for here?"

Syn shrugged. "You were in no shape to be left alone. And I wasn't looking for anything, although I will admit to snooping around your paintings. They're quite remarkable."

His compliment appeared to thaw the ice around the edges of her expression. She lowered her gaze and assessed the forkful of food.

"I don't appreciate people snooping around my work." She sniffed the food. "But thank you for the kind words."

"You really don't trust the food. I'll make you another plate and you can watch, if that'll make you more comfortable."

Briella shook her head. She held out the fork to him. "You take the first bite."

Syn obliged. He held her gaze as he took the fork and brought it to his lips. A faint blush rose across her cheeks as he took the food from the fork and chewed it leisurely before handing the fork back. That blush spread down her pale neck and got lost in the thick waves of dark red hair that curled around her shoulders and collarbone. Soft, silky waves that drew his eyes to the lacy hem above her subtle cleavage.

He swallowed his bite of food. Almost choked.

"All good," he said, his voice thick and raspy.

She waited several long minutes. Apparently satisfied when he didn't keel over, she scooped up a small amount of eggs. Syn barely realized his fingers had begun to curl into fists when her full lips pursed before she slipped that fork between them. Thank Goddess for the table. He had no control over other parts of his anatomy.

Briella swallowed and nodded. "Not bad."

"Glad you approve."

She made a sound, something that may have been a snort if it wasn't so delicate. "I make better."

"Next time, I'll let you do the cooking."

Her eyes snapped up to him again. He offered a smile.

"You seem so sure there will be a next time." She scooped up another fork of food. "You seem so sure of a lot of things."

"Perhaps I am."

"Such as?"

Syn leaned forward on his elbows. He folded his hands together, his smile growing. He cast the unfinished painting a curious glance before shifting his attention back to Briella.

"Tell me about your paintings. Tell me about the voices you hear in your head."

CHAPTER 7

Briella fumbled the fork, but managed to lower it to the plate without looking like a fool. The succulent scent of the meal enticed her, but her stomach, already queasy from her binge at the bar, revolted at the thought of food as the weight of Syn's request settled universe-heavy on her shoulders.

"I'm going to make tea. Want a cup?" she asked, trying to distract herself from his probing gaze and the uncanny warmth that filled every inch of her body as he stared at her. She climbed to her feet and filled the kettle with water. "Or coffee?"

"Whatever is easiest for you."

His voice matched his name in every possible way—sinful, from the rich, deep tone to the slight accent. She couldn't pin that down, but it rolled from his lips so smooth and sexy and definitely worked an unseen magic on her.

Magic. There was something very magical about Syn. Magical and fierce. That much she was sure of, but she was not going to be quick to fall for his charm.

Your good looks aren't going to buy you respect, buddy.

Good was a poor descriptor for Syn's appeal. He was drop-dead gorgeous. She recalled noting his handsomeness the night before, but today, mind a little more clear, eyes a little less impaired, he made her heart stutter and her breaths come in unsteady gasps. His scent alone coaxed her closer, soothed her doubt until she vividly imagined herself shamelessly sidled up against the man. That mixture of spice and campfire and the cool cast of wind. Never in her life had she experienced an addiction beyond that of painting, but Syn?

For crying out loud, you barely know him. She shook her head as she pulled two mugs from a cabinet and set them on the counter. *You know nothing about him.*

He surrounded her. The power of his presence alone assured her she was safe. A stranger. She would have balked at the idea had it not been rooted so deep in her subconscious.

Still, the things she heard him say and think made her mind wage war with her body's reaction to him. There was no discounting the stream of visions she suffered when their fingers brushed. There was no denying he was the man who stopped her on the sidewalk. The man she shocked. There would have been no link, no evidence, in that simple touch otherwise.

She rapped her fingers against the counter. Her gaze pulled toward the painting. The moment she got home, the ache to paint sprang to life with such a ferocious demand there was no denying it. She barely saw what she created, her fingers and wrist working at the instruction of something far stronger than her own imagination.

The haunting voice from that terrifying night, the same voice that struck her after the touch, resounded in her head.

"Get her when she returns."

One thing she knew for certain—that voice did not match Syn's. But either Syn was the bad guy, or the bad guy was an unknown entity she had yet to come in contact with.

Scalding heat tingled along her spine. It streamed down each vertebra in thin, sensual ribbons until it pooled low in her belly. A deft pulse followed, then a flush of warmth coasted up to her face. Her knees melted. She leaned against the counter to keep from swaying.

Damn the man for being so…so…

She shook her head again.

Get your bearings, Brie. You have a damn stranger sitting at your kitchen table. This is about as careless as careless gets. Mom would have a coronary.

She'd kick herself in the butt for this oops later. Hopefully there would *be* a later and she wasn't about to take tea with a murderer.

The whistle on the kettle began to pitch. She poured out two cups of bubbling water and dunked a tea bag in each mug.

"Do you take milk? Sugar?" Briella asked, keeping her gaze averted. She feared her inability to mask the arousal she suffered in Syn's presence, now that her anger and adrenaline had abandoned her. "Honey? Lemon?"

"Why don't I help you?"

She spun to face him, eyes wide. When did he come up behind her like that? And without a sound? Or was she so far gone in her thoughts she hadn't heard him?

Either way, her mouth dried and her body zinged with recognition as Syn reached past her to pick up the mugs. His eyes locked on hers. Eyes that held no fire, but a stunning dark brown that lightened to amber and gold around his dilated pupils. His nostrils flared and his jaw shifted beneath the neat trim of his scruff. It was far from a beard—she wasn't a beard girl anyhow.

Her gaze lowered to his mouth. Her breath hitched and her vision spun. Clearly, her reaction to him the night before had nothing to do with how many drinks she had consumed. Her reaction was primitive and visceral. Her body and her soul knew him, understood him, connected with him on an unseen plane, a place where she longed to be.

Her fingers curled. In his shirt. Heaven help her, when had she reached one hand up to touch his shoulder? And was that all…muscle?

"Briella," he murmured, his voice spreading down her nerves, caressing every ache into a frenzy. His hand molded against the side of her face, warm and rough and strong. His thumb lifted her chin and tilted her head back. Her eyelids fell shut, her body becoming near flaccid. Her heart thundered and raced, making her dizzy. "Sweet."

The heat of his breath preceded the fiery touch of his lips across hers. An airy brush. A test. A tease. A key that unlocked every wild and sensual need dormant in the deepest recesses of her soul. She leaned into him, his arm slipped around her waist and drew her close. She didn't want to touch him. Didn't want him to think he could have his way…

He kissed her again, chaste, sweet and tender. His lips lingered.

Her plan to not touch him backfired. A palm splayed against the hard ridges of his abdomen. The hand curled around his shirt at his shoulder, flattened and found its way to the back of his neck. Her fingers tingled, her arms lost their strength. She trembled beneath this taunting kiss.

Syn combed his fingers into her hair, tipped her head back a little more, and kissed her the way she badly needed. His tongue slipped past her pliant lips and swept into her mouth, filling her with the heady taste of man and fire. His kiss sang to her soul. The hint of possession behind each lazy sweep poured into a void that opened when he touched her. A void in the center of her heart that grew and grew until *he* did his magic to fill it up.

Briella drew up onto her toes, demanding a little more of his kiss with a quiet moan. He delivered, from completely possessing her mouth and her mind to pinning her to the counter, their bodies flush. Oh, sweet glory, having Syn so damn close, feeling every little—*Oh, definitely* not *so little*—detail of his arousal. If she ever fit so perfectly with a man, it was here, now.

Lost. She was completely and entirely lost to Syn.

A buzz shattered the euphoria that had built to suffocating proportions. Syn stole one last kiss before Briella lowered her head to catch her breath and find her flagging control.

Her gaze landed on his hand, gripping the edge of the counter like his life depended on it.

And dark, curved—

Briella shrieked, shoving Syn away. "Holy shit!"

She stumbled from the kitchen, still dizzy and weak and utterly stripped of fight. Her eyes widened and she gasped when she caught Syn's gaze.

Fire. Liquid flames consumed the man's irises.

"You-you're...you're..." Briella slapped a hand over her mouth, blocking the stuttering words. Holy crap, the room spun. Her legs threatened to give out beneath her weight. That hand, those *claws*, still bit into the countertop.

The edges of her vision grayed.

Don't do it. Don't pass out. Don't, don't, don't...

The doorbell buzzed again, the sound hollow and distant.

"Damn it," Syn snapped.

One moment, there were feet between them. The next, he cradled her against him, both of them sitting on the floor.

Tremors rattled her muscles and made her teeth chatter, but she still managed to bite out, "Dragon."

Those fiery eyes flooded her mind. The rain pricked at her skin as she bolted into her apartment.

"Briella, listen to me."

"You *did* attack me."

Tea with a murderer.

"No. I tried to stop you from coming in here."

Realization chilled the arousal. "You've been watching me." She tried to shove away from Syn, but his arms remained steadfast around her. "Stalking me."

"I've been watching *over* you. Protecting you. You're in danger and you haven't any idea what that danger is."

"Yes." She growled in frustration and outrage and put all her strength behind her next shove. She deliberately slammed the heel of her palm against the hard mound in his jeans. He barked a shout of pain, released her, and she scooted away. Instantly, her soul ached at the separation and she felt guilty for causing him harm. *You're so screwed.* "I do. And I understand deception, as well."

She scrambled to her feet and jerked open the door at the top of the stairs. Syn swiped for her as he shot up off the floor, and missed. She barreled down the stairs.

"Don't open it!"

Like hell she wouldn't. She had a dragon at her back. The last thing she planned to do was *listen* to it.

She snapped back the bolt lock and threw the door open.

Steel slammed into her back, bringing her to the floor in the corner of the entryway. A dull crash echoed around her as the force of the weight pressing her down into a ball snarled and she realized Syn had tackled her. Her bare arms slid against hard, hot metal, or what she thought was metal.

The weight lifted and she flipped onto her ass. Shock jolted through her as she watched a man as large as Syn lunge up the front steps behind a slender man holding a sizzling orb of blue light.

She gasped.

What the...?

The orb-wielding stranger pitched the ball of light toward her and vanished as Syn and the other big man grabbed for him.

She shrieked, ducked. There was a booming sound. The plaster over her head cracked, powder and larger pieces sprinkling down on her hair and shoulders.

When she straightened, she came face-to-face with the man who'd thrown the orb at her, a grin so cold spreading his thin lips that she could feel her blood chill beneath his fathomless black gaze. Specks of silver danced in his eyes like the tips of knives waiting to spit into her skin. She goggled. She could have sworn he'd blinked out of sight and back again.

"Dear little Keeper," he said, his voice as icy as his gaze. Every bit of knowledge about self-defense fled her as she pressed into the corner of the wall.

Abruptly, something flung the man off his feet. His body smashed into the ceiling and dropped down.

A whimper escaped her as she watched Syn catch the guy by his throat, claws extended from the tips of his fingers and drawing blood. Unnaturally dark streams of liquid trickled down the man's neck to disappear under the collar of his shirt.

"Leave her alone," Syn warned. Briella shuddered. If she thought the stranger chilled her, the threat in Syn's voice could have frozen Hell.

"Or what, Dragon? You have no power in this world, only your scales. And what happens when they fail?"

Slowly, Briella pressed up from the floor, keeping her back hard against the wall. The trickle of blood flowed faster as Syn's claws burrowed deeper into her assailant's throat. The amused look on the man's face faltered and his eyes widened.

"I'm not as generous as my brothers. I *will* kill you and whoever else you bring to threaten what is mine."

A hand fell on Syn's arm and squeezed. Briella's stricken attention jerked to the other guy, who eyed her curiously before he said to Syn, "Not now, brother."

Syn kept his hold for several long breaths before he snapped his arm back, releasing his captive.

In front of Brie's disbelieving eyes, the man with the bloodied neck began to fade out of sight—until the man who'd called Syn brother snatched him in the same hold Syn had released him from. He snapped something shiny around the man's neck. "I don't have to protect anyone's sensibilities, so let me finish what he started." The guy winked at Syn, flashed Briella a big smile, and dragged the magic man through the door. She heard him say, "I have a witch friend looking for a guinea pig. Guess you'll have to do."

Breath labored, her mind spinning in shock, Briella stared through her front door as the big man dragged the orb-wielder down the short pathway to the iron gate. A few pedestrians stared, confused, as the two men moved past them, then turned their attention to Briella's garden and to where she stood, clearly visible in her skimpy clothes, just inside her doorway.

She instantly wrapped her arms around her body. Syn slammed the door shut and reached toward her.

"Stay the hell away," she warned. He obliged and stepped back.

"I want to make sure you're okay."

"You're kidding, right?"

Briella looked at him. More specifically, his arms and hands. The claws had retracted. His tanned skin was marred by points of burnished red that slowly disappeared. His eyes—sweet heaven, those eyes—glowed like coals, defining very vertical slits for pupils.

"You can't stay here." If a man could speak and growl in the same breath, Syn perfected that sound. She hated that it played teasingly along the vulnerable nerves that hummed from their kiss. She had just been attacked by a light-holding stranger who could disappear in a blink, and saved by a dragon. She had to get a grip on her libido. "I think we should have an overdue conversation."

Briella observed the indentations in the two walls and the ceiling. Plaster continued to float in a choking cloud of powder. "You think?"

The high pitch of her voice made her brows furrow.

She looked back at Syn in time to see his eyes transform from those of a mythological creature to the enchanting dark brown with those strange rings of amber and gold. He remained at the foot of the stairs, his dark gray shirt dusted with white plaster, a thin coating lightening his hair.

"Care to tell me what fucking portal I just stepped through?" Briella shook out her hair and huffed a breath to get the mussed strands out of her face. She rubbed her nose. The dust made it itch. "'Cause this isn't where I started my day."

"You started your day hung over, but that's beside the point. I want to make one thing exceptionally clear to you, Briella." The seriousness in his tone held her still. "I am *not* your enemy. That sorcerer was, and there are many more where he came from. They're hunting you, hunting me, and will not stop until they have what they want most."

"Dare I ask?"

"Dare or not, this is your life. A life they want to steal from you."

"And you're protecting me. I find that hard to believe." Though the idea of having Syn as her bodyguard was far from distasteful. "I'm twenty-nine years old. I've never been in danger in my life. This was a fluke."

"It doesn't get more premeditated. Your apartment was broken into. They were searching for something. Perhaps a stone or a jewel." He paused and Briella had a suspicion he was waiting for her to react. Well, she had no idea what jewel he was talking about. "You are the icing on the cake, so to speak, and they want you as much as the next female."

"Great, go from chivalric to chauvinistic." She scowled. "There are plenty of females for them to choose from. I'm off limits. I'm not weak. I can protect myself."

Syn's expression hardened. He leaned toward her, thrusting an arm toward the door. "You were as good as dead the moment you opened that door."

"But I'm not," she snapped.

"Because of *me*."

Briella snorted, then laughed. "Man." She shook her head. "Apparently, I'm in this *because* of you." The cold laughter died on her lips and she pierced Syn with her frustration. "Look at my place. Look at what you've brought in here. Just look, Syn, and tell me what the hell I'm supposed to believe."

"I did not bring that slayer into your home, Briella. I tailed him. He found you and, luckily, I wasn't far behind. It's evident you have no idea what pursues you, or the dangers that follow who and what you are."

Briella jammed her fists on her hips and glowered. "Tell me, Syn. *What* exactly am I?"

Syn stared at her, unblinking. But in those few breaths, she watched the hardened man soften. It was barely discernable, but his shoulders relaxed a fraction, and the residual glow of his eyes faded. His jaw stopped grinding.

At last, he tilted his head a little. *"You're in line to be my Keeper. But most importantly, you're my lifemate."*

Briella tried her hardest to muster another disbelieving laugh, but something in his words hit an unknown target within her memory. That he spoke directly *into* her mind didn't upset her as much as that niggling feeling she had heard that term used before. She sought the truth of his claim. Keeper. Didn't the light wielder call her that? And now a dragon man insisted she was this Keeper person.

No, she had heard the term used before. Not recently, but somewhere in her past.

The dangerous turn of Syn's demeanor began to ease. He brushed a hand over his hair, sending another fresh coat of powder and plaster chips plinking to the floor. He dusted off his shoulders. Briella could do nothing more than watch his fluid motions while she desperately tried to make sense of the last ten minutes.

Try the last two days.

"I can help you pack—"

"Like hell you will. I'm not going anywhere." There was no fight behind her words. Syn sighed, his eyes turning up to the ruined ceiling. As if *she* was the unreasonable one. She scowled. "And now I should probably get on the phone with the landlord and a handyman to fix this mess."

"Briella, I'll fix it. It's not on you. But right now I need you to come with me."

She should have swatted his hand away, but the second his fingers touched her face, she lost the drive to fight him. The strong woman inside her groused and grumbled, but the tender motion, the gentle sweep of his fingertips over her brow and along her cheek, turned her into a pansy fool.

His touch *calmed* her.

"Bring all the weapons you want. Bring *anything* you want. I'll help you pack, but we need to get out of here."

"And go where?"

"Taryn, the man who took the sorcerer, has a place on Esplanade. Not far from here. Plenty of bedrooms. You can have one to yourself." His thumb caressed the corner of her mouth before he lowered his arm to his side. "I'm sorry if what I thought of as protecting you was misinterpreted as something malicious. I'm not entirely in sync with the do's and don'ts of this world. My concern is you, and whatever I need to do to keep you safe."

Briella promised herself a really good ass-kicking when her brain emerged from the fog. She was taking a practical stranger at his word. Didn't matter how right it felt. For now, Syn's promises were everything she wanted to hear from a man, and it was somewhat lowering to realize how quickly he'd won her over. The sincerity in his voice and expression was genuine. There was not a nudge of doubt anywhere in her intuition to say otherwise. If anything, her damn mind was practically throwing her at him.

Moistening her lips, she nodded once. "Okay." Her shoulders dropped. "Okay. I'll come with you, but I can't leave any of my paintings. And I don't have a car."

"I borrowed Taryn's pickup. We have plenty of room."

She lifted her arms slightly and sighed. "I need to shower first."

"Tell me what I can start packing, and I'll get moving on that while you shower."

She lifted her eyes to his again. Her body yearned to weaken a little more, just enough to allow herself to step forward and lean into Syn's warmth and strength. She was all about excitement, but this was stretching her boundaries.

Syn's mouth curled in a sympathetic half-grin. *"I know this is hard. You're not going to go it alone, sweet. I promise you."*

"Aaaand you can speak to me telepathically," she muttered.

"Yes."

"Can you hear thoughts, too?"

"Yes. But I haven't invaded your privacy." Syn pressed his lips together. "Your gift is the gift of Keepers. A survival mechanism. But I'll get into all of that when I get you settled at Taryn's place." He held out his hand. She didn't hesitate to take it. The spirits knew she needed some sort of support right about now. Why not from Syn? "Come on. I don't trust we'll be safe for long."

Briella followed Syn up the stairs. There was a feeling of disconnect for the first time since she moved to New Orleans. Her apartment, a place she fell instantly in love with, no longer held the comfort and energy it did a half-hour ago. It felt strange, cold, remote.

"If you want, you can pack my paintings. I have boxes folded away in the closet over there." Briella pointed to an accordion door. "There're sheets in there as well to protect each canvas. I have two storage containers for the paints and brushes. Most are kept in there, but I have a few out from last night that need to be stored. I'll pack up my clothes after my shower."

She released her hand from Syn's and started toward her partitioned-off room. "Can you give me your friend's address?"

Syn obliged. She picked up her clutch from the nightstand where Syn must have placed it earlier, a fresh set of clothes, and tucked herself behind the closed and locked door of the bathroom.

Whatever new world she'd tumbled into between last night and now, she wasn't going alone. She sent a quick group message to her friends, informing them she had to go to a new place while issues were tended to at her apartment. She promised to fill everyone in later.

After she turned on the shower, she found one primary contact on her phone who she both dreaded and missed. She was about to open a whole can of worms, but she had no choice. There were only two people in the world she trusted one hundred percent.

Taking a deep breath, she typed in a short text, address and all, and hit Send.

The universe had seams that could tear open, and she was about to watch that event unfold, front and center.

CHAPTER 8

Briella's tension didn't escape him. He choked on the density of her nervousness the entire ride to Taryn's place a few blocks away. Not even the sweet jasmine from her body wash or the lavender essence wafting from her hair could cut through the thickening tension.

Syn turned the truck down a crossroad and slowed. "Do you want something to eat? You haven't had much."

Briella shook her head, the motion stiff. His gaze dropped to her hands, fingers knotted tightly in her lap, knuckles white.

"A coffee?"

Another head shake. This time, she followed it up with an uncertain chew of her lower lip. He tore his attention from the sight, the vivid reminder of what those lips tasted like surpassing the discomfort and igniting a poorly timed adjunct to the tension.

"You'll be okay," he tried to reassure her.

"I'm being stupid."

His brows shot up. "How's that? You're not going to be alone. That's not stupid. That's smart."

A sharp sound blew past her lips, a cross between a half-second laugh and a snort. "I'm with a complete stranger. I'm going to stay in a house with two complete strangers, two men. Any logical woman would run."

"Logic doesn't play a role when it comes to the paranormal."

"Umph." Her fingers tightened more. He feared she'd break those precious digits if she continued to twist them. "Apparently neither does respect for one's preferred lifestyle. I have things, big things, happening to me right now and my entire world has been invaded, dissected, and destroyed in the matter of a day."

Yeah. He couldn't deny that. And the upset was far from over.

"The only reason I agreed to this is because you're a dragon."

Briella had more to say, but those unspoken words hung on the heavy silence that stretched between them.

"I think *that* reason surprises me more than anything. Most people would run in the opposite direction, which leads me to believe you know a little about our kind," Syn surmised. He hoped the opening would lead her to tell him what she knew, and whether her father still lived.

Instead, he felt the heat of her gaze move over him, starting at his face, lowering like a warm caress to his hips, and lifting back to his mouth. His lips burned beneath her attention and a surge of renewed desire flooded him.

"Believe what you want."

"You're not going to tell me anything, are you."

"You haven't told me much, but you've done plenty."

"If you're implying the kiss—"

"Not happening again."

A satisfied grin crossed his mouth. She could deny it all she wanted, but he sensed her desire was as raw and potent as his own. Their attraction went beyond sparks and straight to explosive.

First, they had a foundation to build and information to share, if she was open to sharing.

"I'll be sure to hold you to it."

Two can play this game.

He pulled up to Taryn's house, climbed out to unlock and open the gate, and parked the truck beneath the carport. Briella was half out of the truck by the time he cut the engine. Silence continued to stretch between them. He refrained from trying to break it. Briella had shut down. He couldn't get a read from her mind. She cast him out as quickly as she had accepted his advances.

Syn closed and locked the gate. When he returned to the truck, Briella was staring at Taryn's home, her lips separated and her eyes glowing with awe. The sight of her stole his breath, the long, loose braid of dark red hair draped over her shoulder and the rose cresting her cheeks. The flouncy shirt cinched at her narrow waist emphasized her curves, as did the tight black jeans tucked into a pair of leather riding boots.

Not now.

He shook himself free of the sensual trance she induced and returned to the truck. He'd hoisted one of the boxes of Briella's paintings when she twisted away from the house, eyes narrowed on him.

"This is your friend's place? That other guy?" Briella asked.

Syn nodded. "Yeah. He's a bit extravagant."

"You don't say. These homes run in the millions!"

"I got all the details from him when I arrived here a few days ago." He jutted his chin toward the front door. "Wait 'til you see the inside."

Briella grabbed her weekender bag from the bed of the truck and followed him up the front steps. Syn rested the box between the wall and his side as he dug out the house key from his pocket and let them in.

"Oh my...*wow.*"

Briella moved into the grand living room and stopped. Syn smiled as he watched her spin in a circle, her eyes drinking in every nuance and detail of the Greek revival architecture meshed with a modern flare. The opulence of the home definitely fit Taryn's high-end tastes. A sliver of envy crept through him, and for the first time since leaving The Hollow, Syn wished he had a place of his own in this realm. A place Briella would gush over. A place she wanted to live in, with him.

"This is beautiful."

"And you haven't made it more than ten feet into the house." Syn placed the box of paintings on the floor and hitched his thumb toward the door. "Let me get the rest of your stuff inside and I'll give you a tour. I think I know something that'll really suit you."

Syn unloaded the rest of her paintings and art supplies, followed by the last two bags of her belongings. Each trip into the house, he found her moving about a different part of the ground floor, exploring the layout with growing awe. On the last trip, he closed the door and secured the lock. Briella waited for him in the dining room. She pointed to the pillars that flanked the opening between the living room and dining room.

"These are magnificent. What character. And all the molding? It's stunning."

"I have to agree. He picked a winner with this house."

Briella nodded. She did another turnabout, then met him in the living room. "You said you came here to visit. Where do you live?"

Might as well break the ice. "I kind of live the nomadic lifestyle. Since leaving my home, I haven't found a place I cared to stay more than a few months. Besides, we weren't supposed to lay down roots anywhere. It's too risky." Syn made a single circular motion with his hand. "As you can see, Taryn isn't very good at listening to instructions, but he's always been a homebody. This place has filled the gap abandoning his home created."

A spark flashed through her eyes, a thread of sympathy. "Where is your home?"

"It's called The Hollow. It's a land not of this realm, but cloaked in magic and power and untouched beauty. Nothing compares, and I've seen plenty of this world to vouch for that."

"Sounds like you're the homebody, more than your friend is." She gripped the strap of her purse and cast a glance toward the stairs. A lock of wavy hair fell over her cheek. "Is your friend aware you've invited me here?"

"He's anxious to meet you." Syn curled his fingers to keep from brushing that chunk of soft hair away from her cheek. They'd had enough bumps between them already. He didn't want to create another by being too familiar and possibly making her feel more uncomfortable around him. "So, your turn. Where are you from?"

"New York," she answered, and left it at that. The shadowed side-glance she shot him made him awfully aware of her non-specificity.

He tried again with, "What got you into painting?"

A flicker of a smile transcended her mouth before disappearing. "I needed an outlet for the voices in my head. It turned out I had a talent for it."

"That you certainly do."

"Thanks."

Again, she didn't embellish. He let it slide. There was time for digging. Time for discovering whether his Keeper lived. If Giovani was alive, everything else would fall into place.

"One of the guest rooms is upstairs. I'll bring you to it." Syn motioned with his hand toward the stairs and followed closely as she climbed to the second level. By all that was sacred, why did she have to look and smell so good? Twice, he had to pull his gaze up from her lithe legs and the outline of her ass beneath her shirt.

Twice, he swallowed back smoke that began to rise in his throat and blinked away the shift in his vision from human to dragon. All he needed was to see her thermal outline, detect even a slight increase of her temperature from normal to aroused and he'd be a gonner. "Second door on the right. It has a bathroom attached and plenty of room for you to set up an area for painting."

Briella came to the door and stepped into the airy room. Simply decorated with elegant white furniture and a full-sized canopy bed, her presence alone breathed life and excitement into the room.

Syn stamped down the image of her lying in that bed, her hair fanned out, the rich red of it a stark contrast against the pure white sheets and blanket. He grabbed hold of the doorframe and cleared the lump from his throat. Damn, this was going to be a nightmare to get through, especially if she kept the walls up between them.

"I'll thank your friend for opening his home to me. I'm sure I won't intrude for long." She turned and pinned him with a stubborn look. "I can't live in another's home for long, Syn. My place is at my apartment."

Your place is with me.

The flush along her cheekbones darkened. She'd heard him.

He offered a friendly grin.

"I think I should get my paintings up here. I need to finish up something and see if I can't get it in my show."

"You have a show?" He knew, but she didn't know that. "That doesn't surprise me, with your talent. Is it your first?"

Briella nodded. "I moved here for the opportunity. I had a connection from back home to a gallery here. That fell through, but I was referred to another gallery and offered a debut showing." She cast her eyes down to the floor. "I should really get to work."

She turned her back to him. He stepped into the hallway. "I'll bring everything up."

"Thank you."

Syn lingered in the hall for a few slow heartbeats. What he'd do to turn back time. To have introduced himself before the Baroqueth broke into her apartment. To have hidden his talons when he kissed her.

What he'd do to kiss her again, promise her the world with every sweep of his tongue. Show her she could trust him completely.

Time wasn't on their side. It was only a matter of time before one of those slayers tracked Briella to Taryn's house. When that happened, his lifemate's last roots would need to be torn from the ground if he had any hope of protecting her.

"She hasn't come out of her room in how long?" Taryn asked, handing a beer bottle to Syn. Syn thanked him, popped the metal top off with the tip of his talon, and took a hearty chug.

"Five hours."

Syn had waited patiently for Briella to emerge. He checked on her throughout the afternoon to make sure she was okay. Her answer was the same each time, muttered clearly with no attention to what she was saying other than to end the interruption. "Fine. Busy." The scrape of her brushes over canvas preceded his question and followed him down the hallway when she didn't come to the door.

He looked over the takeout containers spread across the countertop and shook his head.

"She won't come down to eat. Said she's in a zone, whatever that means."

"Any artist I know can attest to 'the zone.'" Taryn shrugged a shoulder, cast a glance at the ceiling over their heads, and flicked a wrist toward the French doors leading to the private courtyard. "She's been through a bit. She'll come down when she's ready. And don't worry about safety. I have connections, and those connections have connections who've placed some powerful wards around the property. I'll know if we're going to get ambushed long before it happens. Take a load off."

If only he could take the load of turmoil off his shoulders. That wouldn't dissipate until he broke through Briella's shell.

The soothing trickle of the courtyard fountain created a relaxing atmosphere. The subtly sweet scents of nighttime jasmine and sweet olive tree blooms filled the air. Taryn had turned the private area into an oasis filled with flowering plants, willowy trees, a square dining table with an umbrella, and wrought-iron chairs and benches arranged around the flagstone patio. Fanciful garden décor spotted the sanctuary. Moss clung sparsely along the side of the rectangular fountain base, ivy creeping up the stones and spreading along the closest vegetation.

Taryn flicked on the outdoor light strands that produced enough illumination without making it overbearing. If he thought Taryn had a romantic bone in his beast, he'd say there was definitely an air of sensuality and seduction about the space.

"How many women have fallen to your suspect charms after you brought them out here?" Syn asked, trying to lighten his own mood. He took a seat in a cushioned chair and kicked out his legs.

"And he dodges to the left, avoiding the cluster down the middle," Taryn taunted, using his beer bottle like a microphone. Syn rolled his eyes. "Brother, the last thing you need to worry about right now is my love life, but I'll put it simply enough. I've had more of the kind of fun that'll make you blush than you care to know."

"Answer enough." Syn raised his beer in mock salute. He took another long pull on the brew. At this rate, he'd finish the beer in the next couple of seconds. "And I'm not dodging."

"Avoiding. Shutting out. Ignoring. Call it what you wish. Your lifemate locks herself in one of my spare rooms for five-plus hours and I come home to find you on the verge of tearing all that pretty hair out of your head. This situation has *got* to be killing you." Taryn tilted his chair toward Syn and sat down, resting his elbows on his knees. "Is she in denial? Or did you frighten the bejeezus out of her?"

"There's nothing to deny because we haven't had a discussion about anything. She's closed me out." Syn pinched his forehead as the weight of his words came down on his head. "Is it even possible for one lifemate to close the other out?"

"I don't have lifemate experience, but based on what I've heard about Zareh and Alazar and their lifemates, the separation won't last long. And when that time comes, watch out, because those little sparks you're feeling now will become dynamite."

"Already there."

"Well, then, warn me when that time comes. I don't need to be in close proximity of anything nuclear." Taryn laughed. "Let me rephrase. I don't *want* to be."

Syn scowled as his groin throbbed. "You're not helping me."

"Face it, there's no helping you. So, she doesn't know she's a Keeper? Or the daughter of a Keeper? Is Giovani alive? What about Saralyn? Where are they? And where's your dragonstone?"

Syn raised a brow. "Was I supposed to write those down?"

"Smartass."

"Jackass."

They tapped the necks of their bottles together in salute and drank.

Then Syn shook his head. "She knows about dragons, but I haven't learned anything else about what she knows and doesn't know. She's from New York. City or state, your guess is as good as mine. I think the Baroqueth were searching for my jewel when they ransacked her apartment, but couldn't find it. She claims she has no idea about any stone or jewel, and her claim was genuine."

"That could mean Giovani is alive." They both pondered that before he shifted the subject, saying, "Cade gave me a shout. Said Gabriel and Emery were joining the party sometime tonight or tomorrow morning. Looks like I'll have a full house." Taryn tapped a foot against the flagstones and a finger against his bottle. "You know, I love this city and I love this house."

"I sense a but coming."

Taryn turned his russet eyes on Syn. A shadow fell over his face. "I'm ready to go home. To The Hollow. I think Cade's plan is good timing. I heard Alazar moved his lifemate and his Keeper back there. Zareh intends to relocate once Kaylae has the baby, unless they've moved up the date. I've already spoken with a real estate agent. I'll be putting this place on the market by the end of the month."

Syn straightened. "Are you sure you want to get rid of it?"

"It's not home." Taryn waved his hand around. "What am I supposed to do with it once I return to our real home, Syn? Sure, I might come for a visit because this city is the best and I'll get lonely watching all of you lovebirds doing your lovey-dovey things. But, really, it just doesn't make sense."

"Get a caretaker or two. You purchased the property outright. It's yours. Damn it, man. I'd even take a vacation from The Hollow to come here for a few days."

"It's not the same as living here."

"We're still going to be moving between here and The Hollow until we locate all the surviving Keepers and any other females there might be. Taryn, your lifemate may very well be out there, waiting to be found."

Taryn nodded, but his eyes dimmed. "You know my Keeper didn't make it out of The Hollow. He had no siblings, which means no genetic link to produce a female Keeper." His lips curled downward as he refocused on Syn. "If I had any hope of finding my lifemate, Syn, I would never have put myself out there in the human world the way I have over the last couple of decades. But there is no hope, so I might as well enjoy my life to the fullest."

Syn reached over to squeeze Taryn's shoulder. "There is always room for hope."

"Hope in death?" He snorted and shook his head. "Even I know better than that."

A gentle chime echoed through the house and into the courtyard. Syn stood up, his brow furrowing. Taryn was two steps ahead of him, heading into the house.

"Are you expecting someone?" Syn asked.

"Other than our brothers, no one." He dropped the beer bottle on the counter as they moved through the kitchen. Syn did the same. "And they wouldn't ring the bell."

"Did your fancy wards falter?"

Syn came up short when he caught sight of Briella rushing toward the door.

Taryn picked up his pace. "Hey, Brie, don't—"

Déjà vu.

Syn shoved Taryn aside and bolted to reach Briella.

She pulled the door open.

His boots skidded over the polished wood floor of the living room. His eyes went wide as he came to a sudden halt.

The woman on the stoop dropped a bag, her expression mirroring his absolute shock. The man's smile dropped from his face the moment his gaze moved from Briella and landed on him.

"Awww, shit," Taryn said. "*Boom!*"

"Syn?" One of the woman's delicate hands flew up to her mouth while the other held her husband's arm for dear life. Her eyes sparkled as they teared up. "Gio, tell me I'm not seeing things."

Slowly, Syn approached the door, acutely aware of Briella's confused attention swinging between himself and the couple.

Her parents.

His Keeper.

Giovanni released the handle of his luggage and crossed the threshold, never taking his eyes off Syn.

"Uh, what's going on here?" Briella asked.

Giovanni paused a couple of feet from Syn. Shock, concern, relief, excitement. The concoction of feelings punched Syn in the gut, the head, and left him reeling. His Keeper was alive. And so was Saralyn.

"Syn," Giovanni whispered. Syn grinned. The air sizzled between them, a familiar electric connection. "Syn!"

Giovani slung his arms around Syn in a fierce hug, one that Syn was thrilled to return.

"You made it out. You and Saralyn," Syn said, clapping Giovani's shoulder before he stepped back. He lifted his gaze to meet Saralyn's. She rushed toward him, and delivered an equally tight hug. "How did you know to come here?"

"Belle texted me earlier today with an urgent request to come immediately," Giovani said.

Syn shot Briella a curious look. He caught her eyes and registered the rush of confusion and horror that expelled from her. He tried to go to her side.

"Don't," she snapped. She threw up a hand and backed toward the stairs. Her gray eyes shimmered, her face paled, and the hurt that came up through the fissures of her hardened expression shredded his heart.

"Briella—"

"I-I don't know what is going on here, but right now, I don't care to find out." She backed onto the first step and paused. "Wait. Yes, I do." Her gaze shot to her father. "How the hell do you all know each other?"

Giovani cast Syn a lost look. "You didn't tell her anything, I assume."

"Apparently, neither did you," Syn retorted. He was beyond ecstatic to see his Keeper, but Briella was his priority. "How did she know about the dragons?"

"I told her stories when she was a child. Saralyn and I both did, but we never divulged our origins. We wanted her to have as normal a life as any human girl. In case…"

In case Syn hadn't survived the Baroqueth ambush and his Keeper had no hope of returning to The Hollow.

After thirty-something years of separation, in proximity proved their connection was as strong as ever. He knew exactly what his Keeper wanted to say, but kept to himself.

Giovani came to Syn's side and held his arms out to Briella, who moved away and up another step. "Belle, come here. We've missed you so much over the last few months. Your mother is lonely in the gardens."

"Sure seemed that way as you two rushed by me without so much as a hi to throw yourselves at *him*. A stranger." Those pain-etched eyes flashed toward Syn before returning to her father. He felt the glance like a damn poison-laced spear through his gut. "Listen, Dad. I don't know what kind of conspiracy you've all got going on, but this is the worst possible joke you could even think to play on me right now. My apartment's been broken in to, I've been attacked twice in two days, and now I'm supposed to trust a dragon who thinks I *belong* to him?"

Her words lanced down his middle, splaying him open.

Saralyn gasped. "Attacked?" She hurried to the stairs. "Oh, I knew letting you come here was a terrible idea. I told you, Gio. Especially this city, with all the activity surrounding it. Oh, Briella."

Syn's chest tightened and his gut clenched when Saralyn reached for Briella, but his spitfire lifemate scowled and ran up the stairs, leaving her mother staring after her, bereft.

"I think you both might need this," Taryn interrupted. He held out a beer to Giovani and a glass of wine to Saralyn. His gaze drifted up the stairs. "Today has been a day for the record books. The day the world came crashing down at our feet. Or rather, her feet."

Syn rubbed his hands over his face, anguish and aggravation warring for control. Aggravation at the universe for thinking this was someone's bright idea of twisted entertainment. Anguish at the pain he'd felt radiating from his lifemate.

"Did you two rent a car?" Syn finally asked.

"No. We took a cab from the airport. Brought one bag each. Belle's text had us in a panic, so we rushed to get here." Giovani sipped the beer. Familiar gray eyes looked Syn over. "I think I'm starting to put the puzzle pieces together. She's your lifemate?"

Syn nodded once.

"I should've told her more about us, but I didn't." His Keeper sighed, his shoulders slumped. "I should have at least told her about you, but you know how young females can be. Get these fairy tale ideas in their

115

heads and can't see past the story to reality. I didn't want that happening to her, but I taught her about her gifts and self-defense, and dragon history."

"Gio, I'm going to speak with Briella. She needs familiarity," Saralyn said. She rested a gentle hand on Syn's shoulder. "I'm so happy to see you again, Syn."

"As am I you."

Saralyn smiled sadly and climbed the stairs.

"Second door on the right," Taryn called after her. To Giovani, he said, "I'll bring your things inside and put them in another room. I think we can celebrate reunions later. Right now, you and Syn need to catch up on current events. Courtyard is open."

Syn nodded, taking in his Keeper with one short glance. The man had aged well, his hair a dark red with only a few lighter strands, his face nearly free of wrinkles and his body fit and lithe. There would be more time for historical updates later.

For now, they needed to address the Baroqueth threat and how to rip the carpet of her old life from beneath Briella's feet smoothly enough so she remained standing strong.

CHAPTER 9

Briella pulled her knees up to her chin and wrapped her arms around her legs, keeping her eyes lowered. She listened to the door click closed and soft footsteps cross the polished wooden floor until her mother sat down on the edge of the bed.

She hated herself in these moments. Hated her weakness and her confusion. Hated her childish response to the performance she watched downstairs. Hated the way she yearned for a stranger who locked away more secrets behind his mysterious eyes and devilish beauty.

She hated that she had lost control of her life.

Briella didn't count the minutes that passed as she and her mother sat in silence. Having her mother's company did wonders for her battered ego, but she still wasn't willing to let anyone off the hook easily. They deceived her, betrayed her, let her wander aimlessly down a path they knew well, if what she witnessed a short time ago wasn't a mind trick.

The shock that her parents and Syn knew each other damn near wiped her off her feet. What were the chances?

She knew it wasn't a coincidence.

Her mother finally broke the silence with a hand on Briella's arm and a softly spoken, "Sweetheart, are you okay?"

Briella wanted to laugh at the absurdity of the question, but as her mother's words sank in, her defenses shattered. She shook her head against her knees.

"I'm twenty-nine years old and I feel like a little kid lost in a storm. I don't know what's happening around me anymore. I'm losing control of my life just when I finally started building the life I dreamed of." Briella clamped her jaw and ground her teeth. Her eyes burned and her throat tightened and ached. She hugged her legs harder. "I don't even know where to begin because I can't make sense of what I've seen. You and Dad and Syn? Dragons? Enemies? Ma, what is going on with me?"

"Oh, my darling."

Briella fell into her mother's open embrace. Tears streamed down her cheeks, but she refused to let the sobs free. Her throat burned in protest.

"Your father and I made the decision before I had you that we were going to give you the most normal life possible, despite our differences from the rest of this world. We had no way of knowing what the future held. We didn't want to feed you false hope in case we could never return to our true home." Her mother stroked her braid and rocked her slowly. "Perhaps it was wrong of us, but our intentions were to allow you to live, not create barriers that prevented you from living your life to the fullest."

"Ma, you've always been overprotective. You fought me about coming here to follow my dreams," Briella reminded, her voice raspy. "You didn't want me to pursue the gallery."

"No, sweetheart. I wanted you to pursue the gallery. My joy at the possibility of you achieving this monumental goal was unbelievable. But I knew the dangers this city might hold for you. With your gifts to hear others' thoughts and the visions that can manifest inside your mind, I feared New Orleans would be too overwhelming. This place attracts paranormal elements, and the possibility our enemies might stalk these streets was very real."

Briella sucked in a shuddering breath and sat up, pulling free of her mother's arms. She wiped her cheeks with the backs of her hands and moistened her dry lips. "For all these years, I knew who I was. Briella Everett, aspiring artist with strange gifts. I knew how to make a garden thrive through patience and perseverance. I knew how to protect myself and guard my heart. I knew I was strong and smart and diligent. I didn't give up. I fought for what I wanted." She shrugged, letting her hands drop to the blanket. "Now, I haven't a clue. I have never felt fear the way I felt it earlier today when I was attacked by that person. I should have felt fear when I saw the impossible manifest before my eyes. When Syn turned into what resembled a dragon. But I didn't. I'm a basket case." She lifted her chin and met her mother's sympathetic gaze. "Who am I, Mom? Because today shook my foundation and I don't know anymore."

Her mother grabbed her by the shoulders. Her gaze hardened. "Yes, you do. You're Briella Everett. You're the strongest young woman I know, and I could not be more proud of you. You go after what you want and fight for what is right. You have the power to make a difference."

A small smile began to crest her mother's lips. A peculiar twinkle lit her eyes. "You are a blessing as much as you have been blessed. Every hope and dream your father and I secretly held are unfolding."

"I don't understand."

"I'm about to tell you the truth, Briella. The whole truth. It is as fantastic as it is real." Her smile widened. "It's been a little over thirty years since we came to this world from another. The dragon realm, The Hollow, was attacked by an enemy so bent on destruction they cared not what or who they destroyed to get the power of the dragons. You see, Syn is a Firestorm dragon. They were already a rare breed before the attack. Only a couple dozen existed. After the attack… I don't know. Your father and I escaped the carnage on the back of another dragon. Syn ensured our safe escape and stayed behind to protect others. We had no idea if he survived. This is the first time we've seen him or heard from him since that day."

Briella blinked. Was she seriously hearing this tale from her grounded, logical mother? Okay, so her gift of visions came from Saralyn Everett, but her mother kept her head about her more than most parents Briella encountered.

There wasn't much to discount her mother's claims, however. She'd seen for herself what Syn was. Or, at least, an impression of what he was.

"Your father and I didn't mean to brush you aside, sweetheart. We were both in utter disbelief that he was here. Here, Briella. With you. My heart can rest easy knowing that you are in his care because he won't let anything happen to you. You see, we are not entirely human. Your father is what the Firestorm dragons call a Keeper. Specifically, he is Syn's Keeper."

Briella stiffened. "A *what*?" *Sweet little Keeper*. The sorcerer's voice mocked her. Her mother's face faded as the attack replayed in her head. "Oh my God. That's what that person called me."

Saralyn's shoulders squared. "What person? Are you talking about the attack you mentioned downstairs?"

Briella nodded. "Yeah. At my apartment. I had thought it was one of my friends stopping by, but Syn... I don't know. He freaked when I opened the door. I had no time to think before he took me down to the floor and shielded me from the attack. The guy looked pretty human, except for the fact he was carrying around what seemed like a sparking ball of blue lightning. He had the strangest eyes. Black with silver specks."

In all her life, Briella had never seen such fear drain her mother's face of color and steal the strength and life from her eyes. She watched her life-loving mother melt into a terrified shell of a person in the space of a few breaths.

"They found you? How did they find you so quickly?" Saralyn's fingers curled into the blanket, bunching the white fabric in similarly whitened knuckles. Briella dropped a hand to her mother's, surprised by how cold her skin felt. "My worst fear, Briella, is losing you. I haven't had any visions about danger coming close to you. None."

A distressed moan fled her mother's lips.

"Ma, I'm fine. But who was that person?"

Saralyn shook her head before she lifted a hand to her forehead. "Our enemies. The Baroqueth slayers. At one point, centuries ago, they were allies. Friends and protectors. The leader of the Baroqueth sorcerers— they didn't adopt the slayer name until after their betrayal—was Keeper for the leader of the Firestorm dragons. Greed made the Baroqueth turn on his own dragon. He killed the dragon for his power and unleashed an evil within our sanctuary. It was defeated, but as all evil does, it came back again and again until it almost wiped us out. We all understood that if we ever had to leave The Hollow because of the Baroqueth, we were to blend into the human world and not attract attention until the dragons contacted us. They never came. Information about the dragons, the number of survivors or casualties, was never discussed. We were told to keep the dragonstone safe, not to open it—"

"Wait." Briella waved a hand, cutting her mother off. "A what? Dragonstone? What is that?"

"The dragonstone?" Saralyn's fists loosened their grip on the blanket and she aimlessly traced the stitching. "It's a priceless jewel unique to each and every dragon. No two are the same. It's magic, created from a dragon's first shedding of his scales as a youngling. It's used to bond the Keeper and the dragon throughout the Keeper's lifetime. Each generation of Keeper bleeds into the jewel. It opens the bond between Keeper and dragon."

"You know how ridiculous this all sounds, right?"

Saralyn let out a small laugh. "To you, I can imagine. To your father and I, it's normal. We were born and raised in a world of magic alongside dragons. My love of gardening comes from my longing for our home. The Hollow is unlike any place you will ever see. The flowers, the fields, the mountains, the waterfalls. Briella, you will fall in love with it."

Briella had always envied her mother's green thumb. The gardens in Briella's childhood home far surpassed magnificent and could easily put many botanical gardens to shame. Her mother spent more time in the gardens than she did inside the house, when the weather permitted.

But her mother's insistence that she *will* love this other world, not would, struck her stubborn self as wrong.

"I'm not leaving here. My art. It finally has a chance to be recognized." Briella tugged her braid in agitation. She sighed, gazing across the room to the boxes of paintings she hadn't unpacked because the drive to finish the dark and sinister portrait of a dragon under a man's skin demanded every molecule of her concentration. "I won't give it up. Not now."

"Sweetheart, things are changing. If the Baroqueth have found you here it New Orleans, it's only a matter of time before they find you again. The dragons have very little power in this world aside from their shifting abilities and the natural protection of their scales."

"And that's fine. Syn and that other guy downstairs can go back. I'm staying here to pursue *my* dreams. I'll figure out a way to protect myself." She shrugged. "I'll befriend a few witches and voodoo priestesses. Maybe barter with a demon or two I've seen lurking in the cemeteries."

Saralyn stiffened, her lips drawing taut. "Briella Isabelle Everett! That isn't funny."

Briella arched her brows. "And neither is your insistence that I'll be leaving the only world *I've* ever known to go back to the world *you* miss. I'm an adult, Ma. I have the right to make that decision for myself."

"The Baroqueth will kill you!"

"Why?" Briella snapped back, her voice rising. "Why are they after me? If they want the dragons and their power, why me?"

Saralyn's eyes gauged Briella for a long moment. The older woman's gaze seemed to pick at the outer layers of her mind, the probing a dull zing that resonated throughout her body. The corner of her mouth twitched.

Silently, she pushed to her feet and crossed the room with leisurely steps until she stopped in front of Briella's painting of Syn. She folded her hands behind her back.

Briella watched her mother, waiting for her response.

"You tried to paint a monster," Saralyn said softly. There was no accusatory hint in her voice, just simple observation. "You tried to create a beast, but your subconscious softened what your conscious mind desperately tried to hold on to. What it wanted the world to see."

Briella scooted to the edge of the bed and hesitated. She played her mother's words over in her mind, dissecting what she heard for the true meaning beneath the surface of obvious statements. That was Saralyn.

Slowly, Briella moved to stand by her mother's side. The hint of rose and wildflowers caressed her senses, calming her roiling emotions. Saralyn brought with her the delightful scents of her garden, and it stirred a bout of homesickness inside Briella.

Her mother pointed to the swirling grays that outlined a sodden hoodie and the broad expanse of night-drenched shoulders. "I see the sharp strokes you initially used, but then you went over them with gentle curls."

She lifted her finger to the shadowy face, a face Briella recalled as menacing the night Syn stood between her and the safety of her apartment.

Briella tipped her head, eyes narrowing on her work. She noticed it before her mother even spoke.

"Here. Again. I see the underlying jagged edges of his face, the gruff, dangerous angles, but you went back and softened them, too. Rather than possessing that threatening component you wanted, something inside you created an intriguing vision. More mysterious than menacing."

Briella felt the curiosity of her mother's gaze before she peeled her focus away from the painting and looked at the older woman. Her blue eyes contained layers upon layers of wisdom and knowledge. Her pretty face, seemingly untouched by time, possessed an angelic component Briella always found soothing. Her blond hair could easily have been a glowing halo.

And right now, all of that soothing, angelic essence poured over Briella, dissolving her resistance.

"Why, sweetheart?" Saralyn asked.

Because…

She turned her gaze back to the painting. To the fiery eyes she had seen more than once. Heat, both deadly and wicked, throbbed in the details of the eyes she had painted. They touched her soul, wrapped her in an unseen strength.

But she had seen those eyes after a kiss. A kiss that claimed her in more ways than she wanted to admit. A kiss she wanted to experience again and again until she drowned in a passion she had never experienced before.

"You know the answer," Briella said quietly.

"I do."

"Then share it with me, because I'm so confused."

"You said he claimed you belonged with him." Saralyn's hands rested on her shoulders and eased her around to face her. The gentle expression on her beloved face further banished Briella's fight. She trusted her mother and father. Trusted them to the death. Right now, she clung to that trust, hoping it would keep her feet steady beneath her as her world imploded.

"Keepers, Briella, protect their dragons as much as the dragons protect their Keepers. You have your gift for hearing thoughts. It's a survival mechanism. A way of filtering your surroundings to locate a threat before that threat has a chance to attack. Keepers and dragons can engage in mind-speak, or telepathy. The dragon can feel what you feel, as well as the reverse, once the bond is made with the dragonstone. However, there is one case when the bonding isn't necessary and it happens naturally."

Briella's heart began to thump. Blood rushed past her ears, muffling her mother's words. A wave of weakness washed over her, starting at her toes until it reached her head and made her vision spin.

Lifemate. Lifemate. Lifemate.

She heard the term in Syn's mind. Heard it as clearly as she felt her mother's hands.

"You are our daughter, and next in line to become Syn's Keeper. One day, you will take your father's place. When that time comes, you will be the last Keeper for Syn."

Briella shook her head, trying to dispel the gray fog that threatened to overtake her mind. Never had she passed out. Never, until earlier today. She sure as hell wasn't making a habit out of it, no matter how much her world cracked, crumbled, exploded. She was stronger than this. She'd adapt.

"Why? Why the last?"

As the word left her lips, a flood of turbo-fast visions sped through her mind, none of which made much sense. Syn was the only constant in each scene, from them sitting at a dining table, standing beneath a lavender and silver tree, a strange rock, flying through the sky, a baby, two babies, her and Syn late in life…

All of this news about dragons and Keepers and dragonstones was taking its toll on her, but there was enough of herself left that she had an inkling of what her mother meant.

The visions supported her assumption.

"In the history of the Firestorm dragons and Keepers, females are seldom born into the Keeper lineage. They are more rare than the dragons themselves. The last time a surge of daughters was born was after the first war between the Baroqueth and Firestorm, when the population was culled to the brink of extinction. Females are born to help preserve the Firestorm bloodlines. Nature's way of saving a race."

"I think I know where this is going." Briella rubbed her eyes with the heels of her palms. "What's a lifemate?"

Saralyn's mouth melted into a smile that set off the sparkle in her eyes. "A soul mate to a dragon, but more. You're Syn's lifemate, Briella. If he survived the attack on The Hollow, as we now know he did, it was only a matter of time before he found you. The pull is irresistible, from my understanding. It is overwhelming. The dragon, who is already supremely protective of his Keeper, will be more so toward his lifemate because you, my darling daughter, are priceless to him."

"Because I'll give him kids and the dragon lives on." Like she saw in that dizzying vision. She wasn't going to be a baby factory. That wasn't in her plans.

"No. Well, yes, but more importantly because you own his heart. And owning a dragon's heart?" Saralyn shook her head, a dreamy glaze crossing her eyes. "Briella, you have no idea how lucky you are. None. If there is ever a man to exist that I feel is deserving of you, Syn is that man. The only man. He will treat you like a priceless treasure. He will forever respect you, protect you, and love you. You, like all Keepers to their dragons, are his equal, not his possession. And you can rest assured that whatever he says and does comes from his heart."

"So when you and Dad realized you were having a daughter, you also realized there was a chance that I would be a dragon's lifemate."

Briella wasn't sure how she felt about this. Okay, so there was definitely nothing appalling about Syn and having the security of knowing they were meant for each other was certainly tempting. However, she lived in a modern world with modern thought processes. Pre-ordained marriages before birth did not exist in her world.

"Yes, but we also knew the significance of being blessed with a daughter beyond the possibility of her being a lifemate because, remember, daughters are rare." Saralyn cupped the side of Briella's face, lifting her gaze. Briella hadn't realized she'd looked away. "Sweetheart, you will find your path on your own, but you need to understand who and what we are. You need to understand the dangers that will hunt us, hunt you, because if the Baroqueth got their hands on you, there is nothing Syn won't do to save you. He *will* give his life for yours, whether you have accepted him or not. The significance of what you and Syn have will be irrelevant because it is you, and only you, that will matter to him in the end."

"What about Dad? I thought dragons protect their Keepers."

"They do, but their lifemate comes first, and your father knows that. He is pleased by it." Saralyn leaned over and pressed an airy kiss to Briella's forehead. "It is a lot to take in, I understand. Know that Syn is not your enemy. Whatever Firestorm dragons survived the attack, none are your enemy." She stepped back and nodded once. "I'll leave you be. You'll learn more in time, but for now, you should relax. You're safe. As safe as any person could hope to be."

Briella listened to her mother's light steps recede from the room, followed by the soft click of the door opening, then closing, leaving her alone.

She looked at her painting. Five hours of work led to this finished product. A masterpiece because her inspiration was a living, breathing, walking masterpiece. The longer she retraced every stroke and detail, the more discrepancies she discovered that fell in line with her mother's observations. She'd tried to create a monster. The monster that attacked her and terrified her.

The end product?

Not a monster, but a mysterious depiction of a man who created as much turmoil within herself as she created on the canvas.

Turmoil. A churning entity alive and well, fighting to make sense of a life she thought she controlled until she learned fate had other plans.

CHAPTER 10

Syn slowed down by his second beer, and his first hour into catching up with his Keeper, taking small sips rather than trying to drown the tumultuous emotions that battered his spirit. The dragon grew more and more restless, the desire to see Briella, to explain to her and beg for forgiveness growing unbearable.

Giovani was his rock in these restless moments, since the alcohol had no effect on Syn physiologically. The drink kept his hand and his mind busy, that was all. And his throat moist against the hot smoke that roiled deep in his chest.

"Who else survived besides Cade and Taryn?" Giovani asked. He had settled back in a chair, taking in the serenity of the courtyard. After two beers, he looked relaxed and a faint flush painted his cheeks, evidence that alcohol certainly had more of an effect on him than it did on Syn.

"Eight of us total. Zareh, Alazar, Emery, Gabriel, and Tajan came out of it, too. Emery and Gabe will be here by morning. Zareh's Keeper was killed a year ago by Baroqueth. It was the first attack since Cade had dragons and Keepers split up to divert attention."

Giovani's eyes widened. "Talius didn't make it?" Then he shook his head and took a sip of beer. "I learned a lot from Talius before the attacks on The Hollow. I find it hard to believe the Baroqueth were able to kill him. Wow."

"His death prompted Cade to search for the remaining Keepers, especially after he learned Talius had a daughter none of us knew about. Zareh's lifemate. Shortly after that, Alazar learned his Keeper had a niece, and she's his lifemate."

"So the surge of female Keepers is true."

Syn shrugged a shoulder and turned his head up to the cloudless sky. Streaks of dark navy swallowed up the brilliant cuts of magenta and gold. The moon made its presence known before nightfall took over, a pockmarked chalky white orb waiting for its time to shine.

"Seems so. After the Baroqueth attacked Alazar, Cade decided we should all return to The Hollow. Our enemies' powers have gotten stronger, as have their numbers, and they are actively hunting us here. We don't have a good lock on exactly how much stronger, or how many of them there are, but enough to be a serious threat. At least on our own soil, we have the magic and power we lack in this realm. We've been locating survivors, but pinning down the whereabouts of everyone has been tricky. Many have moved several times since escaping. Names have been changed. Birth records altered. Essentially, anything and everything the Baroqueth could use to make the connection between the surviving Keepers and The Hollow and dragons."

"Cade never told Saralyn and me whether you survived before he disappeared that night. He ordered us to protect the dragonstone, but to not use it in any way. That was the last contact with anyone from The Hollow. We had only instinct and hope. Neither one of us gave up hope. When we had Belle, that hope grew. We refused to believe the blessing of a daughter by the Goddess was anything less than a sign that you were alive."

"Yeah." Syn took a drink, licked the beer from his lips, and looked at Giovani. "I was one of the last to make it out. I wouldn't leave our people unprotected against the Baroqueth wrath. My wings took a few brutal hits. Tore and burned the membrane in several places. I could get lift off the ground, barely, but couldn't get the speed to break through the portal. Cade eventually got me out."

"You've fully healed since then, I hope?"

"What would've taken a few days in The Hollow took almost a year in this realm. I kept moving during that time, hoping the Baroqueth couldn't pin me down and attack when I was weakened."

Giovani clapped his shoulder, a familiar and missed gesture of their camaraderie. "I'm glad you're okay. You've always had a selfless heart, Syn. You've always been a humble hero."

Pride swelled in the Keeper's voice, but failed to find resonance within Syn. He did not see his actions as heroic. He did what he had to do to save lives. All of his brethren sacrificed so much to save as many lives as possible.

And still, they lost more than they had saved.

Heroes were for the humans.

He was no hero.

Veering away from that particular topic, Syn asked, "Your emergency account was enough to help you survive the last few decades, I hope?"

"More than a lifetime's worth of money. Saralyn and I moved around a bit, as well, until we found a modest place in Upstate New York. A little over three acres of land surrounded by trees and the nearest neighbor about three miles down the road. Saralyn created lovely gardens, similar to the ones she used to keep back home. We've lived quietly, simply, leading as normal a life as possible." Giovani ran a hand over the shorter strands of hair at the back of his head. "I can understand why Cade would keep your survival a secret from us, but why didn't he tell you we were okay?"

"Simple, actually." Syn again rolled his head back to stare at the darkening sky. "He knew I would seek you out to make sure you were safe. That would've been dangerous." Syn extended the tip of one talon and tapped the glass bottle. His scales rippled down his arms, tickling his skin as they brushed the surface of his body. The small door for his dragon to emerge helped the beast settle a bit.

"We believed by being in close proximity to other dragons and Keepers, we'd pique interest and lure the Baroqueth to us. That's why we all separated. Cade remained the link between us all, keeping tabs on the dragons and as many Keepers as he could without direct contact. Like you, though, so many moved around and blended into the human world that he lost track."

"It's in our blood, Syn. To protect each other. These last few decades have been stressful. For us all."

A comfortable silence settled between them. He sensed Giovani was as content as he to be reunited and safe.

"Do you miss flying, Gio?"

Giovani chuckled. "Almost as much as I miss home."

"We'll have to share a ride, for old time's sake."

"Definitely." A strange current disrupted the calm. "You know, Belle is going to have to learn if we plan on returning home."

"In time." *That we don't have.* "Your daughter has her first gallery showing in less than two weeks. I have a feeling she'll resist any talk about leaving right now."

"We were going to book a flight down the day before the showcase. Our trip started early." A muffled scrape against the table between them drew Syn's attention from the darkening sky. His heart instantly sped up and he straightened in his chair as Giovani pushed forward an ornate mahogany box lined with delicate gold around the edges. "I've kept it safe all these years. I know you'll want it. For Belle."

Syn put his bottle down and lifted the box, testing the weight in his palm. Energy and magic thrummed through the wood, reconnecting with him after all these years.

His dragonstone, locked away inside power-enforced walls.

"Here." Giovani held out a delicate key that Syn accepted. "You have no idea how many nights I held the box, desperate to learn if you were alive. I came close more times than I can count to opening it. To reach out to you."

"Cade believes that's how the Baroqueth tracked Talius. He used the jewel shortly before his death." He held Giovani's gaze. "I'm glad you didn't. It may have kept you safe."

Giovani climbed to his feet and stretched his arms over his head. A yawn followed shortly after. "Well, we're all back together again. I should help Saralyn unpack and check on Belle."

"Why do you call her that?"

A thoughtful smile lifted his Keeper's mouth. "Her middle name is Isabelle. I've called her Belle from the moment she came into this world. Our beautiful girl."

"She *is* beautiful. Quite more, frankly."

His body wouldn't let him forget it, either.

"Thank you, Syn." He gave Syn's shoulder a hard squeeze as he rounded the chair. "We'll say goodnight before retiring. It's been a long, stressful day on all accounts."

Syn listened to Giovani's footsteps return to the house, leaving him alone in the courtyard. A welcoming breeze rustled the trees and the plants, stirring the sweet aroma of the flowers that surrounded the peaceful space. The methodical trickle of water from the fountain, the distant echo of music from Bourbon Street, the soft glow of the light strands woven throughout the intimate space added to the magical air.

He turned the box over and over in his hands, tracing the gold filigree, recalling the last time he'd held the box with his jewel. The weight of the dragonstone inside was evident, displaced slightly more to the front than to the center. The wood was smooth, unmarred. Magic protected the jewel. Only the key could open it. Nothing, not the largest hammer or the strongest machine, could gain access to the contents. Only the key, or magic.

If he could only find the key to winning Briella's heart.

"In time," he whispered to himself. Maybe the good Goddess could speed things up for him.

A few minutes later, his dragon stirred and stretched. Heat spread over his back, rolling up his neck and down through his legs. Uncertainty hovered in the deep recesses of his mind—not on his behalf, but that of the woman standing in the doorway behind him. He knew she contemplated the step from the house to the courtyard, from what she once knew to what she was willing to learn.

Syn stopped rolling the box between his hands and leaned forward, elbows on knees. It didn't take long before he caught sight of Briella from the corner of his eyes, moving around him from the right and settling in her father's vacated seat. It took every ounce of willpower not to look at her, drink her in, drown in the sight of the stunning woman who refused to leave his mind.

He didn't want to stare and make her any more uncomfortable than she was.

So they sat in silence, listening to the nighttime orchestra play its natural notes throughout the courtyard. He relished her nearness, even if she was a table away physically and a world away mentally. He could smell her, hear the steady beat of her heart. It was enough. For now.

"You and my father must have a lot to catch up on," Briella said, voice soft, almost timid. "How long have you been separated?"

"Almost thirty-one years."

"Long time."

The corner of his mouth quirked. Her attempt at small talk was utterly cute.

"Yes," he agreed.

"Nice night." She shifted in the seat. A phantom tension touched his legs, one that must have come from the stiffness of her body. "The courtyard is so tranquil."

Syn eased back in the hard chair and placed the box on the table between them. He looked at Briella and immediately regretted doing so. Her memory was potent enough without being refreshed. She hadn't changed out of the flouncy shirt and skinny black jeans. Her hair remained braided, although strands had escaped to fall over her cheeks. He smiled when he spotted a smudge of paint over her temple and along her neck.

"It's a nice place to escape and relax after a hellish day," Syn said. "I had wanted to show you earlier. Figured you'd appreciate it."

Briella chewed her lower lip, her head down. She played with the hem of her shirt, her mind running. He watched the turmoil of thoughts play across her face.

He wasn't expecting the woman to look at him, dead in the eye, regret in her gaze.

"Listen. About earlier. When my parents arrived. I, uh, I guess I looked like an idiot. Almost thirty years old and having a temper tantrum." A strained laugh pushed through her lips. "I'm sorry." She lifted her hands in a sign of helpless resignation before resting them against her thighs. "I was out of line."

"You have no reason to apologize. Stress does funny things to people." Syn offered her a grin. "I certainly wasn't on my best behavior today, either."

Even in the dim lighting, he could see her cheeks darken and her eyes focus more intently on him. Those full lips separated just enough to turn her innocent look into one of a seductress. She had no idea what she did to him in those precious moments. The subtle signs of her persistent attraction satisfied the aching curiosity he'd suffered since leaving her apartment after their interrupted sensual interlude.

Syn opted for another sip of his beer. His throat had gone terribly dry.

"My mother filled me in on things," Briella said. She started to trace the grating in the tabletop with a single finger. "The more important points, I suppose."

"Giving you a full history lesson in one sitting is impossible. Not after the day you've suffered."

"It hasn't been entirely *in*sufferable."

There. That shy little voice again.

"Oh?"

She blinked, then motioned to the box. "What's that?"

"Many things." Syn reached across the table and held out the key he hadn't relinquished. "My dragonstone."

Her eyes flickered and awe filled her expression. She reached to take the key from him. Their fingers brushed. A bolt of heat shot through his arm and down to his groin, taunting the beast and intensifying his poorly controlled desire. The visible shiver that wracked her assured him she felt the same fierce connection.

"Do your eyes always have fire?" she asked.

"When the dragon isn't contained. He's a beast when you're around, so I apologize in advance."

"Do I need to be cautious of the dragon? Is the dragon separate from you? Do you share bodies?"

Syn chuckled. "Precious, we are one and the same. The dragon is an extension of myself. There's only one kind of body sharing I'm aware of."

Had he really just said that? Aloud? Sweet Goddess, if her cheeks could get any darker, they'd soon match the shade of her hair.

"My pitiful attempt at a joke," Syn said. He released the key to Briella and pulled his hand away before he brought her to him. He had the patience of a saint, according to his brothers, but right now he certainly felt the anxiety of the devil in waiting. "It's my turn to apologize."

"Not at all." After another delectable chew of her lip, she grinned. "I'll get used to this, you know. Everything going on. All of these…secrets I'm learning now. I'll be okay." Moonlight glittered in her eyes. "I'm not a fragile human being. I have a backbone."

"I recall, on more than one account." He rubbed his neck where she had used the stun gun, then shifted uncomfortably in his seat at the reminder of her painful move against his groin earlier. Yes, she certainly had a backbone, one he appreciated, even if he suffered a bit of pain for it. He was glad she could—mostly—take care of herself.

"I think I had every right to zap you. You were pretty frightening that night. You can be very intimidating." Briella motioned to the box again. "You mentioned something to me earlier about a jewel that the attacker might have been after. I didn't think about it until now, but the night you tried to stop me from going into my apartment, I heard someone's thoughts about me giving 'it' up. I initially thought the voice was yours and your intentions were, um, sexual in nature."

Syn narrowed his gaze. "I'm sure you know now that I would never force myself on you."

She nodded. "As confused as I've been the last two days, I can tell you're a respectable man."

"Good. And the voice?"

"Wasn't you. Didn't sound like the guy from earlier, either, but it certainly wasn't you." Confirmation that there was at least one other Baroqueth roaming around. "You have a pretty neat accent."

Syn stared at her, then laughed. He ran a hand down his face. Relief rushed through him. She was starting to loosen up. "Ahh, it's good to know I have something going for me."

"More than you know," she said in a barely audible tone.

Whether he was supposed to hear that or not, he kept the little tidbit to himself.

"Was it one of those sorcerers who broke into my apartment?" Briella asked, her seriousness back. Syn gave a single nod. "Do you think this is what they were looking for?"

"Yes. Without a doubt. If they gain possession of a dragon's jewel, they control the dragon. The box can't be opened without the key, but they have the power to unravel the spells protecting the dragonstone. They can access the jewel with or without the key."

"But you keep the jewel and the key together?"

Syn shook his head. "Most Keepers hide the box and keep the key on them, or the reverse."

"What does the jewel do?"

"Many things. First and foremost, it is part of me. It's an important form of communication between Keeper and dragon when the two are separated. My dragon can see and hear through the jewel. I can track my Keeper through the jewel, as long as the jewel is out of the box. But danger comes with opening the box right now. If the Baroqueth are nearby, they can sense the energy from the dragonstone and trace it to the source."

He didn't want to add to her discomfort just when she seemed to be relaxing by telling her that opening the box, and the connection between her and his dragon, could unleash the wild hunger he barely controlled.

"My mother said it's a form of bonding between dragon and Keeper."

"It is. When a new Keeper steps into his place, he bleeds into the jewel. In a way, he becomes part of the dragon and myself." Syn tapped the top of the box. "Generations of Keepers' blood resides within that jewel."

"She also said that I'm next in line to be Keeper. That when I bleed into your jewel, it will be the last time."

Oh, sweet Saralyn. In all of her eloquence, she managed to slip that little bit of information to Briella. Syn held Briella's gaze, gauging his lifemate. Did she really want to hear the truth? Or was she looking for a reason to push him away?

"You are." He let out a low breath. "It will be."

"Does it have to do with being lifemates?"

And there it was. He could have sagged with relief when she acknowledged their match with a hint of hope lightening her tone.

"Yes."

"Why is that? And is that something you want?"

Syn contemplated her questions and his response. "Is it something I want? I think it's something we all want, sweet. It's something that every Firestorm yearns for. Completion. Being gifted with a lifemate. I've lived for centuries. There comes a point in our exceedingly long lives when we realize it's time to put our mortal clocks into motion. It's a barter. Longevity for love." He angled himself toward Briella in hopes of making his point clear. "There is no price tag on love. I would choose love over another half a millennia of life."

A delicate crease formed over her brows and her eyes glowed with something deep and powerful. Syn's chest cinched, his breath difficult to catch. His heart did a strange double-beat that left his head swimming and his body aching. His dragon was in knots.

"However, I'm not the only one who is affected. If you choose to bleed, to accept the lifemate bond, you gain longevity. You will age more slowly and live far longer than the average human. Younglings require decades of parenting to get them prepared to survive on their own, far more than human offspring do."

"I have a choice," Briella said in a musing tone. She settled into her chair, relaxing against the back. She rolled the key between her thumb and index finger.

"Yes. You do." Not that there was much of a choice when the attraction, the pull, turned raw and primal and inevitable. "And whatever choice you make, I will honor it."

"Can you?"

"I will do whatever I must to honor your decision. Simple as that. It will not change the fact that you are in line to be my Keeper."

"But I have to bleed into the stone, and if I do, there will be no more after me. What happens if I choose to be Keeper, but not lifemate?"

Dear Goddess, he hoped she was running through any and every scenario in order to make a wise decision when the time came. The prospect of her denying him would drive him mad. Simple to honor her decision, a completely different story to hold true to his word without losing his mind.

My battle, not hers.

"Your silence speaks volumes, Syn," she said quietly. "If I don't accept, your bloodline dies, doesn't it? There *is* no other option. There really is no choice."

Syn reached across the table and grasped her hand. He ignored the fierce thrum of fiery heat his touch ignited inside him and gave her fingers a gentle squeeze.

"Briella, you have a choice, and that is all you need to know."

Briella's head dropped as she looked at their hands. He half expected her to pull her fingers away. When she turned her hand over and returned his gentle squeeze, peace filled him. If nothing more, they were on the road to being friends. He was gaining her trust.

Her fatigue washed over him in swells throughout their conversation. It peaked then, a hazy crest preparing to crash down. "You must be tired." Syn stood up, continuing to hold her hand, and helped her to her feet. He handed her the box. "Your father returned it to me. To give to you, if you wish to have it. If you feel you want the responsibility of keeping it safe, that is. Keeping me safe."

"Now, isn't that funny. Me, five-foot-four, someone who slips in heels, and responsible for keeping my big, brawny dragon safe. Boy, on a good day that might be a risk."

The laughter they shared lifted the weight of the universe off his shoulders. He didn't miss her small claim on him, either, as *her* big, brawny dragon.

"I think you're deadly with that stun gun."

"Then you should see me with paintbrushes." She made a *whoosh* sound. "I wreak havoc all the time."

Syn's smile grew as he traced a smudge of paint over her temple. "Those lethal brushes left their mark on you."

"Oh geez. I didn't even think to look."

"You wear them well, sweet." He cupped her face, their other hands still joined, and pressed a soft kiss to her forehead. Briella lowered her head and leaned into his chest. "I enjoyed this."

"So did I." She remained resting against him for another few moments before she straightened up with a deep breath. "I should shower and get some sleep. I have a long day tomorrow. I have to start passing out brochures for my showing, and I work tomorrow night at the restaurant."

"Get some rest." Syn stepped back, allowing their hands to slip apart.

She brought the box with his dragonstone to her chest.

"I'll keep it safe." The sincerity in her eyes touched his soul. "I promise you, Syn. I'll learn how to be your Keeper."

Her parting words left a bittersweet air caressing his soul. He hoped for more, but that was her choice. The steady click-click of her boots faded as she moved deeper into the house.

Syn reached for his beer and finished the remainder in a matter of chugs.

This battle may very well undo me.

CHAPTER 11

Briella lay in bed, staring up at the ceiling. She glanced at the dragonstone case several times. The ornate box sat on the edge of the nightstand, capturing the moonlight sifting through the gauzy curtains. For hours, thoughts of Syn haunted her mind, from his scent to his strength. She replayed their courtyard conversation over and over, and how his responses rang with genuine truth.

Comfort, unlike any she'd known. Comfort, and security.

She didn't want to leave him, but couldn't bring herself to stay. She had a life on the runway to her dreams, and the very thing that she dreamed of landed right in front of her.

It was a collision course in the making.

Her thoughts rolled, her mind working to untangle the nonsensical information she learned today from its relentless knot. So much to take in. So much to learn…

She'll give it up.

Briella gasped, but the air that filled her lungs was anything but reviving. Thick and tenacious, it seemed to settle deep in her chest as she fought to breathe. Panic speared through her with adrenaline on its tail. She grabbed her throat and tipped her chin, trying to suck in air through the dense, suffocating substance.

Sweet little Keeper.

Her scream snagged deep in her chest. She thrashed on the mattress, trapped in the tangle of sheets and blankets. She twisted her head one way, the other, anything to open her throat and get air into her burning lungs.

She saw him. Right in front of her. Felt evil so pure it turned her blood to ice. Dark eyes with their silver blade tips and that menacing face. The room closed in on her. Them. Blackness swallowed the moonlight, stole the white of the bedding, until all she could see was black.

The power that rolled off the creature far more terrifying than the blackness.

Panic soared. She clawed at the bed, the pillows, trying to get away, but the edge of the bed never came.

Neither did the air.

She flailed, arched, fought an unseen binding, magic that trapped her like a sacrifice to this evil creature.

In the darkness, a small pulse of blue began to grow larger and larger with each pulse.

A jewel. A stone.

Oh God, she had to get the box! She had to to—

The blue flashed.

She screamed, jerking away from the orb of energy.

Syn!

"Briella. Wake up."

Air flooded her lungs and she sucked in each breath as she fought the encasement surrounding her body.

"Briella, you're having a nightmare. Wake up."

Whatever spell she was under drew back its inky tentacles, releasing her to reality. Sharp spasms shook her. She blinked several times, grappling for the solid form in front of her until he came into view.

Stark worry glowed through the amber rings of his eyes. He brushed her hair from her face, slow and methodical, tucking strands behind her ears.

"You're safe, precious. It was a nightmare."

Briella's body shook. Cold sweat dampened her tank top and forehead. Her breaths remained ragged. She held Syn's gaze for the very life of her, his unwavering strength drawing her back to herself.

"You're safe."

Deep, rich, and so utterly certain, Syn's voice somehow worked beneath her skin, soaking into her muscles until she relaxed. Briella sank down and collapsed against him. She released her nail-biting grip on his shoulders and let her hands slide weakly down his chest. For a short eternity, she listened to the strong beat of his heart, drawing calm from each one of his slow breaths.

Oh, to stay like this for hours.

As the tremors subsided along with the nightmare, Briella eased off Syn's chest. Her legs remained haphazardly tangled around his thigh and waist. So intimate, and embarrassing had she not been such a complete mess.

"Want to tell me what happened?"

Briella rubbed her hands over her face. "I think everything from the past few days caught up with me." She drew up and looked around the room. No thick black shadows. The moonlight lit the room with a succulent gray-blue glow. Her bedding was still white and the box with the dragonstone remained untouched on the nightstand. "I can't remember the last time I had a nightmare, let alone one that choked me. How did you know something was wrong?"

"Connection, remember? Your distress was almost palpable in the other room." He motioned with a quick wave of his hand toward the door. "I was sleeping on the sofa in the living space outside the room. Heard you scream."

His confession to sleeping outside her room should have sown a seed of unease, but all it did was increase her sense of security.

"Oh, geez. I hope I didn't wake up the house."

Syn's mouth quirked. "You have nothing to worry about."

Briella wanted to sink back into his arms and stay tucked against his body for the rest of the night. She dipped her head, plying her bottom lip between her teeth, and closed her eyes. She'd steal these fleeting moments of distress to relish the warmth of the hand pressed low against her back, skin touching skin where her tank top didn't reach. Capable fingers tangled in her hair, the rough heel of his palm molding against her neck as his thumb swept back and forth along her jaw. The seemingly innocent touches created a low simmer deep in her gut and a subtle burn where she most wanted one and least needed it.

Or maybe she had it all wrong. Want and need had become interchangeable terms since she crossed Syn's path.

She opened her eyes, but her lids remained heavy. Her gaze flicked up to his mouth, those warm, full lips that led her through a kiss so wickedly delicious and addicting she could barely stop thinking about it. All she had to do was shift her hips a few inches closer, her head a few inches up, to complete a connection that would otherwise be...

A faint shiver skated along her nerves. A thrum so visceral gripped her until she caught herself leaning in for a kiss.

Instead, she unwrapped her legs and scooted back onto the mattress, clearing her throat. She went from one level of distress to the extreme opposite side of the scale. From raw fear to raw desire. From burning up with fever to the harsh cold of reality.

Your dreams. Don't lose sight of your dreams.

"I"—she tried to clear the lump from her throat—"I should clean up. I don't think I've ever sweat while I slept before. I don't think I've ever had a nightmare before tonight." She rested a hand on his knee, his leg tucked under him. "Thank you. For coming. I didn't mean to disturb you."

He laid his hand over hers. "Taryn has powerful wards set around the house. Nothing can get in here without alerting him." He leaned forward and kissed her forehead. She could really get used to his tenderness. "I'll leave you be, as long as you're okay."

Briella nodded, forcing a grin. She was far better now that Syn was with her, but she wouldn't break down into a weakened wanton over a nightmare. The pull her mother had mentioned, it was stronger than her willpower to refuse. It was unnaturally strong, an entity of its own devices, forging iron-clad links between Syn and herself. She knew, though, that giving herself to him would be tantamount to letting go of her dream of becoming a recognized artist.

"If I need anything, I'll call," Briella said. The her head jerked up. "*Did* I call you?"

Syn nodded once.

"Telepathy?"

"Yes."

"Huh." She'd have to learn more about how to use this new gift.

Syn climbed off the bed, his gaze dropping to the box on her nightstand. His face was a marvelous depiction of angles and curves, the shadows and moonlight creating their own masterpiece of light and dark with nature's fantastic paints. His profile stole her breath. His dark hair with hints of dark red fell over his forehead. His tilted eyes were mysterious beneath shades of dark gray. His jaw, lined with short scruff trimmed to perfection, shimmered under the moonlight.

Oh, to paint him within the throes of his inner thoughts and emotions. So much played across his face, which appeared rugged and sharp in the same glance as it appeared content and serene.

She could easily sacrifice her dreams to build new ones—

No.

She needed sleep, preferably nightmare-free.

Syn's attention shifted back to her and lingered. He graced her with a sexy half-grin. "Goodnight, sweet."

"'Night." *Handsome.*

Damn her eyes for dropping from his head to his waist and lower before he turned to leave the room. A wash of liquid fire drenched her from head to hips. And here she thought she was bad off. Her utterly controlled dragon might be able to hide most of his desire, but what lay in his pants gave him away. Tremendously.

After her second shower that night, Briella dressed in a fresh set of pajamas and climbed back into bed. Her eyes burned with exhaustion. She was far past tired, but sleep eluded her. She scanned every dark corner of the room, waiting to see something or someone pop out from a hiding spot she knew was not there. Every time she closed her eyes for longer than a few moments, she relived that suffocating terror from her nightmare, the choking sensation, the helplessness. Blue flashed against the back of her eyelids.

Every visual sweep of the room brought her to her painting, and stoked a longing that started in her chest.

An unremarkable ache that grew with each breath and each beat of her heart, spread with each minute spent staring at that painting.

An hour passed. Two. Three in the morning crept in like the fog over the mountains back home. She tossed. Turned. Restless until she threw back the blankets and scrambled from the bed with an inward groan.

Briella scrubbed her palms over her face and blasted out a breath. Strands of hair had escaped the haphazard updo she'd left it in after her shower.

"This is friggin' hell," she muttered.

She jerked her head toward the painting, then over to the door. Was Syn sleeping, unfazed by the events of the day? Did he have the strength to resist what was quickly breaking her down?

Briella crossed the room. Hand on the doorknob, she pressed her ear to the door and listened for any sign of someone's presence in the living space. Did dragons snore? She imagined they did to perfection.

Silence. Not a single sound from the other side of the door. Perhaps Syn finally retired to another room, knowing she was okay.

Quietly, Briella opened the door and poked her head into the open room. Her eyes landed on the hulking figure stretched out over the cream-colored sofa, arms crossed over his chest, ankles crossed and propped up on the arm. Syn's width did not fit on the sofa any better, and his shoulder hung over the edge. He was dressed the clothes he'd worn the day before, dark blue jeans and a black T-shirt, leather boots. The man wore no jewelry, except for a black-banded sports watch. Everything about him appeared neat and tidy and humble. Simple.

There's nothing simple about that man. Nothing simple about what he's created, the havoc tearing you apart.

A sweet, delicious havoc.

She knew she needed to step back, close the door, and count sheep in her own bed, but her legs drew her from the room and to the sofa. The sleeping man. The devilish temptation.

For a long while, Briella stood beside his waist, drinking in the magnitude of who this very man was. Her lifemate. *Her...*lifemate. Those arms could hold her for years to come. Those hands could touch her, explore her, bring her pleasure and comfort.

"Precious, you need to sleep." The gruff rumble of his sleep-filled voice startled her. When she snapped her attention to his face, she caught his eyes, open to mere slits, watching her.

"I, uh, I..." What on earth was wrong with her? She tossed a quick glance back toward the open door to her room. Syn's advice was quite sound. Her inner voice suggested the same. But...

I don't want to be alone.

A crushing revelation for someone who prided herself on her self-reliance, but one that gave her a small sense of relief.

Syn kicked his feet to the floor and sat up in one fluid motion. No man his size should possess that degree of grace.

He patted the seat beside him. "Come here, sweet."

She obliged. Settling down beside him felt as natural to her as producing an art piece. Folding her hands in her lap and hunching forward, not so much.

"I've been listening to you toss and turn for most of the night."

"Tonight's been…trying." A soft breath fled her lips and she shook her head. "I'm not weak, Syn. I can hold my own. I can face my problems and deal with them and come out on top. I don't need rescuing."

"I didn't realize my actions would have been perceived as rescuing."

"They weren't. They're not."

"Then who are you trying to convince of your strength?"

She shot him a hard glance. One that earned her what she was coming to recognize as his signature sexy half grin. Blasted man. He had a point. Again.

After a long, tenuous moment, Syn nodded once and leaned back, spreading his arms over the back of the sofa. He kicked his feet up on the large square ottoman and sank lower into the cushions.

"Briella, I am the last person you need to prove anything to. I know you're strong. I've seen your strength in everything you do. Every expression, every movement, every word. It's beautiful, that strength of yours, and only an insolent fool would try to take that away from you."

Briella looked away from him, playing with the knot of her fingers in her lap.

"That same strength can allow one to admit to the reason behind actions taken," Syn added, his voice lowering, turning into a thick, molten river of words that curled around her and gently drew her closer. Her back heated as she felt his gaze slide up her spine.

"It does."

"Mmm."

Briella closed her eyes. Why had she come out here? What possible reason did she have for coming out here, knowing there was a possibility Syn was on the sofa?

I don't want to be alone.

At last, she resigned herself to listening to the pleading voice she'd stomped down into the pit of her mind since landing in Syn's arms the night before at the bar. No, two nights before. Her fingers loosened and she leaned back, her side resting lightly against Syn's. She could hear the echoing beat of her heart throughout her head, mimicking the seconds as the night slowly ticked away. Mocking her resistance.

"My sweet, let go of the day's troubles and allow your mind to rest."

That sultry voice in her mind washed out the echoing beat and performed magic on her internal mayhem. His arm lowered around her shoulders, a blanket of warmth from his body cloaking her in comfort. Before she could fight instinct, she twisted and curled up against the side of his form, laying her head on his hard shoulder, her arm draping around his equally hard abdomen, and a leg over his.

So, so right.

"Yes, precious. It is."

Ah, that telepathy thing. She'd really have to work on those skills. Another day. Another time.

Right now, for the first time in forever, nestled beside Syn, she could think of no other way to make perfect better.

Syn was perfect. Her perfect.

Syn was her dream within a dream.

CHAPTER 12

Roaring laughter and the sound of loud bangs jerked her from a blessedly peaceful sleep. Briella groaned, rolling to her side, and tugged the blanket over her head.

Her leg fell off the edge of the bed and her body followed.

"Shit!" She scrambled to keep from becoming one with the hardwood floor, and came up short of a painful tumble. Blinking several times, trying to clear her eyes of sleep and slow her frantic heartbeat, she took in her surroundings.

Sofa. Living space. She wasn't in bed.

"That's right." She'd come out here because she didn't want to be alone. She wanted to be next to Syn, and that's exactly where she'd fallen asleep. Curled up next to a dragon.

A grin tugged her lips at the memory. Her soul brimmed with satisfaction over the small step into what she had only just discovered was her destiny.

"I think you might be able to use a cup this morning."

Briella looked up at the man who stood over her from her awkward place kneeling on the floor, her upper body clinging to the sofa cushion. He had a steaming mug in one hand and an arm stretched out to her. An arched brow accompanied his humored grin.

"May I help you up?"

She nodded, taking his hand. Syn pulled her to her feet—to her toes with all that power—and steadied her. She rested a hand on his chest as she gained her bearings, her fingers tingling as they slid over the defined curves of his muscles under the fabric of his shirt.

Ohhh, boy.

"Here, sweet. Have some coffee."

"Thanks." She accepted the mug and took a deep breath of the rich aroma. "How did you make it?"

"A coffee pot?"

Briella laughed. "No. Sugar and milk wise."

"Ah, got a laugh out of you in the first five minutes of being awake." Syn kissed the top of her head, his smile stunning. "I knew what you meant. Two sugars and more milk than coffee. As per your mother."

She lifted a brow. "You asked my mother how I like my coffee?"

His brows furrowed. "I know how bad a day one can have starting off with a bad cup of coffee. Don't think I've forgotten you prefer tea."

"Then why the coffee?" she teased. She took a sip and sighed. "Damn good coffee."

"Because you had a damn bad night."

She nudged him in the ribs. "It wasn't all bad, you know."

He tilted his head to the side, a nonchalant, knowing motion that plucked away another panel of her resistant wall. The morning coffee and his thoughtfulness to take the trouble to find out how she preferred it launched a wrecking ball through an entire side of panels.

A new round of raucous laughter filtered up the stairs. Briella took another sip of coffee.

"What time is it?"

Syn glanced at his watch. "Little after one."

She nearly dropped her mug. Syn shot a hand beneath the bottom to steady it in her grip.

"One? Are you serious?"

"You were up most of the night. And if I were to assume, you didn't sleep much the night before." If she weren't in such a good mood, she'd have a few words about that smug smile. "Who am I to wake a sleeping beauty up?"

"Oh, the compliments." She fanned her face and batted her eyes. "I'm overwhelmed by your charm, but"—all joking aside, she took another swig of coffee before handing the mug back to Syn—"I need to go."

She brushed past him and stalked into her room. Syn followed to the door, where he stopped and made himself comfortable leaning against the door frame like a big, languorous...

She jerked her attention from him and gathered her clothes from the closet and dresser.

"Where do you have to go today?"

"I need to stop by the gallery and pick up brochures, then start pushing my show. Time is ticking away while I'm losing sleep during the night and letting that sleep eat up my days." She paused as another bang and thump shook the house. She cocked her head and scrunched her nose. "Um, should I be nervous about that noise?"

Syn chuckled. "Get a bunch of dragons together in one place, you're bound to have some rattling." He waved his hand in a lazy manner. Briella fisted her clothes to her chest. "I'll let you get ready. There's food downstairs. I'll introduce you to Emery and Gabe. Let me know when you're done."

Syn reached into the room far enough to place her coffee mug on a decorative table, cast her one last lingering look, and quietly closed the door. She let out a sharp breath, her legs growing warm and weak as she stumbled to the adjoining bathroom, plucking her cell phone off the dresser on her way.

She really needed flame-retardant body armor. If it wasn't proverbial fire from a dragon's mouth, it would ultimately be those dark, scalding glances that would cause her to combust.

When she lit up the screen on her phone, dozens of messages, text and voicemail, scrolled up the window. Emma's last text was a panicky threat to have the cops show up at her place if she didn't get in touch with her. Immediately.

That was an hour ago.

Briella quickly put in a call. The last thing she needed to add to her topsy-turvy life was the police assuming she'd been assaulted and kidnapped when they saw the damage to the entryway at her apartment.

"Briella! Where are you? Where have you been? You send us some cryptic message yesterday and don't return calls, texts, leaving us worried sick over you!"

Briella pulled the phone away from her ear and cringed. Only when the phone remained silent for a few seconds did she dare bring it back to her ear. "Hi, Em. I'm okay. There was a freak accident at my apartment yesterday. And then my parents showed up and so I'm staying with them until my place is fixed."

Emma huffed. "That doesn't explain why you've ignored our attempts to reach you since yesterday afternoon."

Damn, was she really going to lie to her friend? How was she supposed to explain this insanity without sounding, well, insane?

"I got caught up in a painting. Really, really caught up in a painting."

A partial truth, but certainly believable. Her friends had experience with her immersion in her work when inspiration had a death grip on her.

"Where are you? What hotel are you staying at? I'm coming down to make sure you're unharmed."

"Hey, no need to do that. I'm leaving shortly anyhow. I have to do some advertising for my show. How about I stop by your place in, say, an hour? You can do a body check and see I have no injuries."

"Briella." The terse tone in Emma's voice made her blush. The only other people capable of making her feel like a scolded child were her parents. "Don't you *ever* scare us like that again, you hear? Mark stopped by your place three times between your text and midnight, hoping you'd be there. Adrienne and Mindy were over here, waiting to hear from you. Girl, you can't *do* that to us."

She rubbed her cheek, shame sputtering around her head. "I'm sorry, Em. Really I am. Things kinda happened. Fast."

"Well." She heard the sound of her friend's long exhale over the line. "As long as you're okay, that's all that matters. But I expect to be filled in on everything when you stop by."

"Will do."

She disconnected the call and slumped against the counter. How was she going to explain everything to her friends? Without creating a story of lies?

Since when did her life turn into the obscured imitation of one of her paintings?

If only reconfiguring life in reality was as easy as it was on canvas.

Syn sank against the wall beside Briella's door and let out a long, ragged breath. There was no term in his centuries' old vocabulary that could adequately describe the torture he'd endured in the last forty-eight hours. The pain he suffered when his wings were shredded by Baroqueth sorcery could not compare to the pain of maintaining control over his dragon, and himself.

But he would continue to endure, even if she curled around him again because she couldn't sleep alone. Even if her hands crept over his body in her sleepy state, making him acutely aware of what her simplest touch unleashed beneath his skin. Even if she looked at him with heavily-hooded eyes and the tension between them ramped up faster than he could launch into the sky.

Her lighthearted attitude in the last few minutes was a slight relief.

The only relief you'll find is either leaving the area for another continent or being accepted into her bed.

With a resigned growl, he pushed away from the wall and headed downstairs.

"Well, well. He's finally decided to join the party!"

Syn laughed, accepting the hard hug and clap on the back from Emery as he strode into the kitchen.

"Ah, man. It's so good to see you." Emery groaned, then backed up, holding Syn at arm's length. "Look at you. Haven't changed an ugly ounce. Amazing."

"I can give you a few pointers." Syn flicked a wave of jet-black hair off Emery's cheek. "You may benefit from my advice."

Emery tucked the chunk of hair behind his ear and winked. "Girls love the longer hair. Feels so good when they tug—"

"Okay, okay." Syn threw his hand up to forestall Emery's revelation. "Don't need to hear about your bed-ventures. Bad enough I got a dose from Taryn last night." He looked over Emery's shoulder and caught Gabe's glowing gaze from his propped-up position against the counter. "You guys are rocking this house off its foundation."

Gabe wagged his brows. "Sad it's us and not you and your missus."

"Watch it, Gabe. I love you like a brother, but your mouth regarding her is to remain clean." Unlike Syn's imagination. He allowed a hint of his dragon to show in his eyes before he switched from dead serious to laidback. Emery dropped his hands from Syn's shoulders and fell into a seat at the table. "She'll put you in your place better than I ever could."

Gabe snorted and grabbed a handful of peanuts from a bowl.

Taryn tsked. "Syn's right. That girl is no joke."

"None of the females are jokes," Gabriel said. "That's why they're Keepers and lifemates. Takes a special kinda person to handle one of us."

Syn glanced around the kitchen. "Where're Giovani and Saralyn?"

"They insisted on going to Café du Monde."

"And you let them go alone? With an unknown number of Baroqueth scouring this city?" Syn's good humor died at the carelessness of his brethren. The three dragons exchanged glances. "Seriously?"

He couldn't have felt more relief when a familiar voice said, "Don't let those guys mess with you. We're in the courtyard. Taryn brought us over to the café earlier," Giovani said, stepping up to Syn. He gave Syn's arm a squeeze before turning his head toward the upstairs bedrooms. "You were still asleep. Saralyn and I didn't want to bother you."

Syn calmed his dragon, and himself, and settled a grin over his mouth. "Very well." He shot the three dragons a scalding look. "I'm going to have a few words with you three later."

"Well, until our scolding"—Gabe pushed off the counter, wiping his hands on his jeans, and joined Taryn and Emery at the table—"who's ready to continue with smoke bombs?"

"That's what all the noise is from?" Syn groused.

The childish antics of his three brethren were unexpected, but not entirely surprising. Emery and Gabriel, true brothers by blood, were two of the youngest survivors of the attack. Their mother had been one of the few female Keepers born outside of a near extinction, and the brothers' births came a couple of centuries after most of them.

Having only a few centuries under their wings, there were occasions when their immaturity came out. However, when it came down to it, the two men could be as serious and lethal as any of them.

Smoke bombs and all.

"Syn, you've gotta see this. It's crazy!" Emery said, flipping a metal bowl upside down. Pinching the rim with the tips of his talons, he breathed a steady stream of smoke beneath the bowl until it started to seep under the edges.

Syn stretched his arm out toward Emery and narrowed his eyes on Taryn. "You're allowing this crazy in your house? And you wonder why I never settled in one place. Insanity follows."

Taryn shrugged. "If he blows out a window, I'll fix it. Oh, which reminds me." Taryn rolled out of his chair and snatched a piece of paper from the counter. "Here are a few people you can trust to clean up our mess at Briella's apartment. Should get it done in the next few days so she can break her lease. The sooner she has no connections with that place, the better."

"Good luck, Syn," Giovani said from where he stood pouring out two cups of coffee from the carafe. "She's got a wicked stubborn side to her. She loves her apartment and won't leave easily. It's her first place."

"Almost thirty and you've never let her out of the house?" Gabe asked. "Geez, Daddy. Isn't that a little extreme?"

Giovani scooped up a handful of nuts and pitched them at Gabe. They rained down over the table and floor, plinking against the metal bowl. Emery coughed out a short burst of flame, toasting some of the nuts before they skidded across the table. Gabriel protected his head with a scale-covered arm. Taryn jumped back, spilling water from the bottle in his hand onto the floor.

A loud bang brought Syn around.

"What the—"

Syn had no time to follow that sweet female voice. He flung up his arm as the metal bowl shot toward him and deflected it to the floor, where it bounced until it came to rest against the wall.

Syn spun around and swallowed back a swell of flame in his throat. Briella stood, pale, wide-eyed and mouth agape, a couple of steps behind him. Those eyes dropped to his arm, where his scales retracted, then around him to all the men in the kitchen. Syn took in the familiar riding boots and a new pair of dark skinny jeans with silver threadwork up one leg, and his eyes trailed up the V-neck shirt that showcased the lush swell of her cleavage. She'd pulled her hair back in a ponytail that left soft waves pouring down her back and over one shoulder.

The woman was damn stunning.

"What are you boys doing in here?" Saralyn asked, stepped up beside Briella. She gave Syn a knowing look before she turned her attention to Taryn. "You're going to have your neighbors calling the police on you, Taryn. The last thing we need is unwanted attention coming to your door."

Taryn's head dropped. "Yes, Mom."

"Don't you Mom me, old man." Saralyn pointed a finger at Emery. "And you. Play a game of Monopoly and stop trying to put holes in this beautiful house." She leaned through the archway to peer around the corner and a disgruntled groan escaped her. "Oh, Gio. I expect better from you."

Giovani threw up his hands. "I swear I had no part of this. Look." He held up the two mugs of coffee. "This is all I came in here for."

"He threw nuts at me," Gabe said casually, leaning back in his chair.

Saralyn shook her head and turned, giving the kitchen, and the chaos, her back. Syn waited for her to give Briella a hug and a kiss, then held his hand out for his lifemate.

"I'm almost afraid to introduce you to these clowns," Syn said. He'd never suffered any form of embarrassment until now. The lick of warmth that touched his face was not overlooked by Briella. She seemed to shake the shock and stepped forward, accepting his hand and her place at his side. Giovani came over to kiss his daughter's cheek.

"Morning. Or afternoon, rather. How did you sleep, Belle?"

Briella rubbed at the back of her neck, rose painting her cheeks. Giovani winked at Syn when his daughter wasn't looking.

"Good, I guess."

"I'll leave you two to face these knuckleheads. Your mom and I'll be in the courtyard."

Syn nodded to Giovani as he followed Saralyn out.

"So, this is the woman of the day," Emery said, getting to his feet and raking a hand through his hair. He stepped forward, extending a hand to Briella, and smiled. "I'm Emery LaRouche. And that pitiful sight there"—he made a careless motion toward Gabe—"is my brother, Gabriel. It's a pleasure to meet you."

Briella took his hand and laughed quietly at Emery's exaggerated chivalric motion of bowing and kissing her knuckles. "Stop that nonsense. I'm Briella Everett."

"Now if that isn't a sexy name."

"Emery," Syn growled.

Briella snickered and rested a hand against Syn's stomach. "Hey, no worries. It's not the first time I've been told that."

Syn groaned, ignoring the implication and the dark swirl of jealousy it inspired. He caught Emery's mind churning with amusement. His mouth opened to say something goading. Syn threw up a hand to silence him.

"Don't you even think about it," he warned on a low rumble.

"You are so easy to tease. Too serious and always the gentleman."

"It's nice to have a gentleman around these days. They're few and far between," Briella said, sidling a little closer to Syn. He looked down at her and caught the sparkle in her eyes as she smiled up at him. Oh, he could definitely kiss her right about now. "I have to get going. I'll be back in a few hours so I can get ready for work."

"Yeah, about that," Taryn started.

All of the sweet admiration drained from Briella's expression. She leveled her attention on Taryn. "What are you talking about?"

"Hey, we'll catch up with you guys in a few," Gabe said. Light on his feet, he snatched Emery's arm and dragged him from the kitchen, leaving Syn in the awkward position of breaking the bad news to his lifemate.

Taryn raised his water bottle in a salute and shrugged. "Things are fun and games, but when it comes down to it, our guards are never down, Brie."

"What Taryn is trying to say is that you can't go out alone. Not with the Baroqueth searching for you," Syn interjected.

Briella's shoulders straightened and stiffened. Her back became ramrod straight and her chest puffed slightly with the deep breath she sucked in through clenched teeth. Her fingers flexed by her sides.

Slowly, she lifted her defiant gaze to him. "Excuse me?"

Syn matched her defiance with unmoving finality. "You cannot go out alone on those streets, day or night, with the threat pursuing you. I can come with you, or if you choose, you can have one of the other guys accompany you, but you won't go alone."

"Ahh, yeah. Okay." The smooth skin over her brow creased. A chill expression coasted across her face. "I haven't needed someone to hold my hand in over a decade. I'm pretty sure I'll be fine. Have you seen these streets during the day? Because there's little to no chance of someone accosting me and getting away with it." She poked a finger at her chest. "I have things I need to do, and you will not tell me I need a chaperone to get them done."

"It's for your safety—"

"If all of you dragons are overbearing to the point where you feel that suffocating a woman is the equivalent of protecting her, then I feel sorry for the ladies who actually let you guys boss them around," Briella said in a scathing tone. She stepped back when he tried to reach for her hand. "Not going to work. I had someone try and do that to me. Ruined my chance at a showing. Put me down for my paintings. I swore I'd never let another man control me. I'll be back. If I need anything, I'll call." She stabbed a finger in the air toward the courtyard. "My parents."

Syn gritted his teeth, smoke sifting through his taut lips, as he watched Briella storm toward the front door. He fisted his hands. Now was not the time for the distraction caused by the sway of her hips in her determined beeline to leave the house. He should be chasing after her, forcing her to listen to reason, because being nice obviously wasn't working.

But, she finally explained her desperation for independence, whether she realized it or not.

"I warned you, Syn. You've got your work cut out for you."

He twisted to catch Giovani's sympathetic gaze from the table in the courtyard. *"Advice?"*

"Your good looks aren't going to divert her from her path. Your best bet? Get her to where she wants to be."

Syn considered his Keeper's advice. Get her to where she wanted to be. That was easy enough.

"Hey, you can't let her go alone. She's a walking target. If not for Baroqueth, then for drunkards who have a thing for gorgeous redheads." Taryn jutted his chin toward the door. "I'll come with you. You know, just in case you need some pointers on people skills."

It was pretty apparent he lacked skills in several departments, and they all had to do with Briella.

CHAPTER 13

Briella winced as Emma's crushing hug forced a cough from her chest and trapped her arms by her sides.

"You had us scared to death!" Emma finally released her and leaned back, keeping her hands tightly clenched on Briella's shoulders. The woman's nostrils flared and her eyes narrowed. She glanced over her shoulder to the rest of their five-man crew waiting patiently in the small living room. In a voice far softer than her worried shriek, she asked, "Why do you smell like a man's cologne? Like really, really good cologne?"

Briella shrugged casually, fighting the urge to take a sniff of herself.

Don't even. You wracked your brain over him the entire walk to Emma's. Stay mad.

She tilted her head. Got a small whiff of Syn on her hair.

The damn man was going to be the death of her.

"Why don't we go in there so I can apologize to everyone at the same time. I'm starting to feel repetitive," Briella said lightly, hoping to deflect her friend's curiosity back to scolding.

Emma linked an arm with Briella's and pulled her into the living room.

She pressed her mouth against Briella's ear and whispered, "If you are keeping a guy a secret from me, you're going to get a tongue lashing."

"I've no doubt, but you don't have to prepare for that."

Mark was first out of his seat. The hug she received from him was just as crushing, but his hands lingered far longer on her back and hip than necessary. She stepped away from him before she could stop herself—was that *guilt* she felt?—and caught the glint of hurt in his eyes not quite masked by a dazzling smile.

Thankfully, Adrienne and Mindy pummeled her simultaneously with hugs, shakes, and a slew of questions.

"Where were you?"

"What happened to you?"

"We thought you were dead!"

"Mark thought you ran off with some hunk."

A sharp laugh burst from her at that last remark. She laughed until her friends released her and gave her a chance to catch her breath.

Oh, if you only knew...

Syn was scrumptious. Briella had never met a guy so unforgiving in his looks. Apparently, dragons had a knack for hot in that respect, because Taryn, Emery, and Gabe were all utterly handsome.

"What was the issue with your apartment?" Emma asked, giving her an arched-brow look. Briella met the challenge with a smile.

"The plaster started cracking in the entryway and my AC clunked." She shrugged. "My parents arrived shortly after. They offered to take me in."

"You're their kid. I'd hope they'd take you in," Adrienne said. Mindy giggled.

"Well, all is fine and I'm sorry for the grief I caused by forgetting my phone. The three of us caught up before I got lost in painting." She offered an apologetic smile. "Truly. I'm sorry."

"Great! That's all wrapped up." Emma clapped her hands. "I think we should get moving on those brochures. Three of us have work tonight."

"Why don't we divide and conquer? We can each take two crossroads to Bourbon. That should cover most of the French Quarter. Tomorrow we can hit up the Garden District." Adrienne wiggled her outstretched fingers. "Let me see what that gallery put together in a day."

Briella handed over one of the brochures she had in the large Vera Bradley bag she'd picked up from her apartment on her way to the gallery. They were simple trifold brochures with full color, showcasing a couple of images of her paintings and a brief biography.

Mindy nodded.

"They look pretty awesome, Brie," she said, accentuating pretty. "How many did Harper give you?"

179

"I have two hundred. He has more coming by the end of the week. Forty each. We should be able to hand them out fairly quickly."

"All right. Let's get to it," Mark said.

An hour later, Briella had made a round of Jackson Square, which nearly cleaned her out of brochures. She stopped at a few of the smaller stores, pleased by the support the owners and staff offered when they gave her permission to either pin a brochure to an events board or tape one to the window. She made mental notes of promotional tools she'd invest in after this experience, such as postcards featuring whatever her hit painting turned out to be. The discussions she had with tourists and residents alike kept her mind off Syn, and her hopes for a solid debut soared.

She came to a voodoo shop and slid into the tight quarters, pinpointing the checkout counter. There were no employees in sight.

"Welcome."

Briella jerked around, startled by the nearness of the soft, seductive tone that greeted her. A woman no older than herself offered Briella a red-lipped grin. Dark eyes gauged her curiously.

Briella smiled and held out her hand. "Hi. I was looking for someone who worked here."

The woman touched a delicate choker and stroked the red jewel sitting perfectly in the hollow of her neck. Her nails, painted black, were a stark contrast to her porcelain complexion, as was her black hair set in a big-curl, retro-type style.

She looked like a voodoo priestess fitted in a look from the Fifties with a gothic accent, and she was stunning.

The woman took Briella's hand and shook once, her grip light. A strange sensation of electrical shocks prickled up Briella's fingers and forearm. Her smile faltered.

"How may I help you?"

"I would like to ask if you'd be willing to hang a brochure in your window for an upcoming event at Stackwood's Gallery of Fine Art next weekend."

The woman watched her closely, those fathomless eyes boring into her skin, seemingly trying to peel back the layers of her mind. Briella stifled a shudder and took a small step back. She didn't believe in the voodoo propaganda she found in the shops, but definitely believed in the art of voodoo. Right now, she had the bad feeling she was about to see how real voodoo could be.

"Do you have a brochure?" the woman asked, slow, soft, deliberate. Briella had the strangest sensation that her voice held a spell, and that spell was trying to work its unwanted magic on her. She pulled out one of the few remaining brochures in her bag and handed it to the woman. A tense silence stretched between them. Briella glanced toward the door, suddenly itching to leave.

The last time I come to a voodoo shop.

"Briella Everett," the woman said thoughtfully. "A debut. How...exciting."

Nothing in the woman's voice supported said excitement. In fact, she sounded condescending.

Briella folded her hands over her bag. "I hope I didn't waste your time. I'll be going."

The woman's chin lifted and her thick-lashed eyes narrowed. "Come. I have tape behind the counter so you can put your brochure up."

Briella hesitated, eyeing the dainty woman as she moved with a steady grace through the narrow path of displayed statues, incense, and herbs. The woman paused and turned back to her. Briella tried to strip her body of its protest and forced herself to catch up with the woman.

"Thank you. I appreciate your support."

"We try to…support our own."

Briella paused beside the counter as the woman slipped behind the register. She glanced around, taking in the dolls dangling from the ceiling amidst bunches of dried flowers.

Movement to her right caught her attention. She stared at shimmering fabric draped over two mirrors. At first she thought light glinting off the threading caught her eye. Then she noticed shadows shifting behind the fabric.

She stepped closer to the mirrors. The shadows grew more defined with each step. She reached forward and hooked the fabric on a finger…

"Oh, I wouldn't do that," the woman said.

For the second time, the woman's unexpected nearness startled her. Briella's arm jerked, and the fabric tugged away from the mirror.

She stared, horrified, at an image that should have been her own. Instead, an older woman bedecked with trinkets banged silently against the mirror as though it were a pane of glass, eyes wide. Her cheeks were flushed red as she screamed and yelled, her sounds silent to Briella's ears.

"You do not listen, do you."

The tingle of magic sprang to life along Briella's back. She spun around, ducking to the side as the woman opened an upheld palm. A smoky leash of purple-gray whipped out, lashing the air where Briella stood a moment ago.

She slammed into a table with several trinkets, knocking them to the floor. The woman turned her serpent-like magic on Briella again. A smoky tentacle cut through shelves, bringing the contents crashing to the floor. Several items shattered, blocking her exit.

"You might as well give in, Keeper."

The pulsing danger that fed her body energy froze. Briella shot the woman a sharp glance. Those pouty red lips stretched into a menacing grin.

The whip lashed out at her.

Briella shrieked, reeling back to escape the tip. She lost her footing, tripped over the merchandise scattered over the floor, and slammed into a glass case against the wall. Her hand smacked through the glass and shards tore into her hand and forearm. The coppery scent of blood assaulted her, but she couldn't spare a breath to look at the damage. The pain told her enough.

The smoky whip snagged her legs with the solidity of any real tether and yanked them from under her. The floor came up beneath her back mercilessly, jolting her entire body, making her bones rattle and the air shoot from her lungs. Her neck burned from the pressure of the sudden jerk as she tried to protect her head, and her chest ached as she struggled for breath.

The woman used the whip of smoke to reel her in, unhindered by the shattered glass and tumbled merchandise pieces Briella slid through. Spears of pain erupted over her back as her shirt slipped up, exposing her skin to the sharp debris.

The woman snapped her arm back.

Briella dug into her bag as her body skidded to a halt at the woman's feet.

"There are only so many places to hide before we will catch all of you," the woman said in that haunting voice. She leaned over Briella, unfurled her other fist, and revealed a small glowing silver orb in her palm. Briella's hand just connected with the stun gun in her bag when she noticed several of those black misty snakes slithering toward her from every direction. "You will come with me until he hands over the dragonstone."

The woman twisted her hand.

Briella yanked the gun from her bag, rammed her arm under the woman's until the end hit her target, and engaged the trigger.

The woman screamed, her small figure flailing backward. The snakes vanished in a soft explosion of black dust.

Air finally flooded Briella's lungs, and she gulped as much as she could. Her vision went briefly hazy, but she struggled to her feet and stumbled away from the woman.

"No you don't!"

Something silver flew toward Briella, expanding into a large oval—

She dropped to her knees and threw her arms over her head, a scream bolting up from her chest.

Hard, unwavering strength cocooned her, pulling her to the floor. The deadly growl that reverberated throughout her body was as welcoming as it was terrifying. She lowered her arms and opened her eyes enough to see a swollen Syn twist around, his large body protecting hers.

The sound that left his chest and filled the small shop snatched Briella's breath. It vibrated through the floorboards and rattled what glass was left unshattered.

A burst of blinding bright fire spewed from Syn's mouth.

The woman cut her arm across her body, a body that dissolved into black mist before the fire reached her. Briella shoved her head from beneath Syn's body as the mist funneled up along the ceiling and disappeared into the wood.

If it were possible for a person to lose their backbone, Briella would've sworn her every vertebra melted into the floor. She lay slack in Syn's arms, items digging into her back, the pain in her arm searing her nerves. Each gasped breath added to the tremors that consumed her arms and legs.

Syn straightened up. Stunning burnished red scales tipped in black covered his exposed skin. Talons retracted into his fingertips, his head reconfigured from the oddly beautiful cross between human and dragon, and the human Syn knelt beside her.

It all took a split second. A split second for her to realize she had been wrong.

A pitiful whimper escaped her as she scrambled onto her knees and threw herself into Syn's body. Tension rode his muscles as he embraced her, his cheek pressed to the top of her head.

"I'm sorry. I'm so sorry," she murmured. "I should've listened to you."

When he finally eased her away, his gaze held a mixture of worry and anger, both flashing flames into his eyes. The same eyes that dropped to her bleeding arm.

"How did you know where I was?"

"You're not the only stubborn one who doesn't like to listen."

Without saying another word, he ripped a strip of cloth from the closest table covering and wrapped it around her wrist, which appeared to have the deepest cuts. The entire time he tended to her, from picking shards of glass from some of the cuts, to washing her arm with paper towels he dampened in the employee bathroom, Briella couldn't take her eyes from him. Emotions morphed constantly across his face as he focused intently on tending her wounds. His narrowed eyes barely met hers. She tried to hear his thoughts and found silence.

"Sweet Goddess in this waking hell."

Briella spotted Taryn trekking through the mess at the front of the store.

Syn cupped the side of her face. She looked up at him and earned her first crooked grin. "How're you doing?"

"I think I made a bad impression here. I don't think this shop will promote my show." Syn groaned and rolled his eyes. She winced as she tried to shift up off her knees. "Ow."

"Wait a moment."

Taryn stepped up to her and shook his head. "Damn, girl. If you have a thing against voodoo, you should've stayed out of the store." Taryn looked around. "How many were here?"

"One," Briella said. "A woman."

That earned her two sets of intense eyes boring into her head.

"A woman?" Taryn asked. A crease formed over his brows. "I've only encountered men."

"Whoever she was, she possessed advanced magic. She had no problem showing that when she misted and disappeared into the ceiling," Syn said. "But she didn't possess the tattoos or the silver in her eyes."

Everyone looked up at the wooden rafters.

"Certain she was Baroqueth?" Taryn asked.

"She called me Keeper," Briella confirmed.

"On that note, I think we should get moving before the keep-away magic she must have set at the front door wears off and people actually start coming into the store. Or more of our pals show up," Taryn suggested. "Guess there will be a clearance sale."

Briella's forehead wrinkled. "What do you mean, keep-away magic? I came in without a problem."

Taryn crouched beside Syn and hung his arms over his knees. "Gorgeous, that's because it was a trap designed to snag you. Obviously, you were being watched."

Briella cut her attention back to Syn. The flames had died in his eyes, but a fierce protectiveness shone in their place.

"You can't underestimate them, sweet. The moment you do..." Syn waved a hand around the shop and exhaled sharply. "Please, I'll help you in whatever you want and need to do, but let me come with you when you leave Taryn's house. I don't want to see this happen again."

Briella's gaze lowered to her bandaged arm as the magnitude of her predicament hit her. Blood had begun to soak through the fabric. "I think I might need stitches."

"Syn, why don't you bring her back to our home? She'll heal much faster there."

"What?" She caught a silent exchange between Taryn and Syn. Syn nodded, and her curiosity was piqued.

"Agreed, but we'll have to wait until nightfall. There aren't many places here to launch from without drawing attention."

"I don't understand."

"The Hollow. But that's something Syn can fill you in on when we get you back to my house. For now, we need to leave."

Briella cringed as pain shot up her back and pulsed along her head as she tried to stand. Syn helped her to her feet, his arm solid and reassuring around her waist.

"Will you be able to walk back to the house?" Syn asked. Concern edged his voice. "We'll need to be as inconspicuous as possible. Don't need any more attention, especially when we step out of here and leave it in such a state. We can't risk your injuries being noticed."

Briella nodded, pressing her lips together. She'd manage. She'd suffer when she was in the privacy of her room, in the shower. Her mother could stitch her up. No need to go to a clinic or hospital.

"I'll be fine, Syn."

Those lips curled into a smile. His grip around her waist loosened. He shook free of his jacket and draped it around her shoulders.

"Keep your arm in the jacket."

"Wait." Briella pressed a hand to his chest, stopping him as he and Taryn started to lead her from the store. She pointed to the mirrors. "I think that woman trapped some people in there."

Taryn stepped around a few objects on the floor as he made his way to the mirrors. He tilted his head as he watched the frantic woman try desperately to say something. Taryn held up a hand.

"Damn it," Syn groused. "Taryn, I hope you know someone who can undo this, since we can't."

"I have a few people in mind, but we'll have to take the mirrors with us. I'm not going to leave them here, in case that woman returns." He flashed Briella and Syn a mischievous smile. "This is going to add a dash of interesting to our walk home."

Taryn covered the mirrors and placed them glass-to-glass to hide the terrified images trapped in them from pedestrians. With the mirrors tucked under Taryn's arm, and Briella tucked under Syn's, they left the store, and another nightmare, behind. Briella kept her arm hidden under the jacket and close to her chest, acutely aware of the blood that seeped through her shirt. She tried her best to stanch the bleeding with pressure from her other hand without knocking the jacket off her shoulders.

To her relief, Taryn led them through a series of narrow alleys and slow side roads, avoiding the dense crowds of the more popular streets.

Briella waited until they were almost to Esplanade before she pulled back the jacket enough to inspect the blood-soaked fabric.

"Brie!"

Briella yanked the jacket back in place and twisted to look back at the street behind them. Syn edged a half-step in front of her, his arm still around her waist. So slight a change in his stance, but the impression he presented was undeniable.

Not a single word needed to be said. She felt the meaning to the marrow, to the light of her soul.

Syn claimed her.

"Hey. I thought that was you." Mark jogged the last dozen or so feet to join them, Emma right behind him.

"Ah, your friend from the bar who has a keen eye for you."

Despite his attempt to keep his observation light, Briella detected his disgruntlement. She ignored it and, clenching the jacket close to hide her wounds, stepped around Syn.

"Calm it, dragon. He's only a friend."

"Mm-hmm. I bet that's what he *thinks."*

Briella stifled a groan and greeted her friends with a one-armed hug. Emma's attention was on Syn as she practically drooled. Her eyes reminded Briella of a cartoon character who finally found something to pine after, all bright and sparkly.

"…who is that yummy morsel of a man? Holy bejeezus. And that other one, too…"

Briella sighed inwardly at her friend's gawking thoughts while she honed in on Mark's resentment.

"…from the bar. What the hell is he doing here? With Brie? I'm not about to compete with a stranger. I knew her first…"

The elemental thought brought her shoulders straight. There was no denying the poignant jealousy in Mark's eyes, or in the taut smile that stretched his lips. He tried to keep his expression friendly, and failed.

"I thought we were supposed to meet for po'boys in a half hour," Mark said, his gaze moving between Syn and Briella.

"Who're your friends?" Emma asked, that knowing brow-arch in full effect. Her sly smile backed up her unspoken assumptions as she crossed her arms over her chest.

Taryn joined them, held out a hand in greeting. His smile dazzled and charmed in the same instant. Unfortunately, it didn't work on Mark, whose face darkened with suspicion.

"Name's Taryn. And here, my friend Syn." He lifted Emma's hand to his mouth and kissed her knuckles in his slick manner, quickly earning a blush from a woman Briella thought almost impossible to impress.

Mark stared at the offered hand when Taryn was through painting on the enchanting prince performance for Emma. Briella cleared her throat when Mark appeared to have forgotten basic manners.

He stiffly shook Taryn's hand.

"It's amazing what friends hide from each other," Emma said, accepting Syn's handshake. Briella caught the subtle flare of her nostrils as she took a surreptitious sniff. "Hmm, what cologne are you wearing? It's"—Emma's sharp gaze cut to her— "familiar."

Briella scowled in warning.

"Some concoction I get from a friend." Syn turned his attention to Mark. "And I recall you're Mark, correct? From The Black Duck."

Briella shut out the slew of cusses that tumbled through Mark's thoughts as he begrudgingly accepted Syn's hand. She was appalled by the degree of his disgust and hatred and jealousy. It was enough to make her reconsider the basis of their friendship, and whether it was built on Mark's false hope of it becoming something more.

"That's correct." Mark wagged a finger at Syn, a feigned thoughtful crease deepening in his forehead. "You were helping Brie."

Syn chuckled and directed a thought her way. *"He thinks he's smooth, doesn't he."*

"Don't stoop to his descending level."

Syn sidled close to her side, hard body brushing against her. His arm slinked back around her waist.

She should've been pissed, but instead found herself welcoming his gesture.

"She tripped. I was lending—"

"What is that on your neck?" Emma interrupted Syn, stepping up to Briella and poking her neck. "Are you bleeding?"

"Scratched myself."

"Huh." Emma sounded disbelieving.

Briella tightened her hold on the jacket covering her injured arm.

"So, I know my friends are heading out on the town in a few minutes, if you want to give them the rest of those brochures to hand out, Briella. Their connections will ensure a fantastic debut," Taryn said in a smooth move to change the subject. "Can't keep them waiting."

At this point, all Briella wanted was to get back to Taryn's and forget what had happened in the voodoo shop. She'd lost her drive to pass out her brochures and meet her friends for a late lunch before getting ready for work.

Not that she wanted to go anywhere alone anymore.

"I'll give you a call in a little while," Briella said.

"Why don't you bring your friends with you for po'boys?" Emma smiled at Syn and Taryn. "We're a friendly bunch. Promise."

"Sounds like a date."

Briella kept her grin as she shot Taryn a warning glance. He winked and turned toward Esplanade.

"Did he really just—"

"Yes." Syn gave her hip a light squeeze. *"Guess we're having a lunch date."*

Shouldn't be so bad.

She caught the glowering gaze Mark pinned on Syn and retracted that thought. Maybe the danger posed by the woman at the voodoo shop wasn't as bad as what could manifest from a jealous man.

CHAPTER 14

Syn swore to himself he'd never leave Briella alone again if he couldn't reach her in a split second. After the incident at the shop, his frustration and fear of what might have happened had he not decided to track her down redlined until his dragon wanted to singe anything in sight that threatened his woman. The entire screwed-up situation had been way too close a call for him to relax his guard.

As it stood, his blood seared his veins and his senses were highly attuned to the slightest noise, shift of air over his skin, and possible black misty clouds pouring into the frame of a woman.

It took several minutes and constant reassurance to calm Saralyn and keep both parents from suffocating his lifemate with their attention. He allowed his Keeper his due words to Briella, but put a firm foot down when Giovani and Briella started arguing about freedom and independence.

"I learned my lesson today, Dad, but I am not going to live in fear of walking out the door every day," Briella snapped.

Giovani, whose face was the same shade of flushed red as Briella's, gritted his teeth. "I knew it was a bad idea keeping this from you. Now I have to contend with a strong-willed, stubborn as sin, independent woman. You are not like everyone else, Briella, and the sooner you accept that, the safer you'll be."

"I think emotions are at a dangerous peak right now. Giovani, give her space. And Briella, please take into consideration his concern," Syn said. He half expected both his Keeper and his lifemate to turn on him, and braced himself.

To his surprise, father and daughter nodded, their heads lowering and the fight draining out of them before it turned explosive. Syn noticed Saralyn's closed-mouth smile of approval before she wrapped an arm around Briella and led her to the kitchen table. She had spread a towel over the tabletop and set out several types of antiseptic, gauze rolls, bandages, and a suture kit.

Syn motioned to the table and said to Giovani, "Please don't tell me she does this often."

"Saralyn never lost the skills she learned before the attack. She knows how to handle just about any injury," Giovani said with pride. Pride and love and adoration. Syn noted that in all the years, nothing dimmed that light of love Giovani and Saralyn shared.

To share that with Briella...

His hopeful thoughts were doused a minute later.

Saralyn pulled back the makeshift fabric dressing and the dragon clawed in fury. He hadn't realized he'd lost himself in the powerful anger until both women stared at him, eyes wide. Giovani rested a hand against his arm. A small plume of smoke curled up from Syn's nostrils as his dragon took over his sight to watch the ladies through thermal, orb-like lenses capable of picking out the finest detail of any object.

That object being Briella's sliced-up hand and wrist, and how deep many of her wounds were.

The growl that drew their attention subsided. He raked a hand through his hair, shaking the dragon down. His vision returned to normal, but his body hummed with tension.

Saralyn cleaned Briella's wounds and stitched up three of the lacerations. After a dressing was placed and a gauze bandage wrapped around her hand halfway up her forearm, Briella left the room to change into a clean shirt. Saralyn gave his shoulder a reassuring squeeze before she cleaned up her supplies and returned to the library with Gio.

Briella returned to the living room a short time later, purse on her shoulder.

"Ready? We're already late," Briella said. Syn nodded, but his enthusiasm to meet up with her friends for lunch was about as genuine as her urgency to leave the house. She didn't want to go and neither did he. "Where's Taryn?"

"He'll meet us there." He cupped Briella's face in gentle hands, tilting her chin up. He stared into her swirling gray eyes, sucked into the ribbons of blue and the swell of emotions that were always alive and vibrant in her irises. He traced her lower lip with his thumb. "Something else is bothering you. You don't want to go."

"My back and my head, in addition to my arm, hurt from the abuse that lady put me through." She nuzzled her cheek against his palm. Her eyelids slid to half-mast. "I have no way of hiding this bandage, which is going to lead to questions."

"We don't have to go, Briella."

"No, we do." She sighed. "*I* do. I put my friends through hell last night with my disappearing act and lied to Emma. It's the least I can do after the time they took to help me out this afternoon. If I stand them up, Emma will know something's up between you and me."

The pleasure he felt at Briella's comment was as genuine as the slow grin that curled his lips. He moved a little closer, until his leg brushed hers and the heat between their bodies was almost tangible. His sweet lifemate rested her hands against his hips, fingers splayed.

"You made it quite clear there was nothing going on between us," Syn murmured. His voice dipped an octave. His lips burned with the rush of desire that crashed through him. He drew one hand along the curve of her neck and shoulder, down her arm. Satisfaction followed the subtle hitch of her breath and the darkening of her eyes.

"That's correct." Sweet Goddess, her voice was soft and husky, pure sexual mayhem. "Nothing."

His gut twisted and his groin throbbed when she licked her bottom lip.

"Nothing," he repeated, dipping his head until their noses brushed and their lips lingered a breath away. He slipped his hand to her lower back and slowly urged her closer until her body settled flush against his. "Then there's nothing to worry about."

Briella's eyes closed, her shallow breaths caressing his lips and intensifying the hunger he suffered. She tipped her head, her forehead touching his. Her delicate hands slipped upward, drawing him taut beneath her touch.

"Syn," she whispered, fingers sliding up his neck and into his hair. He battled the urge to take and claim, to set aside the playful banter and make a resounding point. They belonged together, and the sizzling in the air between them, the merciless burn that consumed them emphasized that. She felt it, and it resonated within him, causing his own stormy desire that much more difficult to ignore.

When her fingers fisted against his scalp, his growl was so primitive Briella gasped. "We've everything to worry about."

Her mouth crushed against his, shameless in her need, and he gladly indulged the desperate sweep of her tongue and the urgency behind each kiss.

Blind to logic and reality, Syn unraveled as quickly as Briella. Every inch of her pressed tight to him, from her legs to the swells of her breasts. He drew his breath from her lungs and fed her breath from his, as one without being complete.

Though they could quickly rectify that.

He dropped his hand from her cheek and hooked it under her knee as she lifted it along his thigh.

"Syn."

He barely recognized the shift in her body before she hopped up, locking her legs around his waist. Any sense remaining fled, leaving him engulfed in fire and wanting Briella. All of Briella.

Now.

Her nails scraped his scalp and he groaned, plundering her with a kiss so hot it reversed control into his hands. He turned away from the door, toward the stairs, bumping into the wall. He reached for her hair, wrapped the silky thick ponytail around his hand, and tugged her head back.

The heady expression of pleasure and desire that consumed her face, from the rose of her cheeks to the swollen red lips parted in want, was more than he could handle and remain a decent man. She pushed the very boundaries that had kept him cordial and proper.

But to see how pleasure painted her, how want and need dressed her in sensuality…it was intoxicating to everything *decent* within him. She screamed to his carnal self, the basic, primal beast he kept locked behind a cage of scales. The very creature who would consume her until she could handle no more, and consume her again until all she knew was sensation.

Syn lowered his mouth to her neck and traced one throbbing vein there with his tongue. A tremor shook her. A delicate crease deepened along her forehead, and a moan filled his ears.

"Dear Goddess, the way you look at me…"

He kissed her, every inch of her neck, relishing the taste of her skin and the soft sounds she made. The determined woman wedged an arm between them and, with one hand, plucked open the buttons on his shirt until it lay open to his stomach. She slipped her hand beneath the fabric, running her warm palm over his pecs, down his stomach, and stopped only when her fingers hit his belt.

"Upstairs?"

Even through telepathy, her breathless question drove him mad. The ache in his jeans became a lifeline, reminding him he could not lose control.

"What about lunch?"

Maybe reason hadn't completely abandoned him, but he sure didn't care for it right now.

He kissed her below her ear, delighting in the way her fingers curled into his side and her nails bit into his skin. He twisted to round the corner to the stairs, prop a foot on the first stair, and press her back into the wall.

"Ow," she gasped, arching off the wall and dropping her feet from his waist.

A bolt of ice-cold worry speared his desire, dousing the heat a degree or so. Enough for him to think more clearly. Syn pulled her away from the wall, gripped her chin in a gentle hold, and caught her eyes. They shimmered with tears that she quickly blinked away.

"What is it?" he asked, more gruffly than he intended.

"My..." She winced. "My back."

Syn eased her around and lifted her shirt. She didn't fight him, a small blessing. As soon as he saw the cuts and bruises on her pale skin he wished she had. Upon closer inspection, he realized why she was in such pain.

"Why didn't you say anything earlier about these injuries? This is a lot more than an aching back." Syn turned her to face him and sighed. "Did it not hurt to change your shirt?"

"I checked my back and saw nothing worrisome."

"You have glass in your cuts, precious." She blinked at him. "I think you need to let your friends know you're not coming."

"We can make an appearance."

"If you were willing to forego lunch for pleasure, I think you should definitely forego lunch for injury."

Briella's gaze lowered, that delicious blush deepening across her face. She lifted her hand and drew her fingers down his chest in caress that was pure temptation. His jaw tightened. Did this woman have no idea the fire she played with? Not even a dive in the Arctic Ocean could cool his blood at the moment.

"Briella."

Her hand dropped to her side and she nodded once. "Okay."

"And work?"

"I'll call in sick." She raised her bandaged arm. "Can't carry trays anyhow. I'll just have to pick up extra shifts to cover the damages at my apartment."

"I've covered those. And anything else you need."

"I can't accept that."

"Why?" Syn traced her brow. "You've accepted it all of your life."

The gentle woman disappeared behind a wall of steely strength and defiance. "I don't like handouts. I work for what I want."

"I never said you didn't."

"You implied—"

"Nothing but the truth." He shrugged. "A conversation for another time when I can show you what I mean."

"And when will that be?"

"I would like to bring you to The Hollow this evening. My homeland, the place your parents were born and raised, a place you have yet to see, but have every right to." He folded his hand around her injured forearm and stroked the bandage with his thumb. "These will be gone in no time. If you'll agree to the trip."

Interest glimmered in her eyes. Curiosity softened the edges of her expression. "How long will this trip take?"

"If I had a choice, I would never want to return. I respect that your life is here, and you have dreams you're about to live. I am not the insolent fool from your past, sweet. I'll do everything I can to make your dreams here come true. The trip should take but a day.

Maybe two. A soak in a mineral bath and the natural magic of the world will reverse the wounds."

"And my parents?"

Syn smiled. "We have four dragons, m'lady. I'll let you have your choice which of us you'd like to ride. Your parents will have transport as well, since I won't allow them to stay here if I'm gone."

"Mmm, who to ride…"

Briella closed the small gap between them, resting her palms against his chest. She pressed up on her toes, tilted her head, and nuzzled her nose and lips against the crook of his neck. He caught himself before he wrapped an arm around her back and held her waist instead, drawing her tight against his aching cock.

"I'll have to consider my choices, then."

"You should definitely consider them."

She dragged those cursed lips along his throat. "I will." The sensual torture subsided. She tucked her head under his chin and sank into him. "And more."

After placing her calls to Emma and her boss, Briella stood in the bathroom and tried to check the cuts on her back. She still couldn't see any glass. Then again, it was hard to look while contorted like a wrung dishrag. Or when her mind couldn't seem to keep from replaying what had happened between Syn and herself. What *would* have happened.

She had no way of explaining what she felt. The only way to describe it was that when she was with Syn, either standing next to him or in his arms, she felt whole. Right. Silly as it was, he completed her in ways she never realized she was missing. Never had she felt so strongly for a man, to the point her willpower and her mind had no say in the pull of destiny. She dug her heels into the figurative mud and stood her ground against him, to no avail. She fought to hold on to the urge to maintain control over what she couldn't explain.

All her efforts backfired a hundred-fold when *she* kissed *him*. Like an elastic band stretched to breaking and finally released, the tension shattered and the natural need consumed what it had long awaited.

Her body continued to ache for him, from the heaviness of her breasts and their heightened sensitivity to the slightest movement against her bra, to the thrum of heat between her legs.

She swallowed, choked, and resigned herself to reliving the pleasure of memory. The feel of his skin against her hands. Hot, hard geography carved with smooth, taut muscle. The heat of his mouth, his kiss, an elixir of tenderness and raw possession. The strength of his embrace, how perfect she molded against his form.

And when he grabbed her hair and tugged…

Briella slumped against the bathroom counter and moaned. "Why bother fighting it?"

Seduction by Syn was going to ruin her in every form and fashion. She craved his kiss. It was a need as strong as the need to breathe. And if she gave herself to him, all of her?

He'll be my next addiction I have no control over. Just like painting.

"*Precious, how are you doing?*"

Cursed dragon.

"*I still don't see glass.*" *I'm not seeing much of anything other than you in my head.* "*I know you're busy with Gabe and Emery, but can you send my mom up here? Maybe she can get the pieces out.*"

"*May I come in?*"

Briella squeezed her eyes shut and sucked in a slow breath. "*Yes.*"

She was asking for another round of torture, but the delicious thought of his presence won out.

The bedroom door opened and a moment later, Syn poked his head into the bathroom. His face darkened, as did his eyes. His nostrils flared and his lips grew taut.

He burned her with his slow perusal, and the only person she could blame was herself. She hadn't put her shirt back on, leaving her standing in her jeans and a bra.

Slowly, she turned her back to Syn. "How many pieces are lodged?"

"Come here."

She caught his reflection in the mirror as he stretched out his hand. God, those eyes burned with more than hunger. She had never seen desire so raw that it possessed her own body, her thoughts, and left her swaying.

Somehow, she managed not to fall and gave her hand to Syn. He led her into the bedroom and motioned to the bed.

"Lay down on your stomach and make yourself comfortable. I'll be right back."

Briella barely heard him leave, but felt the distance between them straight to her core. She climbed onto the bed and settled onto her belly, her feet dangling off the edge of the mattress and her arms tucked under her chin. She considered turning on a light, since the day beyond the window was quickly fading into an array of stark reds and purples.

Syn returned with her mother in tow.

"Sweetheart, why didn't you have me look at your back while I was tending to your arm?" her mother asked, her delicate brow wrinkled with concern. "Thankfully, we'll be leaving soon and these can all heal up."

"I didn't think it was necessary. A few scrapes and such." Briella motioned to Syn. "He saw the glass. I tried to see it, but couldn't."

"It's your back, dear. Of course you'd have difficulty seeing it." Saralyn laid out her medical supplies on the nightstand closest to Briella's head. "I'll numb the areas Syn sees glass, but he asked to care for you."

The smile Saralyn doted on her was one of a mother beguiled by the thought of a potential son-in-law.

"If you'll allow, of course," Syn said.

"His sight is far better than mine could ever be, and with the natural light fading, it might be best," her mother explained, preparing syringes with a numbing agent.

Briella half hid her delight behind her folded arms and nodded. She noted her mother's transparent attempt to leave her care in Syn's hands, which was fine by her. She tipped her head enough to catch Syn's searing gaze. "I think that'll be fine."

"Great."

Syn settled on the bed beside Briella and directed Saralyn to the cuts where he noted glass and other debris. Her mother skillfully injected numbing medication around each wound, a few sighs and sympathetic noises leaving her lips as she did so. For the first few pokes, Briella gripped the blanket until Syn rested a hand over her fist. His touch alone relaxed her to the point she barely felt another prick.

"Okay, Syn. She's under your care. Hurt her, you'll have me to contend with."

"You should know you have nothing to worry about, as long as she's *under* my care."

"I'm under your care from now on. No more venturing out alone," Briella assured.

"Good."

Saralyn regarded him for a few beats before she kissed his cheek and left the room, closing the door behind her.

"Do you have any experience digging glass out of a woman's back?" Briella asked, half joking. Syn reached for a sterile pair of tweezers, a small basin, and a wad of gauze squares.

"When I'm through, I'll let you tell me what you think."

Smart.

"Your dragon is doing the looking, isn't it."

Syn's fingers traced through the maze of cuts and lacerations. Again, she found deep-seated comfort in the gentle touch and relaxed into the bed.

"Yes. If it hurts, you tell me, okay?"

"No."

"That's my sweet."

Syn started the tedious work of digging out glass from each numbed cut, using gauze to clean shards from the tweezers. Between each cut, he worked that calming magic along her spine with those skilled fingers until her eyes grew tired. He worked in silence. She watched him through heavy-lidded eyes, catching his occasional glance in her direction. Dragon eyes, lit by dark fire and slit pupils. There was not a sign of frustration or aggravation in his expression, only the kind of tenderness a man would wear for a woman he loved.

The thought struck her as his eyes lifted to hers.

She could swear he was inside her mind, living her thoughts, relishing her ideas.

A ghost of a grin curved the edges of his mouth. He went back to tending to her wounds.

Strangely enough, Briella found herself dozing off several times during his ministrations. By the time he was through, the sun had set and the noise level on the floor below increased to an incessant rumble.

"Sweet, I'm done." Syn's knuckles caressed her cheek, rousing her from another dip into sleep. Slowly, she pushed onto her hands and knees, rolled out her neck, her shoulders, and settled back on her heels. Her dragon protector looked her over, his emotions masked, and climbed off the bed. "Are you in any pain?"

"Not a bit." She didn't have to lie. Her wounds were still numb, but his gentle attendance to each cut left her in no discomfort. "I think you've done this a time or two."

"More times than you can imagine," he snickered, gathering her mother's supplies in a cloth. Briella laughed. She liked this playful side of the super gentle-dragon-man Syn. It distracted her from…other things. "I'll send you a survey."

"Now how would you know about surveys?" Briella hopped off the bed and crossed to the dresser. She rifled through the shirts she had packed until she settled on a simple, deep red split-sleeve piece.

"I'm aware of my surroundings. I listen to people complain about them after hospital stays. Um, I'd make sure you have something to keep you warm. I doubt Giovani brought riding coats, and I'm certain he never had one made for you."

Briella pulled the shirt on before she faced Syn again. Another piece of clothing between them was a safe move. "Riding coats?"

"They protect you during flight and keep you warm against the colder temperatures at higher altitudes."

"How do I breathe?"

Syn tapped his nose. "In and out."

Briella snorted. "I'd throw a pillow at you if I had one close enough."

"Good thing for a few feet of distance between you and the bed."

He came to the foot of the bed, his gaze drifting toward the covered painting of his shadowy self. She had made sure to lay the sheet over the canvas, otherwise she'd be obsessed with a work of art—when she wasn't obsessing over the real deal.

"Remember, you aren't entirely human, Briella. You're of Keeper blood. Your body will adjust to flight as you adjust to minor altitude changes here. You'll be able to process the thin air and retain the oxygen you need. Trust me. Otherwise, I wouldn't dare attempt it with you." He glanced toward the windows. "The guys are ready downstairs. We should head out soon."

"I'll pack a small bag."

Syn nodded and lifted the bundle of medical supplies. "Let me get these to Saralyn and clean out the basin in the meantime."

"Syn." Briella stopped him a few steps from the door. She pressed up onto her toes and planted a kiss on the corner of his mouth. "Thank you."

"Anytime, sweet."

CHAPTER 15

Briella huddled close to her mother on the edge of a field some thirty minutes from the French Quarter, with only dim streetlights half a mile away providing a halo of illumination above the copse of trees. The trees created a buffer around the field, hiding their small group from the prying eyes of any passing drivers. It wasn't an ideal space, according to Taryn, but unless they wanted to waste another hour to get to a good spot, this had to do.

"Ma, you're bouncing on your toes like a child," Briella noted, nudging her mother with her shoulder. "I'm still not quite over this whole riding a dragon thing. How big are they when they're dragons?"

"Watch, sweetheart. It's a magnificent sight to see them transform."

So, Briella kept her eyes on the five men in the center of the field—her father was in deep conversation with the dragon men—waiting for the spectacle to unfold.

"And to think two days ago I was more concerned about landing my first art show, paying my bills, and

212

being on time to meet my friends for drinks. What a funny turn my life has taken," Briella said, aware of her mother's attention on her as she spoke. She offered Saralyn a smile. "Not that I'm complaining."

"I never said you were, dear. But now that you've brought it up of your own accord, how are you taking everything?"

Briella shrugged. How was she supposed to take the news that dragons were real, she was about to hop on the scaly back of an oversized reptile to fly to a world that should not exist, and that her future was tied to a man who was about to shift into a mythological creature? The moment her gaze landed on Syn's sturdy and confident stance, she couldn't imagine her life before he dropped into it.

"I think I'm adjusting nicely. I guess it helps that Dad filled my head with dragon stories when I was younger, and that I know paranormal entities exist." She winked at her mother. "Thanks to your contribution to my crazy gifts."

Her mother laughed. "Great. I'm glad." She leaned close to Briella and made a faint motion with her chin. "Have you and Syn come to an understanding?"

Briella's eyes widened. "Ma, don't you dare start nosing around our personal relationship. I don't needle for information about you and Dad." She shuddered. "Not that I want to know."

Saralyn stared at her, her face relaxed, but her eyes hawkish as they picked Briella apart. A satisfied smile filled out her mouth and she straightened up.

"That's answer enough."

"Sweet heaven, help me," Briella muttered. Her mother's confirmation meant only one thing. She'd had a vision and saw something Briella had yet to experience. She dared to steal another glance at Syn, and ended up focused on her father instead.

He jogged over, hair mussed, eyes glowing with excitement. "We're ready. Saralyn, Taryn and I both agree that he'd be smooth enough for you to ride. I'll go on Emery and Belle, you're going on Syn. The brothers picked up riding harnesses from The Hollow earlier todday." He turned to Briella. "I'll help you mount Syn and secure you into the harness. His body heat will keep you warm as we ascend. Keep close to his back. And don't forget to breathe. Your body was made to fly."

As her father talked, Briella's brow arched higher and higher. "You mean I'm going to fly on a dragon. Alone. By myself. Dad, did it occur to you that dragons are not horses?"

Damn her father for that mischievous smile and wink. "It's much easier to ride a dragon than a horse. You can communicate with Syn in the air. He'll be in tune with you the entire time, and he'll do whatever he can to ease your concerns."

"Anxiety, Dad. Anxiety."

Her father grabbed her shoulders and leaned close. "Excitement, Belle. Just wait. There is almost nothing to compare to the thrill of flight."

She did *not* want to acknowledge that spark of said excitement. Truth be told, how many people could say they'd flown on the back of a dragon?

Giovani flicked the lapel of Syn's leather jacket hanging over her shoulders. He had insisted she wear it over her peacoat as an extra layer of protection. She swam in the thing, but his pocket secured the dragonstone.

"Make sure you're buttoned up," her father said.

Briella took his advice and watched the four men in the center of the field spread out. Syn cast her his signature half-grin.

"Ready, sweet?"

"Guess we'll find out soon enough, won't we?"

His rich chuckle filled her head and eased her anxious nerves.

Briella wasn't sure what to expect when the show started, or what she dubbed as a show. At the voodoo shop, Syn had swelled to about twice his size, scale-covered and awkwardly contorted between human and dragon. The dragon couldn't be much bigger. Then again, storybooks depicted dragons from fairy-sized to mountainous.

The brothers transformed first, and Briella's jaw dropped. The transition was fluid and smooth and quick.

And they were...huge!

"Definitely mountains."

"What, sweetheart?" her mother asked.

Briella shook her head. "Oh, just their, uh, size."

215

Thankfully those trees around the edge of the field were tall and thick. She wouldn't be surprised if these guys brushed the tops with those spines along their backs, since neither had their heads lifted on their long necks.

Taryn turned dragon next, and Syn last. Briella simply stared as the man who melted her from the marrow of her bones out to her skin disappeared within the majestic encasement of an equally breathtaking creature. All four dragons had similar coloring: deep burnished-red scales with blackened tips that gave them a singed appearance. Their crests differed slightly, the brothers' possessing a shorter row of spines and smaller accents of black compared to Syn and Taryn's, who appeared more matured, with ridges and longer strokes of black. And although the brothers were huge, Syn and Taryn had a few feet on them.

Syn's long neck and large head snaked around until Briella stared into a single fiery orb focused intently on her. *"Come."*

"Now I'm scared," she half-joked. How on earth was she supposed to ride him? She'd need a very tall ladder to get on his back. Then there was the problem of those spines.

Her father jogged out to the dragons, and the pile of leather-like ropes sitting in the middle of their quasi circle.

"I'm not sure if I should be insulted or pleased," he replied with a lightness that eased her a bit. *"Giovani*

needs to place the harnesses on, so we're not ready to leave yet, but I don't want you to fear me as the dragon."

His constant consideration for her feelings stole more heartstrings than she possessed. His concern for her well-being was clear as crystal after the incident this afternoon.

Straightening her shoulders and lifting her chin, she crossed the expanse of field to the dragon awaiting her, that glowing orb watching her with an intensity that resonated throughout every cell. The closer she came, the more she soaked in the beautiful details that created a creature as breathtaking as the man he came from.

Syn lowered his head until his thick chin rested on the ground. She barely reached his lower eyelid, but got a front-seat look at a single white fang that rested over his lower jaw.

"I hope you don't plan on using that," she said, running her fingers over the leathery lip above the fang. A sharp breath shot from Syn's wide, round nostril. A thin curl of smoke surrounded her and she groaned. "Really?"

"Not in this form. And yes. Really."

Briella leaned close to the smaller scales that lined his head and took a deep breath. Campfire. Wild and natural and so sensual. She wasn't exactly sure what to expect, but Syn's scent carried over to the dragon and it filled her with calm.

His scales were hot, but not scalding, and incredibly smooth except for the natural ridges at the centers. She dragged her fingertips along his neck, her nails tapping each scale after she crested the one before it. They thickened, grew larger as she drew closer to his torso. Her eyes dropped to his massive feet and those wicked talons that were about half her size. Dark, shiny, and razor sharp.

"Still scared?"

"Nope. Glad to be on your good side." She flashed him a smile, and caught her own reflection in his eye. She pointed to his back, far above her head. "And how do I get up there?"

Syn stretched out one of his exceptional wings to reach the ground. She observed the structure of the wing, from the arm-like shape and the claw at the peak joint, to the leathery membrane and the venous pathways between each finger. The same burnished red as the rest of Syn, with ashen black along the arm.

Her father joined them a few minutes later, one of the leather ropes slung over his shoulders. "I'll fasten the harness and get you up on his back." He splayed a hand over Syn's cheek and sighed. "Like good old days, Syn."

Syn nudged her father's hand in response. Briella was certain they shared their own telepathic conversation, words she wasn't privy to. She stepped back and let her father work, impressed by the deft ease with which he applied the harness and tightened it around Syn's body.

He gave the double strap on Syn's underbelly one last tug, nodded, and turned to Briella. "All right, Belle. Let's get you up there."

Briella gauged the loops that followed one of the straps from the spiny back down. Her father brought her to the strap. Syn tilted his side closer to the ground, making it possible for her to reach the lowest loop.

"I'll let you go first. It'll be easier for me to instruct you that way. The loops are to climb. Hands first, feet follow. Like you're rock climbing."

Briella rolled out her shoulders, grabbed two loops, and hoisted herself up. She fit her feet into two lower loops and began her climb until she reached the row of spines along his back. A thin trickle of sweat beaded between her shoulder blades, causing her cuts to sting. As her father ascended at a far more fluid and faster pace, Briella took a few moments to try and decipher how the harness worked and came up lost.

"Belle, securing yourself to Syn is quite simple, so don't get intimidated by the straps. I've always used these two spines as my guide, since the top one is shorter and not as sharp as the rest." Her father patted the swath of scales between the two spines the harness split over. A set of similar loops dangled from the top strap. Two additional straps connected the top to the bottom, and what looked like a belt gone bad stretched between those two straps. "Straddle his back, settling on this bottom spike until we get you belted in."

"This isn't bothering you?" Briella asked Syn, kicking her leg between the two spikes and settling on her butt.

"Not at all."

"Well, don't brake too fast, unless you want to take out all my lady parts on this spike of yours."

219

A sharp snort and a sensation of disbelief through their telepathic link were his only response.

Her father, on the other hand, quirked a brow in her direction.

Briella waved a hand toward the spines. "I just told him to take it easy. I don't want to get impaled."

"Uh-huh." He chuckled and shook his head. "There are grips on either side of the top spike you'll hold during your flight. Use the two loops closest to your feet as stirrups. I'll strap the harness around your waist. A few things to remember. First, breathe. It might sound silly, but when he launches, it'll be at bullet speed. Faster than a roller coaster. Your body can handle this, but you can't forget to breathe. You're connected with Syn. He'll be able to tell if you're in distress and talk you through it, but you must listen to him. Stay close to his body for warmth. The jackets will protect you a little, but it is his body heat that will give you the most protection. Your mother and I will commission a riding coat for you, now that you'll be partaking in this more often, I presume."

"Let's get through the first time and we'll go from there."

"Belle, you'll become addicted to riding the moment you're in the air and realize how natural it is." Her father's smile lit up his face. He glanced over his shoulder, and Briella followed his gaze. Her mother sat atop Taryn like a woman born to ride a dragon. She waved to them, then resumed fiddling with Taryn's harness. "Let's get you belted in."

Briella watched her father closely, committing each step in securing the belt around her waist to memory. After a kiss to her cheek, he descended the same way they came up, leaving her to settle into a semi-comfortable position.

"Giovani is headed to Emery. How are you settling in?"

She slipped her hands into the grips on the top strap and held tight. *"Why do I feel like I belong in a bondage movie?"*

Syn's neck jerked his big head around until he stared at her with one eye. Curls of smoke escaped is nostrils. Briella lifted her chin, and her brows.

"Don't get too excited. Not my style."

"Sweet gods." His mental voice rasped those two words. *"I'll never have you on my back with innocent thoughts again."*

"I'm not innocent."

"You're making that a very compelling point more and more each day." Syn shifted on his feet, all four of them, and tested his wings with a half-folded flap. Taryn mimicked him. *"Ready?"*

"What about my father?"

"He'll be ready once we're off the ground. We can't launch all at once. I'm taking lead, Taryn behind me, and Emery behind him. Gabe's taking tail."

Briella tightened her grip when Syn moved again, lifting his head to the sky. He stretched his wings, the width almost reaching from one tree line to the other. He leaned back on his hind legs.

"Briella, trust me. I'll keep you safe."

"You'd better."

"I will. Hold on."

When her father told her Syn would launch into the air like a bullet, he hadn't been joking. A slipstream of air poured over her with the weight of the earth, crushing against her shoulders. She tucked her head into her arm, recalling aerodynamics and remaining streamlined so air could pass over her. She silently concentrated on her handgrips and her feet in the stirrups, the belt around her waist keeping her from injuring more fragile body parts against the lower spine.

She heard a rustle before the pressure of the air went from crushing to that of a steady gentle wind.

When she opened her eyes, Syn's wings were extended and they were flying parallel to the land below.

"Wow."

Briella pushed herself up straight, slipping one hand from a grip to get a better view of the light-splattered nightscape far below. *"Wow."*

She sucked in a deep breath of cold, crisp air and smiled. The extreme altitude had no effect on her ability to breathe, and the icy temperature barely touched her, except for the wind in her face.

Free. She felt free. Exhilarated. Untouchable.

"Ahh, sweet. You're a natural. Not an ounce of fear."

"This is probably one of the best experiences of my life."

"Little can compare to the thrill of flight." Syn flapped his wings. *"Are you holding on tight?"*

Briella fit her hand back in the grip. *"Yep."*

"Want a little more excitement?"

"Sure. Excitement of the good kind is always welcome."

The blasted man chuckled in a knowing way.

Briella gasped when he dove downward, but her surprise quickly melted into astonishment, then a new surge of adrenaline-fed excitement as he took her for a ride like no roller coaster could match. The weightlessness of her body as he spiraled downward. The tingling delight as he curved skyward. She may not be well versed in dragons and flight, but she surmised Syn's skills were without fault.

Her assumptions were put to the test when they picked up speed as they flew through the peaks and valleys of a mountain range. Taryn, Emery, and Gabriel kept pace a short distance behind them.

"Relax, Briella. The Hollow is protected by a magical veil. Like a portal of sorts. There are two ways to break through to reach the land. One is by the use of magic. The other is speed."

"And you have no magic."

"Speed it is." Syn flapped his wings, driving them forward faster and faster. Briella pressed her body flat against his back, her hands numb from holding the grips so tight. He banked to the left, left again, right, through narrow passages of stone that had Briella squeezing her eyes shut and praying they wouldn't crash. *"Almost there."*

"Good, because this is a little too death-defying for me."

They had been flying for well over an hour, and the adrenaline was finally starting to wear off. Her ankles were tight, her legs sore, and the cuts on her arm and back throbbed. She took notice of a small spot of blood on the gauze and worried that during her thrilling flight, she might have pulled a stitch or two.

When she looked up, she started to scream and swallowed a mouthful of wintry air instead. She had no time to react as Syn bulleted toward the mountainside.

Through the mountainside.

A strange electric tingle coasted down her body from her head to her toes with no regard to her clothing, encompassing her as thoroughly as the darkness. Goosebumps formed beneath her layers of clothing. The scent of damp dirt after a fresh rain filled her lungs.

As fast as the sensations hit her, they were gone.

And she found herself soaring with Syn above a dazzling land lit by an enormous silver moon.

Syn's wings shot out, slowing their speed to a calm cruise. Briella pushed upright, opting to hold the connecting straps between the top and bottom part of the harness instead of the handgrips, and drank in the surreal world below. Even beneath a cape of night, she could see the brilliant colors of flowers, the startling green of the grass laced with a silvery glow, the diamond-like glitter that swirled over bodies of water and added a new level of brilliance to the many waterfalls. Mountain peaks stretched into the sky, dozens of them, some capped with snow, some draped with moss, ivies, and numerous other kinds of plant life. The land rolled into deep valleys, and those valleys were untouched by human intervention. No streets. No smog. Nothing but pure nature at its finest.

The hum of power was undeniable. It was like a gentle thrum that poured into her skin, soaked into her blood, and became a living entity within her body. The aches she suffered only a short time earlier began to subside, leaving her feeling remarkably rejuvenated.

"Is this...?"

"Welcome, sweet, to The Hollow."

A world that should not exist. A fairytale come to life.

A sudden surge of emotion unfurled in her chest. She blamed the sting of her eyes on the wind hitting her face and the tightness of her jaw and throat on her laughter from earlier in their ride. Regardless, her imagination burst with renewed urgency.

She regretted not packing a sketchpad and pencils, at the least.

"I-I have no words."

"No words are needed. Your emotions are practically tangible. Wait until the sun rises and the world comes alive." Syn banked right, dipping his wing and beginning a descent between two mountain ridges. The jagged gray rock melted into a soft-looking scape of greenery and lush tropical foliage where it met the upper levels of a valley. A few objects glowed silver,

highlighted by the glorious moon. *"You'll see firsthand where your parents lived before the attack."*

Syn glided in wide circles and controlled S patterns until he brought them to the ground. His landing was as smooth as his descent. She barely felt them connect.

"Do you want Giovani to help you down?"

Briella had already managed to tug off the belt around her waist. She swung her leg over his spine and started her climb from Syn's back.

"Beating him to it."

She jumped to the ground once she reached a safe distance, too anxious to take the time to fit her feet into the loops. She stretched out her back and shoulders, her arms, rolled her wrists, and turned to where the other three dragons had landed over a pasture of swaying knee-high grass. Lavender and yellow flowers dotted the grass throughout the field, and the scent that surrounded her was both subtle and sweet. The night was cool, not cold, and the air clean and crisp. Not even her home in the mountains of Upstate New York could compete with the air here. Each breath she took was like pulling weightless magic into her body.

"If I could capture you in these moments, I would."

Briella spun around. Syn, the human man, straightened from whispering close to her ear, and smiled. The harness lay draped over his shoulder.

Despite the cool breeze, her face warmed. "Why do I feel like I'm going to stay in this state of awe and shock for a while?" She spread her arms to encompass the world around her. "I could never do this place justice with words."

Syn tipped his chin. His chest puffed out as he took a deep breath and a peculiar glow tinged his eyes. "It was never meant for words, precious."

He held her with those eyes, entranced, giving her freedom to forget her world and open herself to the possibilities far beyond. Possibilities and experiences. As she looked him over, so irresistible in his dark blue jeans, leather boots, and black button-down shirt rolled up to the elbows, she wondered how much of those possibilities and experiences would be with Syn.

His gaze shifted over her head. Briella dipped her chin, willing the furious blush away.

"So? What do you think?" A man asked her back. "Flying's pretty awesome, right? Looked like you and Syn were having a blast."

Briella laughed and faced Taryn. Her parents were beside him, with the brothers behind them. Everyone looked pleasantly ruffled from the trip and an essence of post-thrill exhilaration hung in the air.

"Awesome, and more," she said.

"Well, I think you're a natural. Might even put your old man to shame."

"Hey, now," her father protested with a quirked grin.

Taryn rested a hand on Briella's shoulder. "She had no prior experience before tonight and she only panicked once, when we broke through the veil. She gets more points."

"Well, I don't know about you, but I'm starving," Emery interrupted as he walked through their small crowd, rubbing his stomach. "Hey, Gio. Betchya can't wait to see your old home."

Briella and Syn followed the group as they trekked down the slope of the hillside toward three cottages below. Her parents' excitement about returning home flowed from their quickened paces and rapid chatter, but Briella couldn't help stopping every few yards to smell the fragrant blooms. She examined a strange butterfly-like creature with luminescent green wings and glowing silver eyes as it swayed with the grass it clutched in tiny paws. Soft music from nocturnal animals filtered through the night in quiet tune.

As they reached a dirt and pebble path that led to the nearest cottage, Briella leaned into Syn's side and wrapped her arms around his waist. "Thank you for bringing me here."

Syn chuckled. "Thanks so soon and you haven't seen a fraction of The Hollow." His hand slid down her hair and curled around her shoulder. "You're welcome, sweet."

A matter of minutes changed her life, because now she knew she couldn't be without the man by her side. She hoped he was serious about helping her reach her dreams. She couldn't give up on those, either.

The cottage reminded her of something she might see in a fairy forest. Built of wood and some unfamiliar materials with a thatch roof, covered in spindles of climbing greenery and spots of colorful blooms, it didn't seem like a place that could withstand bad weather or brutal attacks. It was larger than she expected, but still smaller than their family home.

No gardens. Nothing that hinted at her mother's touch or her father's design.

Syn pushed the wood-slat front door open and let her pass into the cottage.

She stopped, looked around, stepped back outside, regarded the size of the structure, and returned to the expansive sitting room.

Syn quirked a brow. "Is everything all right?"

Briella listened to the excited shouts and greetings and oohs and ahhs from somewhere within the cottage, but where exactly, she wasn't sure. As far as she was concerned, the cottage should have been a matter of four or five rooms at most. The sitting room she and Syn walked into should have filled the cottage.

"Umm, how is this possible?" She circled her hand in the air, motioning to the room. "The house shouldn't be this spacious from the looks of the exterior. Dimensions are way off."

Syn's grin turned thoughtful as he looked around. "I never noticed that before. Interesting."

She shoved his arm playfully. "Bull."

"I told you, this world is magic." He turned back to Briella, eyes glittering with humor. "It's a defense. The homes appear small on the outside to make them more difficult targets to enemies. But, yes. They're far more spacious once you step inside. Think of it like an accordion unfolding the minute you step through the door. There's a shift of space. Physics at work."

"Don't tell me you're a physicist."

"Far from it, but the importance of it when explaining how things work in The Hollow doesn't elude me." He tilted his head as another burst of laughter echoed through the house. "Sounds like Cade's here." He sniffed the air. "Smells like Alazar's here, too."

"Who?"

"Come. Cade's been eager to meet you."

Briella and Syn passed through the large sitting room and down a hallway where they followed succulent aromas to another large living room with an adjoining dining room and spacious kitchen. She came up short of the archway into the kitchen, her body going rigid when she spotted the monster of a man at the opposite end of an island. With deep red hair and a matching red beard, all fierce angles and thick muscle, the man had to be close to seven feet tall, if he didn't cross that mark. He towered over Syn by half a head, and Syn ate up inches on the height scale. His eyes held a fiery glow, a baseline to his coloring more so than the flames she'd seen in Syn's eyes.

He looked like an ancient warrior who belonged in the history books, not a man leaning against a kitchen island with a smile on his face and taking on the role of a happy greeter. Briella narrowed her eyes. Yeah, that smile didn't fit him at all.

"Sweet, you're gaping."

Briella cleared her throat behind a hand she threw up to cover her open mouth. She ducked her head as a merciless flush filled her cheeks. Leaning into Syn came subconsciously, an instinctive reaction without thought. He settled a hand against the dip of her lower back.

"Well, I must say, Gio. Saralyn knows how to pass on fine genes." The voice that came from the monstrous man was as growly and gravelly as a dragon that tried to speak while in scales. It fit the guy. "Briella, is it?"

Syn pressed her forward gently, urging her closer to Cade. Briella scanned the kitchen, which would have been huge had it not been crowded with dragon-men and strangers she didn't know. Aside from her mother and herself, she spotted another young woman leaning up against the counter beside the stove. Another tall, dragonish man handled numerous pots and pans like a culinary expert.

"Briella Isabelle," her father said, pride filling his voice. He had been talking to someone who appeared fairly human and roughly around his own age. Another Keeper, perhaps.

"I think I'm a bit overwhelmed, Syn. Who are all these people and where are we?"

"This is your parents' home. And these are people who will become family."

"Okay, that's great and all, but honestly? I feel like the odd-woman out."

Syn glanced down at her as his hand slipped to her hip and squeezed gently. *"I wasn't expecting a party when we arrived. Had I known, I would've advised against it."*

Briella nodded, coming to halt as Syn stopped in front of Cade.

Cade held out his hand. Briella regarded it, wondering what damage her fingers were about to incur. She would not want to cross Cade's path in a sunlit alleyway, let along a dark one. She gave him credit for trying to appear less intimidating.

She placed her hand in his and was surprised by the tenderness of his grip and the easy shake.

"Cade Fenryn. Leader of the Firestorm *tatsu* clan. It's a pleasure, Briella. We're thrilled to have you here at The Hollow. I do hope you find it to your liking," Cade said. The more he spoke, the more the underlying rumble in his voice faded. He shifted enough to motion toward the cook, the woman, and the man with her father. "Alazar and Ariah Brandvold, and Mark Callahan, Alazar's Keeper. They moved back to The Hollow a few months ago."

Ariah rounded Cade and approached Briella, the friendly smile and gleam in her eyes touching. Briella was startled when the woman embraced her.

"Welcome," Ariah said. "I hope your experience flying into The Hollow wasn't as terrifying as mine." She cast a sharp look toward the cook, who flashed them a wicked smile. "He forgot to tell me about the veil and I thought we were going to crash into the mountain."

"And he's still breathing. I give you credit," Briella said. Ariah laughed, a light, airy sound that fit her smaller frame. Briella eased away from Syn. "He warned me."

Ariah nodded up at Syn. "I always took you for a decent guy. You haven't proven me wrong yet."

"I have no intention of doing so," Syn said.

Ariah tucked a loose wave from her asymmetrical haircut behind her ear. "Alazar told me Syn fixed up this place a few years ago in hopes that Giovani and Saralyn had survived. I understand most of the homes were destroyed after the Baroqueth attack."

"He's done an amazing job, too," Saralyn chimed in, stepping up to Ariah's side. "I believe Alazar's almost done preparing dinner, but I want to take a quick walk of the property and start plotting out new gardens. Would you ladies like to join me?"

"Ma, it's night."

Saralyn's smile stretched. "The best time to walk. Syn?"

Syn stepped back, leaving Briella to go with her mother and Ariah. Unfortunately, her discontent with these small bouts of separation was becoming more and more intolerable.

"Enjoy, sweet."

For a second, she wanted to hate him. Hate him for being so kind and easy-going. Hate him for being so understanding and generous. She wanted him to say no, to give her a reason to push him away.

No. I don't.

"Nighttime garden plotting it is, then," Briella said, taking her mother's outstretched hand.

As she followed her mother and Ariah to the front door, she wanted Syn to stop her and ask her to come back.

God.

She thought she was starting to fall in love with a dragon named Syn.

CHAPTER 16

Dinner was as raucous as Syn imagined it would be. The reunion of dragons, Keepers, wives, and lifemates was celebratory, to say the least. Cade contributed a cask of wine from the wild grapes and berries he tended on the knoll beside his mountain home, which added to the jubilant atmosphere. Alazar's meal of roasted meats and an extensive choice of sides received accolades and salutes.

Two hours of dining, chatting, and catching up on poignant memories passed in a blink. He kept a keen eye on Briella, content that she had warmed to Ariah. She spent a good portion of the meal learning about The Hollow, lifemates, Keepers, and all the roles she would hopefully embrace. Her questions and curiosity were genuine, as were the subtle soreness and evident exhaustion that seemed to have intensified over the last half-hour. Her eyes had noticeably dimmed when he met her gaze across the table.

Syn threw back the rest of his wine and pushed away from the table, drawing the rowdy crowd's attention. "It's been a long day. I think we should let our guests settle in for the night. There will be plenty of time tomorrow to continue this celebration."

Cade nodded, following Syn's lead. He gathered his plate and cup and looked at Giovani. "We'll clean up from this meal and supply you with whatever you need through this stay."

His brethren caught on quickly, finishing up the last of their drinks and clearing the table of dishes. When Ariah joined them in the kitchen and took a spot by the sink, Syn stayed her hands before she could start washing dishes beside Alazar.

"She's taken a liking to you, Ariah. Spend time with her. We'll take care of this," Syn suggested. "She needs someone who came from her world before learning about this one."

Ariah's gaze shifted to her lifemate's before she nodded and disappeared back into the dining room. Syn moved into her spot, grabbed a dishrag, and took the chore of washing dishes next to Alazar.

"You've got yourself a stunner," Alazar said quietly, rinsing off plates he had washed. "How the heck did your ugly ass manage that one?"

"I should ask you the same thing, but you've got a sense of humor that can draw anyone in, so I know my answer." Syn held up the remainder of a few cuts of meat. "And you cook."

Alazar snickered. "Ri helped me with dinner tonight. Her dishes can rival mine."

"That's saying something."

"I taught her." Alazar smiled. *"That's* saying something."

"Have you spoken to Zareh?"

"We visit every month. Kaylae's due soon. He's come here a couple times over the last few weeks, tidying up his pretty little cave in preparation for the big move once the baby's born." Alazar nodded toward the dining room. "What about Briella? She game for a one-way trip?"

Syn shook his head. "Not yet. Unfortunately, she's being tailed by Baroqueth."

"So I heard. Cade's got a big mouth."

"Cade's big overall."

Alazar dropped the plate he had rinsed in the sink, turned to Syn, and arched his brows. "And how would you know?"

It took Syn a moment to catch Alazar's double entendre, and when he did, he let a short spurt of sparks loose from his throat. Alazar jumped back, laughing.

"Such a gentleman all the time. It's fine to go crazy every once in a while," Alazar said, returning to Syn's side.

Syn rolled his eyes and finished washing the last of his dishes. Gabe and Emery had joined them to dry and put the dishes away.

A short time later, after everyone said their parting goodbyes for the night, Syn and Taryn hung back. Syn felt Briella's growing discomfort from her wounds reflected through his body.

"Thank you, Syn. For everything. Saralyn and I are utterly grateful for this," Giovani said, spreading an arm toward the house. His eyes shimmered with tears. "It's so good to be here, in our home. We've missed it tremendously. We've missed you and the clan."

Syn squeezed his shoulder. "You know this is your home, Gio. You tell me when you want to come here. For good. I'll make it happen."

Giovani nodded. "In time. When Briella is ready. We won't leave her."

"And neither will I," he promised. "Give Saralyn my partings. Taryn and I are going to draw buckets from the mineral pools for Briella to soak in tonight. It would be best for her wounds. She won't rest well otherwise. We'll leave them on the front stoop and I'll let you know when they're outside."

Giovani stared at him for a long moment, more emotions playing across his face than Syn could decipher.

"I've always known that if I was blessed with a daughter, you would give the world to her. I see that, Syn. As a father, I can't tell you how much it means to know you adore her. It's written plain as day every time your eyes land on Belle. I've noticed. And so has Saralyn."

Syn hid the sliver of disappointment that he'd be spending the night alone behind a gracious smile. *"She is a treasure greater than anything I have crossed. And I am grateful she is your daughter, and my lifemate. I hope one day to make her happy."*

"If I know anything about her, it won't be long," Giovani said, his voice low.

Syn nodded once and stepped back. "Taryn and I will be back soon."

Giovani walked them out. A dark ache in Syn's chest pulsed, growing stronger every second he thought of Briella.

She hadn't come to bid him goodnight. Not that he expected her to. She owed him nothing.

"I'm still waiting for that nuclear explosion," Taryn said as they started the climb up the hill to the level field. "If the tension between you two gets any thicker, you'll need a hacksaw to pass anywhere near you."

"Tension is but tension, my friend." *Brutal, merciless tension.* "I doubt it is as great as you suspect."

Taryn snorted. "Brother, Al noticed, and he notices little besides Ariah and any danger that might present itself toward her."

"What did you do, bet him a gold piece—"

"Syn!"

Syn stopped short and spun around. Briella hopped off the front stoop and sprinted up the path toward him. Taryn chuckled beside him.

"Ka-*boom*." Taryn flexed his fingers, mimicking an explosion. "Heed my warning."

Briella slowed as she approached him, her cheeks flushed and her ponytail mussed. Her breaths were labored, but her eyes glowed silver beneath the moonlight.

"Where are you going?"

"We're going to fetch some mineral water so you can soak tonight. You'll feel wonderful come morning," Syn said.

"Not just the minerals, but the power that infuses the water from the land," Taryn added.

Briella's attention cut between Syn and Taryn as she caught her breath. She took another step closer to Syn and brought those sultry eyes back to him, melting him. He caught an irrational request on the back of his tongue before it spit from his lips and made him a complete fool.

"Dad said you weren't staying the night."

Syn shook his head. "No, sweet. I have my home and I'm not going to intrude." He grinned, brushed a strand of hair from the corner of her mouth, and felt her jaw clench. "What?"

"Why are you so…so…" A sharp groan escaped her. "Ugh! You're too understanding."

Syn's grin dropped and a brow lifted. "And I assume that's bad."

Briella shook her head. "No."

"Then?"

Briella's fingers fisted at her side. Syn witnessed an incredible storm of warring emotions cross through her eyes.

"I want to stay with you. If you'll have me."

Syn narrowed his gaze on her, certain he'd not heard her correctly.

Had he?

"You want to stay with me? My home, Briella, is not a home like your parents'. Dragons live inside the mountains."

"That sounds perfect. As long as you're there, it can be in a tree trunk. I just want… I want to be close to you."

Oh, he heard her right, and her confession struck him straight through the heart. The right thing to do would be to deny her request.

"Please," she said, her voice just above a whisper.

Oh, dear goddess. He'd have her.

"As you wish, sweet."

"You weren't kidding when you said you live *in* the mountains."

Syn adored her spark of humor and evident awe when they arrived at his mountain home. They mixed together and created a uniquely innocent yet sexy tone in her voice. The calm of her expression and the glow in her eyes added to her allure, and the idea that she insisted on being with him let him release some of his propriety.

"Each mountain peak is the home of a dragon. We need space to take off and land. Provides immense protection and plenty of room."

It had been a subpar explanation. His brain wasn't cooperating with his usual collected manner. Not while faced with the prospect of Briella and him, alone.

After the short tour of his mountain home—he bypassed the subterranean levels to show her the main living area fitted with many modern furnishings, from beds and sofas and tables to a rustic kitchen with a few modern utilities—he left a safe Briella to fetch mineral water from the underground springs. Taryn had gone ahead and filled a dozen large buckets by the time he arrived.

"And I thought I'd be hauling these suckers back alone." Taryn snickered and placed the last bucket on the rocky shelf beside the others. He eyed Syn through the swirls of steam rising from the crystalline waters, lit a serene silver-blue in the moonlight. "Tell me, brother. Why are you trying so hard to be the gentleman she doesn't want you to be? That *you* don't want to be?"

Syn stared at Taryn. That same question pinged around in his head on the flight over to the springs. Briella had pointed out his gentlemanly behavior, too. Was it really so bad?

Hell, yes.

Syn scowled. "She's a strong-willed woman. I want her to make the decision."

"Um, Syn. I know your sight is spot on, and then some." Taryn waved a hand toward the cave's entrance. "But you're damn blind when it comes to her. She's at your place. What more do you need? Geez, man. Even I heard the innuendo in her plea to come with you."

So had Syn. He'd heard it, seen it, felt it. His dragon rumbled with pleasure.

"You're a damn dragon and she knows that. *Show her* how we treat our women." Taryn shrugged, dragging half of the buckets together. "But hey. I've never been one to drive myself crazy trying to make an impression that's already understood by the other party. She knows you're a gentleman. No reason to keep proving it. Maybe that's not what she wants right now."

"Since when have you taken up sex therapy?"

"Since I've had to deal with my friend walking around with a hard-on while waiting for his period to arrive."

"Aren't you the comedian of the hour," Syn groused, snatching up the remaining buckets with his transformed dragon paw. The water weighed next to nothing to the dragon. "Let's get going."

The trip back to his home was blessedly silent of further criticism. They unloaded the water into the bathtub and Taryn took his leave, giving Briella a hug and Syn a glower.

"What was that about?" Briella asked, following Syn to the bathroom.

"Thinks he's funny, is all." Syn stepped aside when they reached the doorway and motioned to the tub. Briella paused beside him. "Something wrong?"

"This place keeps surprising me. I expected more" — she made a circular motion with her hand — "I don't know. Rock?"

"Not enough rock for your taste? And here I thought you'd appreciate marble." Syn smiled when she cast him a glance. "Let me know if the water is warm enough. It cooled a bit on the way back."

Briella drank in the dark marble floor and walls until she reached the ornate copper tub. "I'll give you points for design. This tub is amazing." She dragged her hand through the water. "It's a bit cool."

Syn figured as much. He crossed the room and stood beside her, submerging a hand into the lukewarm water. The dragon poured heat through his fingers, warming the water until Briella was pleased.

"Perfect."

Thin curls of steam rose from the surface of the water as Syn straightened up. In a matter of minutes, Briella would slip into the tub with not a shred of clothing on. He shook his head and turned away, fetching a towel from the cabinet beneath the sink.

"How long should I soak?"

Syn forced himself to swallow when he faced Briella. Damn the woman for tearing off her shirt, not that he hadn't received a very similar view earlier. The shocking reminder of how creamy pale her skin was and how much his mouth watered to taste every inch of that skin almost knocked him off balance. Her lacy red bra created a perfect ridge of cleavage, too. Taryn's house provided the reassurance of interruption. Here? That wasn't going to happen.

"At the least, thirty minutes. I'd suggest closer to an hour." He kept a small distance between them as he returned to the tub and hung the towel on the hook close to the tub's wall. She started to unfasten her jeans. "If you need anything, I'll be in my room a few doorways down."

Syn barely escaped the bathroom with his sanity intact. Goddess help Briella when she was through.

The gentleman was about to lose his battle with the beast.

CHAPTER 17

The hot water soaked into her skin as she sank deeper into the tub. A constant flow of relaxing energy poured into her wherever the water touched. The aches and pains from her abusive day slowly drained away, leaving her rejuvenated, revived, and feeling utterly turned on.

That, she knew, was only one person's fault. Said person continued to remain absent from her mind. Their strengthening connection hummed with the essence of Syn's thoughts, but nothing clear and certainly nothing that made sense to her.

An hour *must* have passed. Her fingertips and toes were well on their way to becoming waterlogged prunes. The water's temperature had cooled, but not enough to make her want to get out. Regardless, she stood up, trickles of water falling from her skin to plink into the pool around her legs, the sound echoing through the marble-tiled bathroom. She towel-dried her hair before tucking the towel around her chest and stepped out onto the soft fiber area rug. She wiggled her toes, luxuriating in the threads.

In fact, while she waited for Syn to return from the springs, she had luxuriated in his home. She hadn't expected a mountainous cavern to possess such warmth and coziness. Most of the floors were covered with marble, similar to the gold-veined black in the bathroom. The walls and hallways were archaic, carved without much consistency. Some areas of the ceiling hung lower than others, like filed-back stalagmites. The walls weren't smooth and flat, but rather kept as rough as natural rock, giving her the feel of wandering in the mazes of the cave. Fireplaces dotted the living space, each carved into the walls.

She loved it all, the simplistic and rustic feel that Syn softened with thick area rugs, sofas and chairs that swallowed her up, and mattresses that felt like clouds. She checked all three of the guest rooms out, as he had suggested, to choose which she preferred. None of the rooms had doors, or even curtains to act as doors. Then again, who needed doors when living solo?

Briella hadn't been above snooping. She found Syn's room, and instantly fell in love with his quarters. His bed was huge, larger than any she'd seen, and covered with the softest of blankets and furs. Two massive fireplaces flanked the foot of the bed, both burning bright. There was no defined shape to his room, and it possessed alcoves and nooks that he had turned into small sitting areas lined with books or closets filled with clothes. One of the alcoves served as a bathroom of sorts, fitted with a stone-based sink and a shower with an ever-flowing cascade of water from an unseen source in the ceiling. She had been tempted to try it out until she felt the cool temperature of the water.

The air kissed her damp skin with a chill as she quietly moved down a corridor to the room she had chosen. It was one of the smaller rooms, but it was closest to Syn's. The closer to him, the better.

You're here now. Why don't you just take what you want?

Take. She knew all about taking. Take the reins of life. Take ownership of her successes and failures. Take pride in her work. Take responsibility for her decisions.

But take a man?

Relationships were beyond her scope of knowledge. A few passing flings here and there before the guy ran off with someone else. Sex? Once. She brought almost zero experience to the table when it came to that department. She had no idea what came over her earlier at Taryn's when she pressed Syn to bring her up to her borrowed room, but she wanted whatever would have happened in that bed.

She wanted it now. More than ever.

"You've never backed down before. Not when you want something," she told herself as she dropped her dirty clothes on a chair and eyed the oversized button-down shirt she had snatched from Syn's closet. She hadn't considered bringing anything to wear when she chased after Syn.

The upside of wearing his shirt? It smelled like him. It wrapped her in that exotic warmth of fire and spice the minute she slipped it on. She almost moaned, but swallowed it past the lump growing in her throat. The persistent throb between her legs intensified as she buttoned the shirt up her chest. Each caress of fabric sent a faint flutter of anticipation through her.

She went in search of a brush. None of the bedrooms had one, and neither did the bathroom. With an uptick of her heartbeat, she headed down the hallway and paused outside the arch to Syn's room.

Immediately, she shuffled backward and pressed her back to the wall. She choked on the breath that tried hard to escape her lungs. Her entire body throbbed, one violent pulse that shed any chill and left only a stream of hot desire raking through her veins.

Syn, every godforsaken inch of him. Naked. Water cutting over the hard, defined lines of muscle and sinew and everything that made him the living, breathing meaning of his namesake. The smallest movement created a god-worthy canvas out of the tanned skin along his back and the flexing of his arms. The wad of towel he was wrapping around his narrow waist hadn't been placed fast enough to hide the sumptuous curve of his butt or the thick muscles of his thighs.

Briella rubbed her face, the heat in her cheeks overwhelming. God, everything in this place was overwhelming. Her own body was overwhelming right now.

For a few minutes, she concentrated on getting oxygen back to her brain. Each breath cooled her a little, but she was far from tempered.

Okay, Brie. Okay. All you need is a damn brush.

One final breath.

"Knock knock." She waited outside the door for him to answer her mental summons, fingers squeezing the hem of the shirt as she willed the rapid thump of her heart to ease. And the ache in her core. And the heat that licked at the pit of her gut.

"Everything all right?" Syn asked from inside the room. "You don't have to stand out there, sweet."

Briella sucked her bottom lip between her teeth, pushed off the wall, and stepped into the archway. Her gaze immediately latched onto the cut planes of his chest and abdomen. Her fingers tingled with the urge to touch him and learn him.

"Briella."

She shot her gaze up to his face. Those eyes glowed with a simmering fire that burned straight through to her marrow.

"I should let you dress."

Her voice *shook.*

She was on the verge of hyperventilating. The pull to Syn was all-consuming, right down to her own brain bypassing her conscious instructions for control.

Syn's chin tilted ever so slightly up, and his eyes narrowed.

Briella caught the fierce tent of his towel before her gaze scattered around the room to land on a brush and comb. She pointed to the dresser. "I was hoping to borrow a brush. May I?"

She was halfway to the dresser before she finished speaking. She snatched up the brush, then spun on her heel and practically ran toward the hallway.

"I can let you run, precious, but I'll catch you in the end."

Oh. My. God.

That deep, husky sound that spilled from Syn's lips made her trip over the air tangling around her feet. She steadied herself with a hand on the wall and stilled. She felt his gaze burn a path along her back, slowly and leisurely, from the top of her head to the base of her heels. She thought she heard him growl, but the furious beating of her heart drowned it out.

"You came here with a purpose and I allowed it...for a purpose."

Her fingers tightened around the handle of the brush until her knuckles ached. This was the side of Syn she'd prodded to come out. The dangerous, devilish, unyielding and ungentlemanly man. The other side of him that she craved to experience. His voice was raw with sexual desire. His gaze merciless on her simmering body.

"But..."

Briella swallowed. Hard. She clenched the brush to her chest. The wall in front of her faded and returned as the pull of want and need flooded her.

And Syn. His voice lowered still more, and his accent thickened. The air at her back grew heavy with heated tension. "But I will offer you one chance to walk away tonight. I will offer you the final decision. You know what it is you want, after all."

She lowered her head. Yes. She did. She knew exactly what she wanted. So why did she want to run?

"I will give you until the count of five. Should you walk from this room, I will let you go. If you remain, well…"

A whoosh sounded. Briella jerked her head toward the fireplace. Flames shot up and out, then shrank to their previous size. She'd do best to remember that Syn possessed magic in this realm.

"By the way," he purred, "you look damn good in my shirt."

Briella cautiously shifted her head to meet Syn's glowing eyes. Oh boy. The man was more than delectable and hypnotic. He dripped with the promise of sexual prowess. Oozed sensuality from every unseen pore of his skin.

"I'm sure you'd look much better without it." A dark, carnal grin curled his not-so-innocent lips. "One."

Briella didn't move and his expression turned to one of pure challenge.

"Two."

He took a step closer to her. The air thickened between them, electric with unspent energy.

"Three."

She turned away from the archway and straightened her shoulders. Syn continued his slow, predatory advance.

"Four."

"Five," Briella said, dropping the brush to the floor. She closed the last few feet of space in a heartbeat and splayed her hands over his abdomen. Her fingers traced and molded the curves of muscles. "I made up my mind this afternoon."

"You weren't in a dragon's den this afternoon."

"No, but I was in *my* dragon's arms." She closed her eyes and lifted her head, the tip of her nose brushing the valley between his pecs. Her lips grazed across his warm skin and she flicked out her tongue for a small taste. Clean like spring water. Sultry like spiced smoke. Utterly addictive. "The only place I care to be."

CHAPTER 18

The weak, uncertain woman from moments ago fled, leaving the confident, anticipating lifemate in her stead. She chalked it up to intimidation. Syn was every inch intimidating. *Every* inch. Her lack of experience when it came to anything sexual didn't help.

His seething gaze, however, gifted her with a sense of empowerment that she gladly devoured. It thrummed along her skin, so scalding hot and intense it should have burned the shirt to cinders. It burned everything else in its path.

Syn touched a thick lock of damp hair at her temple and slowly followed the wave down to her shoulder. His fingertips brushed over her collarbone, tracing the bone to the small dip at the hollow of her neck. His gaze flickered, dropping from her face to follow the path of his finger's light, taunting trek to the first engaged button on the shirt.

With a skilled snap, Syn had the first button undone. Briella's breath hitched. Could he feel how fast her heart pattered in her chest? Did he know how aroused she was, standing there like an offering for him to feast upon?

The second button popped open, swiftly followed by the third.

She drew her bottom lip between her teeth and chewed.

"That" — he lifted his hand, pressed his thumb to her chin, and gently tugged her lip free — "is mine."

His nostrils flared as his thumb traced along her moist lip. She could practically taste his mouth on hers and tipped her head up in silent want.

Instead of indulging her, he resumed his chore of unfastening the buttons on the shirt. With each button undone, a breath of cool air caressed another inch of her skin. Her breasts ached. She squeezed her thighs together to contain the furious throb in her groin only to have it return with a vengeance, wrenching a fleeting moan from her throat.

"Easy," he soothed, though his voice was far from calming. It launched her into a new level of turned on. One that left her shameless as she wrapped her fingers around the top of his towel and drew his narrow hips close.

The moment the last button fell open, Briella pressed herself flush to Syn, tugging the towel from his waist. Oh, sweet heavens. The skin-to-skin contact was enough to rip any last logical thought from her mind. The press of his cock against her belly flushed her body from head to toe in molten arousal. Curls of smoke fluttered up from his nostrils as his hands slid along her torso to rest on her shoulders.

She dropped her arms and Syn slipped the shirt off. It pooled around her feet.

"Where to start," he murmured, drawing his knuckles up the center of her belly. He dipped his head and breathed heat along her neck. "What to indulge first."

"Everything." The word escaped on a breath as his lips brushed her pulse. She felt his deep chuckle in her marrow as it sent a bolt of tremors along her muscles.

His answer came with the rough flick of his thumb over her hard nipple, plucking nerves she had no idea existed. At least, not with the degree of pleasure that shocked her now. She clenched her teeth as he rolled her nipple between his fingers, then tugged gently.

"Syn," she hissed.

She'd lost track of his other hand until his fingers sank into the damp hair at her nape, tugged her head back, and forced her to look into his feral eyes. Eyes that flickered with embers of fire and pupils that stretched into slits.

"You think you can handle everything?" he challenged.

Briella gasped when he tugged her nipple again. She had to fight the urge to let her eyes roll back and close as she died with pleasure beneath his touch.

Instead, she coasted her fingertips along his hip and wrapped her hand around the hilt of his cock.

Fire exploded in his eyes.

His upper lip pulled back in a fierce curl.

Burnished red scales rippled over his face and disappeared, but the prick of his talons against her scalp and the scrape of them over the sensitive flesh of her breast remained.

And it drove her crazy with desire.

She pumped his cock once, taking her sweet time running her hand to the tip of his thick erection and back. "Can you?"

He twisted around, pressing her toward the bed until her legs hit the mattress. "Guess we'll find out."

She was less than graceful falling into the bed as he climbed over her, his mouth crushing down on hers with no mercy. He wrapped an arm around her lower back, even in passion careful of the injuries she barely felt, and lifted her deeper into the bed. The powerful drive behind their crushing kiss, the desperation to be closer and closer, made her blind to any doubt and inhibitions that may have plagued her.

Syn slid his cock through her seam. She moaned as he teased all the pleasure points craving his attention. Wet, throbbing, needy. She needed and he found pleasure in taunting her with each slide against her clit or tug of her nipples. He wound her up like a toy until she could barely breathe with the dire craving for release.

Briella shoved at his shoulder, breaking their kiss and forcing him onto his back. The grin that followed her climb over him was anything but innocent.

Syn caught her hips before she had a chance to scoot lower along his body, and gave a tug. She gasped, almost falling forward at the sudden jerk.

"Even better, love." Another tug, and a little shift from Syn, and she found out exactly what he meant when his tongue licked her throbbing core and began to suck on her clit.

"*Syn.*" The word fled on a rush of breath preceding a violent tremor. His hands cupped her ass and squeezed, arching her hips forward just enough for his mouth to devour her with possessive suckles and deep probes of his tongue into her body.

"You taste amazing, love. I could feast on you all day. All night. Forever."

As the tremors grew more frequent the closer he drove her to release, the harder it became for her to keep steady on her knees. She tried to rock her hips, the need to move and deliver her over the edge hammering against every frazzled nerve.

She would tear apart, splinter, shatter.

Her heart was going to rip from her chest in the best possible way.

Her body coiled and tensed.

Her back hit the mattress.

Before she could open her eyes against the throbbing pulse of impending climax, Syn's hot mouth closed around her nipple and suckled gently...at first. His tongue curled and licked.

Then he nipped.

Briella cried out, arching into his mouth, his body, as sparks exploded through her vision.

"Sweet Goddess, are you sensitive," Syn murmured, the prickle of his day-old scruff across her skin setting off another round of trembling muscles. Damn him for taking his sweet time. Damn him for his control. Damn him for knowing just how to play her body in ways she herself didn't know.

As he nuzzled her other breast, he drew a hand down her body, the careful scrape of his talons wrenching whimpers of raw delight from her throat. She wanted more, wanted less. The sensation overload was about to deliver her to the sweetest death, if his lazy foreplay didn't first.

"What happened to the desperate man from a few moments ago?" Right now, she wanted that man, that beast, to claim her. The slow, tender, lovemaking part could come later.

Syn chuckled, the deep, gravelly sound resonating down to her bones. His teeth scraped back and forth along her breast.

"Oh, he's still here. Trust me."

"Well, I want him. Now."

Syn lifted his head and caught her eyes. The dragon never subsided, and his eyes glowed like fire. The glint of scales appeared in patches along his shoulders, neck and chest, and a few smaller ones over his face.

Never in her life would she have expected to find scales on a man beautiful. On Syn, she didn't want anything less.

"No, you don't."

Briella dropped her arm, reached between them, and barely brushed her fingers over his cock before he shackled her wrist in his hand and pinned it over her head. He caught her other wrist in his iron fingers as his nostrils flared.

"Yes." She ran her foot along his thigh, higher and higher, until she locked her leg around his waist. "I do."

"You've no idea what you're asking."

Briella tipped her hips. The wide head of his cock settled exactly where she wanted it. Exactly where she needed him to be.

"I bet you'll show me."

Hooking her other leg around his waist, she lifted herself enough to draw his tip into her body. They both gasped.

Damn. The dark shadows that crested over his expression and the carnal desire that lit his eyes plucked more than her satisfaction.

"Briella…"

She barely recognized his voice.

He gave her no time to ponder. He released her wrists. His fingers dove into her hair, fisted against her scalp until she whimpered, and his mouth possessed her with more than a desperate kiss.

Syn poured his soul into her with that kiss.

And thrust deep inside her body.

Briella cried out into his mouth, her back bowing off the mattress as he stripped her mind of grounding and unleashed that precariously stacked explosive pleasure. She writhed from the intense splitting of her body as her climax consumed her. With each thrust, he delivered her to a higher level of sensation. Sensation that consumed more than her nerves and her body. It strummed the cords of her soul and made her hum with overwhelming delight. She was light. She was sound. She was the essence of all.

Pleasure rocked this new level of being. Waves of relentless delight crested and crashed. All she saw was the bursting brilliance of white light as her body shattered and shimmered and throbbed in the best possible way.

And as she began to return to reality, as her mind slowly sank back into the physical form of her being, she tightened her legs around Syn's waist as he claimed her as his.

He reared up, grabbing hold of her hips.

Fire burst from the fireplaces, mirroring the ferocity of his climax as a roar tore from his chest.

Briella fisted the blanket at her head as he pulled another low-frequency dose of pleasure from her recovering self with the power of his own release. He filled her with heat as his talons sank into her skin with only an intense jolt of bliss accompanying the marks.

Somewhere in the span of time between Syn's climax and her own spent return to reality, Syn sank down beside her and drew her into his embrace. They both struggled for breath, hearts racing, skin sheened with sweat that made his remaining patches of scales slick. She clung to him, never wanting to let him go. Never wanting to separate.

His lips brushed over her forehead. He sucked in a controlled breath and let it out slowly. "You're bleeding."

Briella somehow managed to tip her leaden head down to the talon marks on her hip. Two spots had thin trails of red from the marks where the others merely glistened with single drops welling up from the small punctures.

"I barely felt a thing. Besides, I don't mind that you've left your mark on me."

Syn chuckled. "My sweet Briella. I've left more than a mark on you, and I think we both know it."

She met his eyes, which were now the beautiful brown she knew so well. The scales had disappeared. When she traced his brow, she was surprised by how much her hand shook. He'd stolen the energy and strength from her, and she would change nothing.

"That was a claiming," she whispered. Oh, the warmth that curled through her chest at those very words. Her lips tilted up of their own accord. "You've claimed me."

"And I plan on claiming you over and over all night long."

CHAPTER 19

There would never be a better way to spend his time than holding the woman who claimed his heart tucked like a precious package in his arms.

Syn hadn't slept, his mind too engulfed in wonder and his heart swollen with love. He lay silent for hours, listening to the soft, even breaths of his sleeping lifemate, occasionally disrupted by a short bout of snoring. Her hair fanned wildly around her head, hiding most of her face. Her body draped over his, all silky smooth and pliant. She might be small, but she had curves he had thoroughly enjoyed with both his hands and his mouth.

There was nothing more perfect than that first time he claimed her, every inch of her. His dragon had roared with delight as his body raged with storm.

And now?

Contentedness filled him to the brim. Wholeness and rightness. He had satiated the beast, if only temporarily.

He let another hour drift by before he eased himself from beneath Briella. She barely stirred through the shift in position, the shower he stole, and the time he spent in the kitchen preparing her a meal and tea.

That meal sat on a tray at the edge of the bed, growing cold for over thirty minutes before he nuzzled her neck, placing airy kisses along her tender skin until she moaned into wakefulness. She stretched her arms over her head, arching her lithe body, then settling back against the mattress with a sleepy grin.

Syn nibbled her earlobe. "Afternoon, sweetness."

"Mmm." She sank her fingers into his hair, her nails scraping his scalp. "Lay back down."

Oh, the temptation. "After you eat."

Briella rolled onto her back and looked up at him through sleep-hazed eyes. Her face glowed and her lips were still swollen. He hadn't been entirely gentle with her, but neither had she been with him. The furs and pillows scattered over his floor was proof of how untamed their mating had turned.

"And get out of this bed?" The woman couldn't sound any sexier if she tried. Syn brushed a thick chunk of hair from her face. "Hello, my dragon."

"Hello, my precious." He sat back and motioned to the tray. "And no. I brought you brunch in bed."

"Really?" She pressed up on her elbows. Her smile grew. "Thank you."

Syn arranged the pillows against the headboard and waited for Briella to get comfortable before he set the tray over her legs. When he looked up, he caught her staring at his hips. Or, rather, his cock. He hadn't bothered to put clothes on.

"I'm absolutely in awe of you," Briella murmured. She let her fingers stroll down his stomach. Such a simple touch to fill him with so much desire. He caught her hand before it reached any lower and raised her fingertips to his mouth. "From man to dragon to something in between."

"You seem fascinated with the 'in between.'" He chuckled at her blush and nipped her fingertips. She gasped. "Eat, love. Gain your strength. I took much from you."

"I still have some left, you know."

"Your invitation is most welcome. But if we return to your parents and you're sporting more scrapes, bruises, and exhaustion than you had when we left, I don't want to be on the receiving end of their disappointment."

"I thought your scales were thicker than that." She snorted, picking up a chunk of cooked meat from the plate. "Scared? Of my parents? Ha!"

"Respectful." He set her hand down only after he looked over the stitched areas on her arm. Most were almost completely healed, with the sutures either dissolved or close to. He stood up. "We'll take a trip to the springs so you can get another good soak before we meet up with everyone. Looks like your bath last night did a wonderful job."

"You know, you really need to either sit down or put some clothes on. How the heck is a woman to eat without choking when you're all gloriously naked so close by?"

Syn laughed as he went to an alcove with his clothes and pulled out jeans and a T-shirt. "Now you know what I've been going through with you so close. And to think, you've *always* had your clothes on, until last night."

"Oh, the torture."

"Sweet, you can't even begin to imagine."

Briella wore her jeans from the previous day and a T-shirt of Syn's that sagged hideously over her shoulders. He promised to stop at her parents' place and pick up a change of clothes for her after they returned to his home from the spring. He was subtly amused by the sight of her swimming in his shirt, as proven by the hint of a grin and the sparkle in his eyes. The rugged beauty of his face seemed softer today, a characteristic she duly noted and tucked away. All these little nuances that comprised Syn were fascinating and captivating at the same time. She wanted to explore each one, and when he wasn't around pull them out of her memories and ponder them some more.

"Will you be okay to walk? The springs are underground, and the closest one in about two miles away."

The gallant Syn had returned, but the beast remained loosely restrained below the surface. She caught the flare of hunger in his eyes and the shadow in his face more than once since they started out.

"If you're implying that I might be sore from last night..." Briella snickered. Her legs ached, as did other parts of her anatomy she had no clue existed. The memory of what they had shared made every aching inch well worth it, and more. "I'm ready to walk."

"Pity." Syn's fingers tightened between hers. "Guess I'll have to try harder tonight."

As if she wasn't treading a tightrope of control with thunderous plumes of lava beneath her. He gave her a proverbial shove, but somehow she managed to keep on the straight and narrow.

"You'll have your work cut out for you." She giggled and leaned her head against his arm.

"Sweet, I love a challenge."

And so the battle to douse the flames of this insatiable hunger began on this new day.

They walked hand-in-hand, their strides slow and leisurely up the hillsides, down into ravines, through forests thick with foliage and plants that were nonexistent back home. The air was light and fragrant. Flowering plants and vines created extravagantly picturesque views. Leaves were all shades of green and silver and gray, the latter two glittering like precious metals in the stunning sunlight.

Streams cut through the geography as they moved along the rough mountainsides. Syn pointed out other dragon lairs until the distant haze swallowed them up.

Briella paused as they crested a rocky hill, drawing Syn's acute attention.

"Do you need to rest?"

Briella shook her head. "No, but the view…"

She closed her eyes for a moment, picturing the view in her mind. God, she wished she had her paints and a blank canvas right now. She'd set up shop and paint the beauty of Syn's world. Paint something she didn't pull from an impression, but that she actually saw with her eyes.

Movement off to her left caught her attention. She stepped closer to Syn, waiting with bated breath until a glint manifested from behind a thick patch of brush. Her lips parted in awe as she stared at a creature she couldn't name. Stag-like, but far bigger. The glint came from the shimmering silver of its thick coat. A huge rack of antlers protruded from its wide head, snowy white in color. Silvery mist danced between those antlers and was mirrored in the beast's large black eyes.

The creature was majestic, if not a little frightening.

"What is that?" Briella whispered.

"That, my precious, is a *cervus*. He is a guardian of the forest." Syn pointed in the general direction of the creature. "He moves on the clouds between his antlers once he becomes mist. He is a kind creature, and one you will not see often. He remains hidden, his purpose beyond the trees." Pride resounded in his voice. "He is like us. Rare. We don't hunt the *cervus*."

"There must be an untold number of creatures here that aren't in my world."

"There are."

As they continued on, Briella received a front-row seat to The Hollow's exotic species, from luminescent winged insects to creatures that appeared to embody Nature's experiments in mixing breeds of animals. Long-haired beasts with horns and three-fingered claws for feet. Others that resembled wild cats, but with longer and often hooked snouts. Birds that sported fur instead of feathers.

"Spectacular," she breathed. So many fascinating creatures came and went, Syn naming each one.

"We hunt higher up. Predators reside away from the mountain peaks, which keeps our Keepers safe."

"Predators are aware of predators. I'm sure those predators know they don't stand a chance against you dragons." Briella looked up at Syn, whose gaze was locked on a cavernous arc about a quarter mile away. "Is that the spring?"

"Yes."

Briella resorted to holding Syn's arm with hers snaked around his biceps as they entered the dark cave. A few steps later, Syn shifted beside her. She shrieked, her voice echoing through the cavern, when he scooped her off her feet and cradled her in his arms. She smiled, tucking her head against his shoulder. She didn't think it possible to shake Syn from her system. Ever.

I don't want *to shake him. I want to keep him.*

A brilliant blue light reflected against the rocky tunnel walls as they drew closer to the spring, the gently rippling water creating a mosaic of movement against the dark brown. Syn set her on her feet when the tunnel opened into a cavern. A pool of silver-blue water glowed with an inner light, brightening the cavern with a sensual and relaxing ambiance. The temperature of the air between the tunnel and the cavern was markedly different, the warm humidity in the cavern fed by licks of steam that floated up from the water's surface. The walls shimmered with gems and stones that added a soothing and colorful design.

"Wow," she breathed. "Are all of the springs like this?"

"They differ depending on where they're located in the mountains. This one is a favorite."

Syn followed as she moved closer to the edge of the water. It didn't drop into a hole, like she half expected. Instead, water lapped up along grainy obsidian stone before it dipped to deeper waters. Although small, it was still the size of a big swimming pool. There was no obvious source of illumination as she listened to the sound of water trickling along rock somewhere within the cavern.

Briella sighed in delight when Syn's hands slipped under the ridiculous shirt and his palms slid over her belly. He nuzzled his mouth against the side of her neck, his scruff tickling her skin while his airy kisses tantalized her hormones.

"You're coming in with me, right?" she asked, leaning back into him.

Syn teased that sensitive area below her ear with a lazy swirl of his tongue. "That wouldn't be a good idea."

She wiggled her hips into the curve of his, smiling at the carnal growl her movements drew from him. "I think it's a perfect idea."

His hands slipped lower, thumbs hooking in the waist of her jeans. "What are your intentions, sweet?" His head dipped. He nipped along the curve of her shoulder, each delectable pinch unleashing a spear of pleasure straight to her core. "Because mine wouldn't be to soak."

He emphasized his meaning by plucking open the button on her jeans. His fingers traced the top of her panties before moving lower. Her breath hitched and her head dropped back.

"I think I like your intentions."

"I think I do, too."

Syn made quick work of stripping them of their clothes before carrying Briella into the pool. She lost sight of herself, where she ended and where Syn began. When they were together, they were one, and for her, that's all that mattered. She couldn't determine when he had become the entity that stole into her soul, held her heart, and made her life worth every breath she took. She couldn't determine when her dreams of hitting it big with her paintings took a backseat to the dreams of building something with Syn.

As they soaked in their post love-making glory, the hot water of the pool relaxing and soothing to her muscles while in Syn's arms, her mighty dragon whispered, "Know this, Briella Everett. My heart is yours. I'm playing for keeps."

Somewhere in this dream-turned-reality twist of life, her heart pattered and her lips curled into a smile, and she heard herself respond, "Your heart is safe with me, as I know mine is with you. And play for keeps all you like. I may be your Keeper, but I want *you* to *keep* me."

Chapter 20

Syn needed to get them around others sooner rather than later if his damn libido had any hope of cooling off. The lifemate pull was insatiable, contrary to what he'd thought only a few days ago. He believed he had some semblance of control over it, but quickly learned how wrong he was the instant she gave herself to him.

He batted down the beast once more as he watched Briella, dressed in the change of clothing he'd picked up for her only a short time ago, brush her hair. Tasting her once had been pure heaven, but the desire never relinquished its maddening grip. It sank its claws deeper into his soul with each roll or tumble they took.

"How many different stairwells, hallways, tunnels, whathaveyous are there in this place?" Briella asked.

"Enough to get lost in, if you don't know your way. It's a defense. I know when someone crosses the threshold into my territory. The labyrinth of my home allows me time to determine the level of threat." Syn led her off one spiraling stairwell to a platform and deeper into the mountain. With a thought, he lit each torch they reached as the glow of the ones left behind dimmed, giving Briella pause. Syn smiled, his vision wavy and thermal as his dragon took over his sight. The lines of warm red and orange that framed his lifemate made her even more stunning. "Remember, love. We have power and magic here. I only have to look at something and will it to catch fire."

"So you're looking at the torches and lighting them through magic."

Syn shrugged, a pleased curl of his lips responding to her awe. "Yes."

"Now, if that isn't friggin' cool." Her gaze narrowed, her fingertips brushing his cheek just below his eye. "Just like the fire in your eyes right now. I'll never admit it, but I love seeing it."

She smiled at the lighthearted tease.

"I guess I'll never know that you love it so much, because you'll never admit it."

"That's right, dragon."

They laughed as he looped his arm around her waist and continued forward. After a few more turns, they reached a stone wall. He extended his talons and located the first lock in a false fissure. With the tip of one talon, he unlatched the covering for the lock into the vault. Fitting both taloned hands into two grooves, he released the locking mechanism deep in the stone and the door slid open. Briella grimaced as stone scraped against stone, the sharp sound echoing in the small quarters.

"I hope you don't think I've earned time in the dungeon."

"Unless you consider my bed a dungeon, then no." He stepped back, ignited the torches along the inner wall of the vault, and drank in the sight of Briella's apprehension melting away to a shade of incredulous. Never in all his years would he have believed that shock actually looked good on a woman.

Briella wore the expression damn nice, from the way her full lips parted to the glitter that lit her eyes and reflected the torchlight. Her cheeks deepened in color.

She twisted around, pinning him with that piqued stare. "You steal things in your spare time?"

"I'm a dragon, sweet. What do dragons do best?"

His darling woman's cheeks turned deep red. "Like you don't know. But" — she turned back to stare around the room — "I never considered hoarding gold and gems a reality. How much is in here?"

"I'm a few hundred years old and I started fairly young." He leaned against the rough edge of the doorway. "Enough for generations and generations after us to live very comfortable lives."

And that was being conservative.

"You do recall when I said that the damages in your old apartment and all else was covered?"

He jutted his chin toward the neatly stored bars of gold, chests of gold that contained his coins, displays of jewels both polished and raw. He had more gold fashioned into candlesticks, frames, sculptures. Silver gleamed beneath the torchlight. Original tapestries from monarchies that had long since perished warmed the walls. Relics from ancient civilizations caught the eye. He had a deep affinity for antiques.

"We take care of our Keepers. By that I mean we provide for them. Your father always kept a stash of gold from my hoard in case of an emergency. Enough to live in extreme comfort for many, many years. Now that we are reconnecting with our Keepers, resources will be replenished. It was never meant as a handout. It is a responsibility that all Firestorm dragons take with pride. The ability to support our Keepers, give them what they need to survive comfortably when they are displaced."

Syn took her hand and led her into the vault. Several centuries of collecting had filled an otherwise overly large space except for pathways. The torchlight created the illusion of a sea of gold that glinted and glittered as they moved between parted waves. Briella's fingers dragged over chests and bars and jewel-encrusted furniture.

"Sweet heavens. This can't be real," she murmured, pausing to looked over her shoulder. "Does this room never end?"

Her admiration gave his ego a small boost. Pride was not a prominent characteristic of his, but he did pride himself on his hoard.

"Of course. But as you can see, you, just like Giovani and Saralyn, have nothing to worry about. Not a handout. This is what comes with me." Slowly, he turned to face Briella full on. "If, of course, you *choose* to have me."

"Even without all this"—she spread an arm out and swept it around the riches—"I'd have you."

Ahh, and there it was. Admittance without hesitation. Without the strain of doubt or question in her voice.

Tucking her confession away, he smiled with a small nod. "I'll be sure to remember that."

Syn's attention snapped to Taryn when he heard his friend snicker for the third time in less than ten minutes. As soon as his gaze leveled on the laid-back dragon, Taryn looked away and rocked back in his chair. His mischievous grin never dimmed. Emery and Gabe were too busy bickering over their latest flight race to lend their share of taunts to the discussion.

Taryn dropped a hand under the table so only Syn could see and flicked his fingers out from his fist sharply, imitating an explosion.

Syn growled under his breath.

"Everything okay?" Cade asked, returning from his kitchen with two jugs of his homemade wine.

"I'd say." Taryn tossed a casual glance at Syn. "Right, brother? Everything okay?"

Syn scowled. He ignored Taryn and followed Cade's enormous self with his eyes until their leader sat across from them. "Where's Alazar?"

"I suppose Alazar's excuse for being late would run parallel to the reason behind that glitter behind Taryn's eyes." Cade poured out three glasses of wine. "You and Briella must be doing well."

Syn held the base of the goblet with two fingers and swirled the wine in it. "Yes."

"Are her wounds healing?"

"She soaked in springwater last night and I brought her to one of the springs today. Her wounds are practically gone."

"And why do I have a feeling she wasn't soaking alone?" Emery chimed in. Syn rolled his eyes and leaned back in his seat.

"You're lucky she isn't here to listen to your wretched mouth," he said.

Emery laughed, far from intimidated. "I'm sure you have some neat tricks up your sleeves to distract her."

Gabe chuckled, but Emery and Taryn burst out laughing. Cade's dark brows hiked, his hand staying his pour.

"It would be nice to leave whatever happens behind closed doors there. And that means no prying into business that doesn't concern you," Cade said. Syn raised his glass to their leader in silent thanks and earned a slight nod. "For Briella's sake."

"I rescind my appreciation," Syn said. Cade shrugged and finished his pour, a smirk lifting his beard. Syn couldn't stop the half-grin that twitched the corner of his mouth.

"I'm sure you do. Your eyes have been fighting back fire since you arrived."

Cade pushed the two jugs of wine to the center of the table as Alazar burst into the room. He hurried to the empty seat beside Syn and fell into it, a contagious smile brightening his face. Since his friend found Ariah, the guilt from his past after the untimely death of his previous Keeper didn't appear to weigh as heavily on his shoulders. For that, Syn was grateful. Alazar did not deserve the guilt he suffered for decades.

Alazar reached for the goblet of wine Cade poured out for him. "Thanks. Sorry I'm late. Dropped Ari off with Briella and Saralyn."

"Don't try and tell us you didn't steal an extra half-hour in the sack," Taryn said.

Alazar winked.

Syn tossed back his entire glass of wine in one gulp.

The brothers roared with laughter.

"Children, it's time to get serious," Cade finally interrupted. "We have to address the Baroqueth presence in New Orleans, as well as successes in tracking any other Keepers and civilians to their hiding spots."

"I say we just torch the suckers and be done with them. Why bother collecting our enemies and locking them away? At least the witches where Zareh's living gave us a form of entertainment by capturing the slayers in those stones," Emery said. He tapped a finger thoughtfully against his chin. "I wonder if they feel it when we pitch them into the walls?"

"When this damn war is over, and over for good, I have plans for those we've captured," Cade said, the primitive rumble of his voice deepening. His eyes flashed with dark red flames and the nails that performed a single rap against the table had tapered to the tips of his black talons. "There will be no Baroqueth left to carry on their breed's curse on the Firestorm *tatsu*."

"Now we're talking," Gabe chimed in, shadows darkening his face. Syn narrowed his gaze on the man, wondering when his brother had acquired a taste for death. None of them were keen on the idea of genocide, but when the dragons weren't the only ones suffering at the hands of the Baroqueth, it was time to take a stand. "Give us the okay to do away with them as they come at us, Cade, and you'll see a depletion in their numbers faster than you can blink."

"Tasted blood, have you, Gabe?" Taryn asked.

Gabe simply shrugged a shoulder and drowned his answer with a heavy gulp of his wine.

"I won't have this turning into a bloody slaying. We're not stooping to their level. Do you understand me?" Cade's hard gaze skimmed over everyone at the table. They all nodded. "Very well, then. Remember, we can't cause fear in the humans for the sake of other dragon breeds. I certainly don't want to drag our reputation through the mud, either."

"Reputation? Cade, we're lore's lore," Alazar said. "You've said so yourself numerous times. We're the Atlantis of dragons."

Cade folded his large hands on the table and nodded once. "Yes, and we'll remain so. Use stealth and good judgment when you encounter any Baroqueth."

"Boss, if you don't want us to draw attention to ourselves when we're leaving trails of dead Baroqueth behind us, we'll need to figure out a way of disposing of them here. Without any powers in the mortal realm, our slayer ash piles will be like cookie crumb trails," Emery said.

"Book of Realms," Alazar said.

Syn pressed his lips together and helped himself to another glass of wine. He had almost forgotten Alazar's Keeper possessed one of the last copies of the Book of Realms. There was a time centuries ago when each Keeper possessed a copy of the magical book. The Baroqueth, in their quest to suck the Firestorm dry of power and life, destroyed all but a few. The exact number of books still in existence was unknown, as was the number of surviving Keepers and Baroqueth.

Everything was a damn mystery.

"I wouldn't traipse around with that book, Al," Syn warned. "If it's the last one left, it'd be foolish to expose it for something as mundane as covering tracks."

"I wouldn't put mundane and Baroqueth ash piles in the same conversation," Taryn said.

"I just find the idea of toting that book around the human realm dangerous and foolish." Syn took a sip of wine. "We'll fare well enough without it."

"Um, I wouldn't have fared well without it," Alazar reminded him. It was true. The Book saved their lives only a few months ago, and landed a bunch of Baroqueth in Cade's magically reinforced dungeon. In this world, their powers far exceeded the Baroqueths', unless they were descendants of those original betrayers who syphoned power and life from their former dragon companions.

The woman.

Syn straightened in his chair. Something in his expression must have drawn Cade's attention.

"What is it?" their leader asked.

"There's a female Baroqueth." Syn pushed his wine glass away, aware of Cade's probing gaze. "Taryn and I came across her in a voodoo shop by Jackson Square. She's responsible for Briella's injuries."

"Female?" Cade asked, his voice sharp, lethal. "Baroqueth are male. Half-breeds might be female. Was she a half-breed, like Miriam?"

Miriam, the spawn of a Baroqueth sorcerer and witch, seduced Alazar's Keeper into marriage. The deceitful creature stuck around for ten years waiting for Mark or Ariah to drop the ball on their Keeper bloodline.

Syn wondered if Baroqueth females were as rare as female Keepers, and if they experienced a similar breeding surge during dangerous times.

Unfortunately, the woman they crossed paths with in the shop was no half-breed. "No. I haven't encountered a Baroqueth with her power and capabilities. She appeared young, maybe Ariah's age or younger, but the energy that rolled off her was something I've never felt from a male."

"Quiet, Taryn," Cade growled.

Taryn threw his hands up in the air, his eyes wide. "What? What did I say?"

"Nothing, but I saw it coming." Cade snorted, dual plumes of light gray smoke exploding from his nostrils. He shook his head. He asked Syn, "Did she give you any clue as to who she was?"

"No, but she trapped two shop employees in mirrors and misted to escape. She didn't just vanish, like the others do, which means she is confident in her abilities and can linger without being harmed. She put a concealment spell around the shop to ward off prospective shoppers. All except for Briella, which leaves me to wonder how long she's been tracking my lifemate."

"What was Briella doing in the shop?"

"She was handing out brochures for an upcoming gallery show of her paintings. Trying to push...promote..." Syn's brows came together as his words trailed off. His thoughts shot back to the afternoon in the shop, Briella and her bag of brochures. Syn looked at Taryn, who stared back at him with a spark of confusion. "Did you see if that woman had one of Briella's brochures?"

Taryn's lips pursed. He shook his head. "Not that I noticed, but I wasn't looking. The damage to your woman was more concerning."

Syn shifted in his seat, his skin burning under the intensifying gazes of his brothers.

"Sweet, did you give the woman in the voodoo shop a brochure?"

It escaped him how he hadn't thought to ask sooner. Then again, as Taryn said, her injuries had taken precedence.

"Yeah. Why? Don't think she so much as glanced at it."

Syn's gaze focused on Cade. "Briella has a debut showing in a week. She gave the information to the woman at the shop. Date. Time. Place. Her name."

Cade combed the tips of his talons through his beard, his eyes hardening. "Perfect opportunity for an ambush. Now we have something to work with."

As realization flooded Syn, so did dread. "And we have a problem if we try to stop Briella from attending."

He had promised to support her in following her dreams.

He feared he'd have to break his promise and watch her dreams shatter instead.

CHAPTER 21

Briella couldn't shake the uneasy feeling that had settled between Syn and herself. She couldn't put her finger on what was off. He held her as he had before, grinned, chuckled, laughed, but everything fell a hair short of genuine. She tried her hardest not to let it get the best of her as she enjoyed the rest of the day with Ariah and her mother.

As the day came to a close in a fiercely luminescent display of colors that streaked the sky, the guys gathered in the field they had first landed in. A heavy weight seemed to settle on her heart.

She didn't want to leave yet. Not when there was so much she wanted to explore and experience. But her wounds were healed and she had work to do at home.

The day of her art show was quickly approaching and she'd missed a full day of promotion while she frolicked in The Hollow.

Crazy thing is, I didn't give my debut more than a passing thought the whole time I was with Syn.

It should have bothered her, that her dreams had slipped somewhere behind Syn and her family and this whole new world on her list of priorities. That her upcoming debut as a new artist, a promising painter, had been nothing more than a flittering idea, a wisp of a whisper.

What bothered her as she pressed her chest tight to Syn's hot scales as they bulleted through the night sky back to New Orleans was the strange disconnect that shocked their strengthening bond.

"Syn, please tell me what's bothering you."

It was the fourth time she'd nudged, and this time she practically begged. She wanted her dragon back. The one who burned her up from core to skin when his gaze landed on her. The one who nuzzled and teased and touched her without the hesitation he'd acquired since his meeting with the other dragons.

"Now isn't the time, sweet."

Her heart twisted and her stomach knotted. This was the closest he'd come to a confession that there was something wrong. It made her feel worse.

"Why? What happened at your meeting? You've been...off since you returned to my parents' cottage."

The merciless wind that cut through the seams of her clothing began to win out over Syn's body heat. She squinted against that same wind, although she knew her eyes were protected from the danger such speed could cause. The icy air that filled her lungs seized her breaths every few inhales, but she knew it was in her head.

She was made for this. For flight. The freedom and the closeness, all shared with Syn.

Yet that closeness was hindered by something dark, threatening, and she didn't like it.

"We'll discuss everything when we reach Taryn's house."

"Now."

"No."

She wished she could pinch him, but the thick armor of his skin beneath his smooth scales was as impenetrable as those scales. Instead, she stewed in building anxiety until Syn coasted to a soft landing in the field they'd launched from the night before. Taryn arrived before them, the dragon having morphed back into a man to stand beside her mother.

She climbed down from Syn's back and was tempted to go to her mother, but decided to wait until Syn transformed back into a man. It was impossible to decipher any expression on his dragon face, but the expression he wore as he shed his scales for skin and clothes was filled with a mixture of hardened determination and sympathy.

It didn't bode well for the unease in Briella's gut.

"Will you tell me something?" she implored in a hushed voice. The thrust of wind as Gabriel and Emery coasted down for their landings rustled the treetops. Strands of hair blew over her face.

He caressed her cheek, catching those strands of hair and tucking them behind her ears. He took her face between his hands, lifted her up, and placed a lingering kiss on her lips. Damn the man for his tenderness while she roiled in turmoil!

"You're beautiful. You're wonderful. You're talented and smart and stubborn as all hell." He kissed her forehead. "I think I love you for it all."

Briella blinked. Did he…? Was that…?

"Syn?"

A ghost of a grin touched his mouth. That hard, lethal edge in his eyes softened. "You heard me right."

She stared up at him as his confession sank in and made her own heart thump hard against her breastbone. His arm slipped around her shoulders as he looked over her head. Caught up in a new cloud of wonder, she could barely comprehend the conversation that started around her. While her parents and the dragons discussed their flights, the bittersweet return to this world, and the prospect of another trip soon, Briella sank against Syn's side, emotions twisting and churning inside her.

"Let's get out of here before we draw attention to ourselves," Taryn suggested, heading toward the parking lot where they had left his pickup truck. Briella and Syn took up the rear, following the others at a slower pace.

"It's not uncommon," Syn said quietly, his hand slipping from her shoulder to her waist. He squeezed gently as he glanced down at her.

"I don't understand."

"You're doubting my confession. Things happen much faster between lifemates than they would normally occur between two humans. The emotions run high and hard and fast, love. And they never dim over time." He made a faint motion with his hand toward the group in front of them. "Look at your parents. They may not be dragon and Keeper, but for Keepers and the residents of The Hollow, Gio and Saralyn were a match. Are a match. They love each other as much now, if not more, than they did thirty-one years ago."

She rested her head against the side of his chest. "It's hard for me to grasp, is all."

"I understand. You weren't raised in our ways."

"Sounds medieval."

Syn chuckled and she looked up at his shadowed and utterly handsome face. "I'm pretty sure you had a taste of exactly how not medieval we are."

Yes, she certainly had. And if she were to admit it, she was eager for more.

"So, you love me? You sure you can handle me?"

There was no forewarning when Syn twisted and scooped her up in his arms. She gasped, swallowing back a shriek as she settled into his hold. He kissed her temple.

"I've handled plenty in my years. Question is, can *you* handle *me*?"

She traced his bottom lip and giggled when he nipped her fingertip. "Nope, but I always like the challenge. And I kinda like you, too."

"That's good to know."

"All of this talk about love hasn't made me forget how off you've been since returning from Cade's place." She preferred this playful side of Syn, but love or not, she wanted to know what transpired during the meeting. She also needed a distraction from her own strange swell of...well... "It has to do with my debut, doesn't it."

"Yes." A heavy breath left him and he lowered her to her feet. "Please. Let's discuss this when we get back to Taryn's. There's much that we need to talk about. All of us."

Briella resigned herself to his request with a nod. A sickening ache pulsed in her belly, one that left her wondering how badly her new life was going to shatter her old dreams.

Ten minutes after they arrived at Taryn's, Briella was cringing over the volume of text messages she received from her friends as soon as she turned on her phone. Most were from Mark. Emma had left a few, teasing Briella about her new beau. Adrienne and Mindy's texts at first conveyed concern, then took on the same taunting nature as Emma's, leaving her to surmise Emma had let the beans out about Syn.

Gabe and Emery left to get some beignets and other snacks before they started their "talk." Briella kept busy with her mother in the kitchen, preparing two pots of coffee and boiling water for tea. Syn must have purchased tea for her, gauging by several brand new tins filled with loose-leaf teas and the new steeper she spotted in the stockpile of coffee. His thoughtful gesture made her heart flutter despite the impending disappointment she feared was to come.

Not even her mother's jubilant talk about The Hollow could lift her spirits.

"Do you ladies need help?" Briella's father asked, poking his head into the kitchen. Her mother waved him away with a bright smile.

"I think we can handle this. Taryn has trays." Trays they were loading up with mugs, sugar caddies, and milk servers. "Are the others back?"

"Should be here any minute. Then we can get this show underway."

Briella managed a tight grin when her father winked at her before disappearing. As she turned back to the tray she was fixing, her shoulders slumped.

Saralyn rested a hand over hers. "Everything will be fine, sweetheart. You'll see."

The doorbell chimed throughout the house. Briella placed the spoons on her tray, napkins on her mother's, and paused when she heard a strange voice echo down the hallway.

Her spine went ramrod straight. No, not strange. Just strange here, at Taryn's.

"What on earth…?"

Briella spun on her heel and hurried into the hallway. Her eyes widened when she spotted Mark in the living room, shoulders stiff and chest puffed out. His expression was shuttered, but his eyes lanced

Taryn as the dragon chuckled and settled into his usual casual stance.

"Mark, what are you doing here?" Briella demanded. Mark's attention cut to her.

"You've no business in this place with these creeps."

Briella came up short as the volatile thoughts practically bellowed through Mark's head. The force of his anger and disgust sent her reeling back a step when he took several long strides toward her.

"Brie! Dear God, I was so worried about you. The ladies haven't heard from you all day. We were expecting to do more promotion"—his arms swung around her in a possessive embrace that she found herself trying to kindly push free of—"and no one could get in touch with you. Between your absence and not showing up for lunch and calling out of work, I didn't know what to make of it."

"Uhh…"

Mark leaned back to look down into her face, but kept his hands low on her hips. Uncomfortably low. She mustered an awkward smile and eased his hands away only to have him capture her hands with his.

"I'm glad I found you. Your friend," he nodded his head at Taryn, "told Emma where he lived and I figured I'd try here."

Her brows quirked. "Oh?" She glanced at Taryn, who wore his humored smirk like an egotistical brute who was thoroughly enjoying this game. "Well—"

"Sweetheart, who is this?"

Relief rushed through her at the sound of the calm, reasonable question. Thank heavens for her mother. She tried to pull her hands from Mark's, but he refused to let her go.

And where the hell was Syn during all of this?

She twisted as her mother came into the living room, wiping her hands on a dishrag. Mark's expression morphed into something utterly charming and engaging.

He released one of Briella's hands and extended it to the older woman. "My name's Mark Heddleman, ma'am. I'm a close friend of Briella's. You must be…her mother?"

Briella took the opportunity to gently twist her other hand from Mark's grip and step back, folding her arms over her chest. She watched in a mixture of horror and fascination as Mark tried to sweeten up her mother with a kiss on her knuckles. Taryn snorted from his position propped against the wall.

"Hmm, I think I need to give him a few lessons." Syn's presence purred through her mind. The sound of his deep, accented voice instantly put her at ease. *"But I'll let him continue to try."*

"Where are you?"

"Courtyard, love. Would you like me to come in and save you?"

"I can save myself, thank you. Continue stargazing while us women handle the problem."

Syn laughed, the sound so rich and delicious inside her head that she barely caught the end of what Mark was saying to her mother.

"...assured, she is safe. I've been certain to make sure of it." Mark came to Briella's side and draped his arm around her shoulder.

Briella cleared her throat as she once again rolled away from him. "Mom, I think I hear the kettle whistling."

Her mother cocked her head at the lie, but nodded. "Oh, yes. Let me take care of that. It was nice meeting you, Mark."

Briella watched her mother disappear into the kitchen. When she turned to face Mark, she found him glowering in Taryn's direction.

"Call me Mr. Chaperone," Taryn said.

"Taryn, give me a minute with him, okay?" Briella asked, lifting her brows to enforce the command behind her request. He groaned, pushing off the wall.

"You're no fun."

"Sorry to disappoint." As Taryn headed toward the courtyard, Briella grabbed Mark by the wrist and dragged him to the front door. Once out on the stoop, she closed the door and hissed, "What are you doing here?"

His charming demeanor melted into disgruntled defensiveness. "Me? I should ask you that question. What's gotten into you, Brie? The last few days you've shoved me off like I don't matter anymore. I don't get it. I don't like it. And I certainly don't like how cocky that guy is."

"Jealousy doesn't play well with you, Mark."

"And flamboyance doesn't play well with you. You've know that guy, what? A couple days? And isn't he that other guy's friend? What are you doing with them?"

Briella flexed her fingers at her sides. She couldn't stop her lip from curling. "What are you implying?"

Mark jabbed an arm toward the door. "You're in a house with a bunch of strangers!"

"Um, Mark. Last I checked, my mother isn't a stranger."

Mark raked his hands through his hair and scowled. "Where's the other guy?"

Briella's spine went straight. "The 'other guy' has a name. And he's here as well. I think you should leave, though. You're drawing conclusions—"

"Conclusions based on what I'm seeing! Guys like them are after one thing, Briella. One. Thing. And if you're going to be so blind as to give it to them, maybe you deserve what will come to you."

"Excuse me?"

Anger darkened Mark's face until she barely recognized him. "You heard me. I thought you better than that. Than *them*. I've been nothing but kind and caring to you. I've given you my time, my concern, my worry, my help. What have they given you? A few screams in the sack?"

The clap of her splayed hand connecting with Mark's cheek stung her ears as much as it stung her palm. She stepped into him, pointing a finger at his face when he stared at her in disbelief.

"You listen to me good, Mark. You have no idea who those men are. You have no idea what goes on between me and anyone behind that door. If you think so little of me as to come within a breath of calling me some foul name because you're *jealous*, you don't deserve my time, my friendship, or the time I'm wasting on you now. But because you're so damn *concerned*, I'll fill you in on something. Those men are friends of my parents. Very, very good friends. So, not only have you insulted me in one of the worst ways a *friend* could, you've insulted my parents, our friends, and someone I care deeply about."

She stepped back as Mark's face fell. His cheek flared red from her slap. His eyes glinted with a potent storm of hurt and hate. She fisted her hands against her thighs, her arms tense.

"You need to leave. Now. Before your mouth causes more damage. As it stands, I've seen a side of you I'm not sure I ever care to encounter again."

"Brie—"

She jerked her finger toward the gate to the sidewalk. "Now."

Mark's jaw locked. He sniffed, his chin lifting slightly, and hopped off the stoop. Briella watched him throw open the gate and storm out of sight. Before she could return to the house, Gabe and Emery slipped through the gate, their gazes cutting between Briella and the direction Mark had taken. They each held several pastry boxes.

"Is it safe to come in?" Emery asked, flicking a wave of hair from his forehead.

Briella snorted and opened the front door. She came up short when she found Syn perched on the arm of the sofa, one brow arched, arms folded over his chest. The half-grin on his mouth was smug and proud and too damn sexy under the circumstances.

Gabe sidled by her. Emery paused to point a finger down at her head.

"Bro, she scares me," he told Syn, giving her a wide berth as he rounded her. He held his hands up when she shot him a hard glance. "I'm on your side. I promise."

Emery's antics managed to crack through her anger enough for her to blow out a sharp breath and shake her head. "Sorry you heard that."

Emery winked and kicked the front door closed. "Hey, I'm all for it, as long as I'm not on the receiving end of getting smacked. At least, not that—"

"Hey, hey, hey," Briella cut in, eyes wide. "Too much information."

Emery laughed and followed his brother's path to the kitchen. Briella rubbed a hand against her cheek before looking at Syn.

He reached out for her. "You okay?"

"Yeah." She shuffled over to him and melted into his embrace. "Thanks for not coming out and doing some cliché kiss or something to show him who I belong to. I appreciate you letting me handle it."

"How's your hand?"

"I think I slapped him harder than I intended." She lifted her hand and showed off the bright red of her palm. "At least he didn't get kicked in the groin."

Syn grumbled something inaudible, then placed a kiss on her palm. "He got off easy. And he's lucky he was able to control his tongue."

She perked up at that. "You think he controlled his tongue? I thought he was out of line."

Syn chuckled. "Oh, sweet. He was on the verge of sinking to name calling, and that's one thing I wouldn't have stood for. Bad enough he implied you were being shared." Fire licked through his eyes before dying out. "I don't share."

Briella sank her fingers into his hair and pressed her forehead to his. "Good. Neither do I."

"Hey, love doves. Wanna get this meeting going?" Taryn called from deeper in the house. Briella laughed when Syn growled and tipped his head to the ceiling. Taryn yelled, "Faster we get moving, the faster you can go to sleep." The deliberate way he said the last word made his insinuation obvious.

"If I didn't like him as much as I do, I'd slap him next," Briella teased, straightening onto her feet. Syn pushed off the sofa arm and led her toward a casual sitting room down the hall. Gabe was helping her mother arrange the beignets and cookies on a tray while everyone else helped themselves to coffee. Briella asked Syn, "Did you buy the teas?"

Syn smiled and gave her hand a squeeze. "I hope you like some of them."

"Thanks. I'm sure I will."

"So, we ready?" Taryn asked, settling into a wingback chair and balancing a cup of steaming coffee on his knee. His usual humor had subsided to semi-seriousness.

Briella took a spot on a plush sofa while Syn poured cups of coffee and tea for them. Only after he sat beside her was she able to feed from his strength and support in the face of threatened disappointment.

She raised her mug in salute. "Let's get this over with."

CHAPTER 22

Syn was not one to sleep much, not that he needed it.

Yet sometime after taking Briella to bed and washing away her disappointment as best he could with passion, he nodded off.

A methodical scraping sound drew him from sleep. He opened his eyes to slits and pinpointed Briella in front of the window, back to him, draped in an oversized T-shirt, painting. The moon lent enough light to illuminate the dark strokes of paint while a dim clip light mounted on the easel over the canvas added a depth of color.

Syn rolled onto his side, tucked his arm beneath his head, and watched in silence as his beautiful lifemate found solace in her artwork. She worked with methodical precision for hours, unaware of his attention.

It wasn't until he caught the first signs of the approaching dawn as the sky outside the window began to lighten that Briella sighed, dropping her brush into the cup of water, and resting her palette on the narrow shelf beneath the canvas. Paint covered her fingers and hands as she used the back of her wrist to brush hair from her face.

She turned to the bed, her face sallow with exhaustion. Dark circles surrounded her eyes as her gaze landed on him. Shock rippled through her expression, but quickly disappeared behind her fatigue.

"How long have you been awake?" she asked, voice thick.

"Long enough to watch you work."

"I didn't hear you move."

He shrugged. "I haven't moved. I've been captivated by how you paint. Your muse possesses you."

Briella nodded once, stifling a yawn behind her forearm. "Let me wash my hands."

She rounded his side of the bed and went into the bathroom. The water turned on. He sat up in bed and dropped his feet to the floor, focused on the painting. From the little bits and pieces he'd gleaned from her thoughts, he knew what inspired her in the deep hours of morning. Although far from complete, there was no doubting what, or rather who, he stared at.

The eyes of the mysterious Baroqueth woman drew him more than anything else. Briella captured the phantom bottomless pits of darkness exceedingly well, and a chill fluttered along his skin at the essence of that woman staring back at him.

"I usually don't like people watching me work."

Syn tipped his head enough to catch sight of Briella approaching the bed behind him. "My apologies. I couldn't help myself."

Briella climbed into bed and walked on her knees until she settled behind him, arms draped over his shoulders. She rested her chin on her arm. "She's haunting. Beautiful in a lethal way. I haven't been able to shake her image. Painting has always helped. She's the second person I've painted who hasn't been a mere essence of thoughts and emotions."

Syn wrapped his hands around hers and nuzzled his nose against her temple. "Who's the first?"

"You."

"Ahh."

She leaned into his chaste kiss to her cheek. "I've worked so hard and for so long for this debut. Are you sure this is going to work?"

"I can't promise anything. There are too many variables that we just don't know. If it were up to me, you know I'd say to forego this event, but I understand what it means to you. We all do."

Their meeting had revolved around plans and strategies to keep Briella safe during her show, since the Baroqueth more than likely were brewing up a plan of sabotage and ambush. It took a hell of a lot of convincing for Cade to actually give his approval, as begrudging as it was.

In the end, they would do whatever it took to protect Briella.

His lifemate sighed, turning her head into the crook of his neck. "You've thrown my world into a shitstorm, you know that?"

"I take the blame. For some of it."

To his surprise, and delight, Briella climbed around him to straddle his lap. Her palms pressed over his cheeks, her fingers tracing his brows.

"I'm exhausted," she said softly, pressing a kiss to the corner of his mouth. "I'm going to sleep late."

He tried to capture her mouth on her next chaste kiss to the opposite side of his mouth, craving more than her taunting brush, but she leaned back too fast. When he started to slip his hands beneath the hem of her shirt, she skimmed off the item with one quick, fluid motion. His hunger erupted like a blast of lava. The growl that bubbled up from his chest couldn't sound more feral than if he were a mindless beast.

"Stay with me?" she whispered, the heat of her skin unleashing the dragon. Through the thermal lenses of his beast, he watched her body heat as he drew his talons gently up her back. The fierce shudder and the delightful whimper that followed had him flipping her over, tucking her beneath him, and settling in the cradle of her thighs.

"Anything for you, love."

Syn didn't sleep. He couldn't. Not when he held his world in his arms, bed mussed and sexy as hell, and each day dished up a new challenge to keeping her safe. Her lips, slightly parted in sleep, were swollen from their kisses, and he had no regrets over the fierceness of their claiming.

She barely moved until it was closing in on noon. Her fingers splayed over his chest and the leg curled over his waist slipped down against his leg. A breathy moan fled her lips before her thick lashes fluttered briefly and her eyes opened.

"What a perfect sight," she said, voice thick and husky with sleep.

"I've had one for hours now." He brushed a few strands of hair away from her mouth and kissed her forehead. "How are you feeling this afternoon?"

The satisfied smile that crossed her mouth as she stretched—sweet Goddess, he didn't need any more temptation—spoke of her delight. As did the twinkle in her eyes and the flush on her cheeks.

"Never better." She cupped the side of his face. "Think we're missed?"

Syn chuckled. The last thing he wanted to do was move, but there would be time for lounging in bed after many magnificent nights when Briella's debut was done. For now, he regretfully sat up and stretched his arms over his head.

Damn the woman for snaking her lithe body around his and coming up in front of him to place a delicious kiss on his lips.

"I think the guys know exactly what's going on," he said.

"Not much privacy when it comes to what happens behind closed doors." She rolled her eyes as she shifted over his lap and climbed off the bed. He grappled for the T-shirt she had shed earlier and left at the foot of the bed, and tossed it to her. She laughed. "What? You've seen me naked."

"Good gods, woman. Put the damn shirt on before I pull you back in this bed and refuse to let you go until tomorrow." The dragon made himself known in the rumble of his voice. Briella's pupils dilated. She took her sweet time pulling it right-side out and unfolding the hem. "Briella. It's *your* exhibit we need to work on. *I'm* perfectly okay with blowing the entire thing off."

Briella finally pulled the shirt on. "Can I say something?"

"You've never refrained in the past."

She turned to him as he shifted to the edge of the bed, keeping the sheet around his waist for Briella's sake. She watched him for a long, haunting moment until he stood in front of her, sheet fisted in his hand.

"What is it, sweet?"

She chewed her lower lip. He gently pressed his thumb to her chin and she stopped. His eyes narrowed.

"Briella?"

She laughed. "You know what? I'm going to let you simmer in curiosity for a while. I should jump in the shower and get ready for what's left of the day. I want to stop by the gallery real fast before it closes."

Syn stewed, thinking of any and every way to get her to spill what she was keeping secret. If the vulnerable glow of her eyes had anything to do with it, he wanted to know sooner rather than later.

He'd just pulled his jeans up to his waist when there was a brisk knock on the door.

"Syn."

Syn crossed the room at Taryn's urgent tone and pulled open the door. Taryn gave his poorly presentable self a quick glance, a quirked brow, and a hint of a knowing grin.

"Where's Briella?"

He hitched his thumb toward the bathroom. "Finishing up in the shower. What's going on?"

Taryn's eyes narrowed on something behind Syn's shoulder.

"When did she paint that?"

Syn followed his gaze. "During the night."

"You realize we have no photographs or sketches of the Baroqueth, right? That Brie was able to capture this with such detail, the female Baroqueth… I've gotta get in touch with Cade. He needs to see this."

"Ask Briella first, but the painting isn't what's got you in a knot."

"No knot. I've been entertaining Emma downstairs for the last hour in hopes you two might crawl out of bed sometime today. She wanted to have lunch with Brie."

Syn folded his arms over his chest and stared at his friend. "Don't even think about working your charms on Briella's friend."

Taryn threw up his hands. "No charm, but I enjoy her company, which says a bit. It's been a long while since I've enjoyed a woman for her personality over other skills. I think we might become friends."

Syn was skeptical. "Do you even know the difference between friend and bedmate?"

Taryn winked. "We'll see. So, you think you two would be up for a late lunch? You should probably replenish your woman's strength after spending most of the night depleting it."

"Taryn."

He shrugged. "Hey, I warned you it would be explosive."

"What would be explosive?" Briella asked, stepping out of the bathroom. Syn was glad she'd had the foresight to bring a change of clothing into the bathroom. Briella, fully clothed, roughly scrubbed a towel over her damp hair. "Hey, Taryn."

"You look quite magnificent today." Taryn dropped a quick kiss on her cheek. "Emma's downstairs asking to take you to lunch."

"She'd like all four of us to go," Syn corrected, catching the gleam of joy in Briella's eyes.

"That would be wonderful. It shouldn't take me long to get ready. Has she been here a while?"

"Not long," Taryn lied.

"An hour," Syn said.

Taryn scowled before it melted into his signature smile. Syn shrugged.

"I should hurry up." Briella nudged his arm. "You, too."

"You heard the boss," Taryn said. Mimicking Briella, he nudged Syn's shoulder before he turned and hurried out of the room.

Syn ran a hand over his face.

"Hey, he's not going to do anything with Emma." Briella gave his shoulder a squeeze before taking up a spot in front of the dresser. She started to brush out her damp hair. Syn moved to her side and she smiled at him in the mirror. "Trust me."

"By the looks of your friend, she's pretty enamored. I just don't want something that happens with them to cause problems between you and your friend."

"Nothing will happen. I've seen it."

He quirked a brow. "Ah, Saralyn's convenient gift of sight."

"Yep. Beside which, I thought the plan was to return to your homeland."

Syn stared at her in the mirror, observing the lovely gray of her eyes threaded with ribbons of steely blue. A flicker of excitement slipped into them.

"You're scrutinizing me."

He stole a glance at his own expression to find his eyes narrowed and his head tilted in a curious manner. "I might have been." He gently relieved her of the brush to take over the task of brushing her hair. "Why does it sound like you're contemplating a change of heart?"

He took care with the knots in her hair, easing them loose until the brush made its way through each parted lock without difficulty as he waited for Briella's answer. A shadow of pleasure moved over her face and the hint of a grin curled her lips. Her eyelids lowered.

"I like you brushing my hair."

"I see that." He dropped a kiss against her temple. "But you still haven't answered me."

She shrugged. "I don't want you to leave me, and I don't want to be separated from you. So if you plan on going back to your world, maybe... I don't know. Maybe I can still do my painting there? After all, it's part of me."

Syn's hand paused, the bristles of the brush lodged in her hair. "You'd be willing to give this up, all of your hopes and dreams, to come with me?"

A blush touched her cheeks. "Maybe."

"What brought this on?"

She caught his gaze in the mirror without a speck of hesitation. "You'd be willing to give up everything to make me happy." She reached back and clasped the hand he'd rested on her shoulder. "I want you to be happy, too."

Syn set the brush on the dresser and turned Briella to face him. He cupped her face and kissed her forehead. "*This*, Briella, makes me happy. Having you accept me."

"You're going to make me all sappy and emotional," she joked with a strained laugh. When Syn leaned back, he saw her eyes were glistening. She wiped a finger beneath her lashes. "Damn you."

"I'll take that as a high compliment." He brushed his thumb over her lips before taking a step back. "I should start getting ready and leave you to finish, sans the sappy and emotional part."

He chuckled when she shoved his shoulder playfully. "Go, you torturous beast."

Oh, he had a comeback for that one, but decided it was best to keep that to himself. The feel of her eyes on him as he went into the bathroom set his skin on fire and taunted his insatiable dragon. There would be plenty of time for them once this debut was through.

That couldn't happen soon enough.

CHAPTER 23

Tonight.

It's here.

And it could all go to hell at the hand of orb-wielding maniacs.

Briella took one final look at herself in the full-length mirror. Her nerves were on edge. She couldn't believe the clock counted down to her debut. A lifetime of dreaming of this moment for it to finally manifest before her eyes.

The last week had been intense, between promoting her show and tweaking plans to make sure she had the opportunity to enjoy the thrill of the evening without the interruption of crazy sorcerers who held grudges longer than a bitter ex. Now, as Emery, Gabe, and a dragon she had yet to meet by the name of Tajan set up a security perimeter around the gallery, and her father finalized their plans in the library with Syn, Taryn, and Cade, Briella worked to shed the excited tremors that coasted over her from head to toe.

"Oh, sweetheart."

Saralyn stood in the doorway, hands over her mouth and tears shimmering in her eyes.

"Mom, don't start with the tears. My makeup's on," Briella said, her voice faint. She pulled the lacy silver and black skirt from her legs. "It's not too much?"

Saralyn crossed the room and took her by the shoulders. Her gaze was firm. "Nothing could ever be too much for my little girl."

She pointed to the door. "Have you seen Syn?"

They shared their laughter as Saralyn fiddled with the single shoulder strap of Briella's dress, then the thick, flouncy curls in her hair. She readjusted one of the two diamond-studded barrettes on the right side of Briella's head. Syn had gifted her with the beautiful accents earlier that day.

Saralyn let out a sigh. "You are a sight, Briella. You are everything I've ever hoped and wished for. Everything your father and I could ever dream of. I cannot tell you how *proud* we are of you."

"Ma, no *tears*." The back of her throat tightened. "Later, all the tears you want, but not now."

"I'm sorry, sweetheart." Saralyn sniffled and pressed two fingers to her lips. Briella kissed her mother's forehead.

"Cade's driving us over, right?"

Saralyn nodded once, sucked in a sharp breath, and tipped her chin as if determined to put aside her weepiness. She put on one of her signature smiles. "Yes. I believe he's downstairs."

"Well, then. Let's not keep him waiting."

Briella and her mother made it out of the house without a hitch, which meant Syn and her father remained crammed up in the library with Taryn. Cade, the perfect gentleman beneath an extremely intimidating shell, walked the women to their waiting ride—a rented Range Rover capable of fitting Cade inside. He looked pretty close to human in his dress pants and button-down shirt, though his bulk seemed to threaten the seams along his shoulders and biceps. Even his dark red hair had been semi-tamed, pulled back in a neat ponytail at the nape of his neck. Briella thought his beard appeared to be shorter, completing his transformation.

"You ladies look lovely this evening. You've remembered a change of shoes in case of an ambush, correct?"

Briella lifted her oversized crossover bag and nodded. "Good old running sneakers for us both."

Cade chuckled, his amusement a deep, dragony sound. "Good. Hopefully we won't have to worry about those, but with Baroqueth, anything is possible. I'll escort you ladies into the gallery and keep out of the way. Emery, Gabe, and Taj are in place. Your father will come with Taryn. Syn will arrive separately. For better visual coverage."

"You have the jewel?" Saralyn asked Briella, twisting in the passenger seat to look at Briella in the back. Briella's lips tightened and she nodded once. She didn't like the idea of carrying Syn's dragonstone with her, but they had discussed over and over that it would be safer with her than left at Taryn's house. It also put the dragonstone in near proximity to the dragons protecting her, who would protect the jewel. "You'll be safe, dear."

"I don't doubt that."

She didn't, if the two times she witnessed Syn and Taryn battling their ancient enemies said anything about their capabilities, magic or not. None of the dragons had survived centuries on their good looks alone, although if someone were to suggest such a thing, Briella might be apt to believe them.

Cade found a parking spot and cut the engine. He turned in his seat and split a glance between Briella and her mother. "When we get out, don't make an effort to find the others. If the Baroqueth plan on attacking tonight, they'll most likely suspect we're aware of their plan. Don't for one second believe that a public event like this will keep them from spilling blood if the opportunity presents itself."

That left a bitter taste in Briella's mouth. Her paintings might lean heavily on the dark and mysterious side, but she didn't need a nightmare to come alive during her debut.

"Got it," she said.

Briella took her cue to leave the car when Cade walked around the vehicle to open the passenger doors and hand the women out. The three of them walked along the sidewalk, tension high despite the lighthearted conversation they fronted. Cade wore sunglasses, and from behind the lenses, Briella saw him ever on guard, scanning their surroundings. As frightening as he appeared, there was an utterly masculine handsomeness to him she hadn't noticed before.

Cade opened the door of the gallery. Saralyn followed Briella inside. Cade made a final check of their surroundings, looking up and down the street before finally coming inside and closing the door.

"Ms. Everett! Oh, I certainly hope you're excited for your debut," Mr. Harper greeted, his brisk strides bringing him from his office to the front of the gallery in moments. He beamed as he held out his hand. Briella shook it, her excitement boiling up and melting the tension away.

"I've had a wonderful response to the invitations I mailed out to my VIP clients," he continued. "The phone has been ringing for the last week with potential clients asking for more information about you and your work. I do believe tonight is going to mark the beginning of something grand for us."

"I certainly hope so," Briella said, her jaw aching from how ridiculously big her smile had grown. "Mr. Harper, I'd like to introduce you to my mother, Saralyn Everett."

A flush colored Mr. Harper's cheeks as he held out a hand to shake her mother's. It took a bout of willpower not to roll her eyes. Her mother was a stunner, and she'd seen that look in a man's eyes far more times than she cared to acknowledge.

"Mrs. Everett. A pleasure. Your daughter has a very unique talent, and I'm certain she is going to succeed in reaching her dreams." Mr. Harper held Saralyn's hand a shade longer than necessary. Until his gaze shifted over Briella's head. His hands dropped to his suit jacket and he nervously adjusted the buttons. She guessed he'd finally noticed Cade. "Well, then. We should be receiving guests within a half hour. Can I offer you a drink? Refreshments? Oh, Ms. Everett, that piece you added to the collection earlier this week? I found the best wall to display such magnificent art."

"May I see it?" Briella asked.

"Of course. Right this way."

Briella and her mother followed Mr. Harper down one side of the room until they reached the end of the divider wall. There were three separate walls at the back of the gallery, and the middle one hosted her most prized painting. The placement was such that it was as if the entire gallery funneled eyes to this very place, this painting.

It was perfect.

"Are you sure you don't want to offer this one for purchase? I can assure you it will go quickly, and for a very high price," Mr. Harper said.

Briella shook her head. "No. This one is from my personal collection. It'll come home with me, but I want guests to see more than shadows."

Staring at the painting made her heart hurt and her mind yearn for the nearness of Syn. She was lost in the fiery eyes, that mysterious glower, and wanted nothing more than to run back to Taryn's house and fall into Syn's arms.

She cleared her throat, shaking herself free of the strange, submissive thoughts.

He's done a job on you.

There was no doubting that. Syn Terravon had claimed her, body, soul, and heart. She no longer felt herself unless he was nearby. Not only did he wreak havoc on her hormones, he filled the gaps inside her spirit, gaps that tore open the first night they met.

The night that inspired the painting she couldn't tear her eyes from.

"Dear?"

Saralyn's quiet concern and gentle touch on her shoulder grounded her and returned her to the gallery. Briella cleared her throat and smiled at her mother, not missing Mr. Harper's piqued interest.

How long had the painted Syn entranced her?

Briella held the strap of her bag. "If you have a glass of water, Mr. Harper, that would be great."

Anything to clear the sandpaper from her mouth and cool her insanely hot libido.

The second closest place to heaven was seeing her dreams come to life.

The first place would always be with Syn.

Briella lost count of the number of people who approached her about her work. Names melted into one another. Handshakes and faces were a blur. Even the dizzying mental conversations she tried to separate in her head forced her to tune out of her survival mechanism to bask in this small taste of success. Her never-empty glass of champagne certainly helped ease her nerves.

She spotted Cade at different points at the front of the gallery throughout most of the evening. Her father and Taryn joined the crowd about a half hour after the event began. Taryn, ever charming and quite the ladies man, engaged the single women in conversation as his sharp eyes kept watch for anyone suspicious. Emma, Adrienne, and Mindy arrived an hour late, and once Emma showed up, Taryn took a place by her side.

Mark's absence came as no surprise, but it still hurt that he'd thrown away their friendship because she didn't see him "that way."

"Six of your paintings have been sold, Ms. Everett," Mr. Harper said in a hushed tone as he sidled up to her. The gleam of success shone in his eyes. "And I'm certain you'd like to know one of your pieces is the subject of a bidding war between three of my loyal clients."

Briella's eyes widened. "A bidding war? How is that even possible?"

Mr. Harper winked. "Anything is possible. Are you enjoying yourself?"

"Exceptionally," she said. And she was. Except for the missing component needed to complete her evening.

Forty-five minutes before the end of the event, and Syn was nowhere to be seen. Taryn and her father both assured her he would arrive shortly. She relieved her father of her crossover bag and slipped away to the bathroom, locking the door behind her. A glance at her watch made her anxiety jump. The only way she wanted this night to end was with Syn beside her.

And if it took opening the box holding his dragonstone to accomplish that, then so be it. He was never late, too organized and careful to toss her debut to the wind. He didn't respond to the few telepathic inquiries she sent, which left her more nervous, fearing that something had happened to him.

Briella wasted no time fitting the key into the keyhole and popping open the latch.

When she lifted the lid, shock flooded her. Her eyes widened and her lips parted on a gasp.

She had no idea what to expect when she laid eyes on the dragonstone, but it certainly wasn't the sheer, stunning magnificence of the object resting in a bed of satin. The oblong, asymmetrical jewel swirled with obsidian black and shimmering gold laced with deep ruby red.

Heat and a faint current of energy tingled along the finger she drew over the strangely smooth surface. The textures she saw were all encased within the jewel—this was certainly no *stone*. The most unusual stroke of warmth curled around her body and wrapped her in a sense of security. A trick of the mind, most probably, but comforting nonetheless.

"Where are you?" she asked the stone in a hushed voice. "Why aren't you here?"

Syn had said the dragon could see and hear through the stone, but he never said whether he would answer her back. After a few minutes of silence, she secured the stone in its luxurious bed, placed both box and key in her bag, and returned to the event.

Her father gave her a suspicious look when she handed her bag to him. "Is everything okay, Belle?"

Briella forced a grin and nodded. "Of course. I should keep mingling. There isn't much time left."

She made another round of the gallery, accepting compliments and giving thanks, but failing to engage in conversations. Her heart broke more with every minute that passed. Would Syn miss this, knowing how important tonight was for her? How much she wanted him to share in her success?

Fighting to keep her increasingly sullen mood at bay, she returned to the painting of the man in the shadows. The man who so many clients inquired about. The offers she'd received for Syn's painting were more than she could have ever dreamed, and yet she would never part with the essence of her first encounter with the man who shattered her world and convinced her to build a better one. With him.

Her shoulders sagged.

A sigh escaped her lips as her throat began to ache with sorrow.

She lost herself in the fiery gaze of his painted eyes and the reminder of the warmth of his arms. Her rock, her foundation. The earth beneath her feet and the air in her lungs.

An arm snaked around her waist. Warm lips pressed to her ear.

"I would never miss this for the world, my love."

CHAPTER 24

The instant Briella opened the box, his dragon roared within his mind. He hated himself for staying hidden for most of the event, but they'd decided the Baroqueth would not attempt an attack if he was near.

Gabe, Emery, and Tajan stationed themselves on nearby rooftops and obscured their presence with the help of amulets commissioned from Taryn's witch friend, Amelia. The magic was true, if temporary. If Syn didn't have his dragon vision to aid him, he would have traced them in circles before locating their positions.

Cade, Taryn and Gio were inside the gallery with Briella and Saralyn, of course.

Syn was at the gallery ahead of everyone else. He observed Harper for almost an hour before Briella arrived, watching his every move to make sure there was no sign of Baroqueth influence over the man. He was a pro when it came to cloaking his presence, and the shadows in the corners of the gallery helped him.

That's where he remained when Cade arrived with the women, while the guests arrived, and as his lifemate's anxiety over his absence mounted. An essence in the shadows, watching the crowd, using his dragon sight to detect suspicious activity. It was a battle to keep himself away from his lifemate when she beamed with a glowing light that faded as the night wore on. Not to mention the fact she was lethal to his logic in that dress.

You had to go and open that box.

The *hunger* was painful. The separation was excruciating, like an icy cold saw hacked straight down his middle. He'd tried to prepare himself for the day she would open the box, but when she touched his jewel, that sweet, innocent caress…

Syn tamped down his dragon and fought a war to gain control of himself. The smoke in his throat made him choke and the knot in his chest almost caused him to double over.

Oh shit.

Briella circled the gallery until she came to stand in front of the painting that was her first impression of him. He couldn't hold back any longer. Escaping his secluded corner, he moved smoothly to stand beside his clan leader.

"Let me know if you need me," Syn murmured. Without waiting for Cade to respond, he bee-lined straight for the woman whose shoulders slumped in disappointment at his perceived absence. He slipped his arm around her waist, wanting to do so much more, and dipped his lips to her ear. "I would never miss this for the world, my love."

Briella started to twist to face him, but he tightened his arm around her waist, fingers biting into her hip as the fierce evidence of his arousal pressed into her lower back. Heat flushed over her skin and her breath hitched. Her body temperature shot up, as did her heart rate.

He kissed the sensitive patch of skin beneath her ear, delighting in the way she tensed.

"You opened my box, love."

Her lips pressed together. *"You're very late. I was worried."*

Syn chuckled, lifting his head to rest his chin on the top of her head. He wrapped his other arm around her waist and beat back the dragon, the need, and the hunger that wrenched his gut. Her sweet scent of shampoo and floral perfume, and the underlying scent of the woman he had become so familiar with made it near impossible to not drag her from the gallery, debut be damned.

"As I said, I would never miss this. I know how much it means to you."

"Where were you?"

Syn stared into the eyes of his dragon. Eyes Briella had painted. "I've been here. Watching you stun the guests with your artistic brilliance. On top of that, no words can possibly describe how beautiful you look tonight." She settled her hands over his. "I watched you walk in tonight and sweep over the floor for the last hour and half."

"And you haven't come over to say hello."

"Part of the plan, love. But I do have a surprise for you once all of this is over."

Briella laughed quietly. "A surprise, huh?" When she tried to look up at him this time, he loosened his arms. "You're just full of surprises."

He fingered one of the barrettes in her hair. The diamonds sparkled. "Mmm." He drew his finger down her cheek and over her lips before he kissed her temple. "Sometimes."

"He *did* make it!" Emma's accusatory tone turned them both around to find all three of Briella's female friends coming straight for them. Taryn looked highly amused as he followed the charging women. Emma stepped up to Syn, brows arched and hands on her hips. "You had better have a very good excuse for coming so late."

"Oh, I think he's forgiven," Adrienne said, her gaze shamelessly perusing Syn from head to toe. "It took him some time to look *that* good."

"What a way to make a good first impression on Brie's boyfriend," Mindy scolded her. "Not that I can argue. Girl? Where have you been hiding this fine specimen?"

Syn somehow dodged the many prying questions from Briella's curious friends, despite their attempts to ask essentially the same question numerous ways. To say he was thrilled he had only a half hour left of stepping carefully was an understatement. Besides, he wanted to deliver his surprise to his lovely woman.

The event went by without the arrival of unwanted guests and ended as a huge success for Briella's debut. More than half of her paintings sold, with additional work sold on conditionals through the end of the following week.

The Everetts appeared at ease with their daughter's triumph.

Syn?

He didn't like the fact that not one single Baroqueth tried to step foot through the door of the gallery. Not when the woman at the voodoo shop had the information to ambush Briella. Cade voiced the same feeling. It left a sharp hook in the pit of Syn's stomach. He was not one for surprises. The last thing he needed was a surprise of the deadly sort popping up over dinner.

After a congratulatory discussion with Mr. Harper, Syn led Briella from the gallery and toward Bourbon Street. He and Cade had discussed performing a sweep of the Big Easy for any sign of Baroqueth laying down plans for an attack.

"What is this surprise of yours?" Briella asked, her eyes glowing.

"I was under the impression a surprise is a surprise because you don't know what it is until it happens," Syn teased, giving her hand a squeeze. "By the way, you are stunning in that dress. I'm not sure I can handle you and Saralyn going shopping without me."

"Just think of all the *surprises* my mother and I can come up with."

Syn chuckled. "You'll be the death of centuries of control."

Briella got a half-step in front of him, pivoted, and pressed flush against him. "Darling man of mine, I think that has died a very pleasant death, if what I felt earlier in the gallery had anything to do with your *control*."

Syn growled deep in his chest. He grabbed her by the waist, making sure she knew just how out-of-control he felt, and lowered his forehead to hers. "Be careful how you stoke this fire, sweet."

"I have no fear of your fire."

"I'll make sure you remember that later."

One quick tip of her head and Briella caught his bottom lip with her teeth and tugged gently. The motion burned him up. "I'll be looking forward to it."

Briella was flying higher than ever. A successful debut, more than half of her paintings sold to eager clients, and now she was on the arm of her man. She couldn't ask for more than these perfect moments where the music of Bourbon Street bars wafted through the warm night air, the clip-clop of a horse-drawn carriage passing by, and the smells of Cajun cooking as the restaurants reeled with business.

"I couldn't ask for a better night," she said aloud, her smile growing. She wrapped her free arm around Syn's arm and rested her head against his biceps. The scent of his subtle cologne mixed perfectly with the underlying fire scent she had come to love. That, and the heat that came off his skin, the hardness of his body, that dangerous look in his rugged face, his mouth...

He was bone-meltingly gorgeous in his black pants, dress shoes, and dark gray button-down shirt. His hair had been combed back from his face, but their walk had caused strands to fall over his forehead again.

"God, I love you."

Syn stopped abruptly and turned to her. Briella blinked. This natural high had some very serious side-effects, diarrhea of the mouth being one of them.

"Uh..." She turned her head down, heat searing her cheeks. Syn caught her chin and brought her gaze back to his. Those warm eyes flashed with fire, fire solely for her.

His mouth lifted in one of those sexy half-grins that won her over every single time. "Do you, Briella?"

She pressed her lips together.

"Because I love you, too, my sweet. Love you more than you will ever know." His fingers slipped over her cheek until he held the side of her face in his rough palm. "From the beginning."

"Syn," she murmured, throwing her arms around his neck and pressing a hard kiss to his lips. *"Yes, I love you. A love that makes my heart hurt when you're not with me."*

"Mmm, kiss me like this when we get home."

Briella tore away and narrowed her gaze. "Why don't we go home now?"

"Because I have dinner planned for you. And a surprise, remember?"

"Dinner isn't the surprise?"

Syn chuckled as he glided his thumb along her bottom lip. "No, love. It's not."

"Well, damn."

When they arrived at the restaurant, Briella gaped at the long line out the door and the crowd of patrons clogging the sidewalk. Syn held tight to her hand as he made a path through people to get into the restaurant.

"We're not eating until tomorrow night, you realize that, right?" Briella asked.

"Doubt me, do you?" Syn shook his head. "I have my ways."

He surprised her again, not only with a trip to the highly acclaimed eatery, but with the forethought of a reservation. A hostess led them through the packed dining room until they reached a smaller room off the main dining room lined with quiet booths and candlelight.

She brought them to a corner booth, placed the menus down and left. Briella leaned against the table and took in the room, from the sensual drapery that decorated the walls to the glinting chandelier and fine tableware. She never believed she'd dine in this place. The menu prices were astronomical, but worth every dollar, according to what she'd heard.

Syn handed her the wine menu. "You choose. It's your special evening."

Briella shook her head. "I'm not really a wine connoisseur. I believe you might have a better idea of what's good." He arched a brow. Briella pressed the menu back to him. "Red. Something, I don't know, that matches the mood of the night."

"You really enjoy playing with fire," he said softly, his voice an unmistakable blend of his usual fluid accent with the rumble of his dragon. It played her humming nerves like a master musician. His gaze lingered on her as he opened the menu, and lowered to look over the list. "Ahh, I think I've got one."

"Good. I'll pick the appetizer."

Briella and Syn placed their orders. Once the server left, Syn braced his forearms on the table and folded his hands.

"How much do you like this city?" he asked.

Briella furrowed a brow at his unusual question. "Why?"

"I'm curious."

"Really? I think you know the answer." She loved New Orleans, but she loved Syn more. Wherever he went, she'd follow. She'd paint at The Hollow and come back for art shows. It could work. "Where is this coming from?"

"Let me rephrase. Would you like to live here?"

Briella couldn't help but laugh under her breath. "You're cute. I live here now."

"Belle—"

"Oh no you didn't." She straightened up in the booth and wagged a finger at him as his smile grew. "Don't you dare pull that nickname out of the bag. That's for my father only."

"Of course… Belle."

"I'd throw bread at you if we had any at the table."

"Good thing there's nothing but knives and glassware."

Briella stared at him before laughing. "Okay, okay. Would I like to live here, long-term?" She shrugged. "Depends."

"On what?"

She leaned forward, mirroring Syn's posture. Their knuckles brushed. "Spill the beans, because I can't hear your thoughts. What's the surprise?"

Syn reached for her hands. "Taryn is going to be putting his house on the market at the end of the month. I made him an offer."

Briella opened her mouth to say something, but the words were lost.

"He loves the house, but he misses The Hollow."

"For good reason. That place is beautiful." She couldn't wait to return.

Syn nodded. "It is, but this is the world you know. The world you're familiar with. My world is not, and the last thing I want to do is rip you away from your roots. So Taryn and I were discussing the house and I offered him half of the value."

"Um, okay?" She tipped her head, uncertain of where Syn was going with this. "So you made a poor offer on his house?"

"No. We're going to be joint owners of the house. This way we can travel between The Hollow and here and have a place to settle down. He doesn't want to give up the house, but he doesn't want to stay here full-time any longer. After tonight, you'll have more shows to look forward to, and we'll need a place to stay for you to flourish with your art."

"But…" She shook her head. Was Syn truly willing to stay here? For her? "I thought you wanted to go back home."

He gave her hands a squeeze. "Why do I sense disappointment?"

"Because." Briella struggled with the mixed emotions roiling in her belly. Geez, where was the wine when she needed it? "Well, it's just that I was maybe hoping that we could spend more time back at your home."

His shoulders straightened slightly. "The Hollow?"

Briella nodded.

"The last thing I want to do is take you away from here. From everything you've told me you worked so hard for. Your success."

"I think my priorities might have changed. I think that what I once saw as dreams and life paths were things that led me to where I am now." She glanced around before meeting his gaze again. "To you, and everything that comes with you."

Syn's gaze did numerous things to her, from warming her blood to making her wonder what was going through his mind. His thoughts were shuttered, and she turned down the internal volume of the conversations around them. She didn't care for inspiration or eavesdropping right now.

In fact, if she were honest with herself, her interest in her old source of inspiration deserted her the night

Syn stepped in front of her outside her apartment. That night, *he* had become the source of her inspiration.

After a long moment of silence, Syn climbed out of his side of the booth and slid onto the seat beside her. He surrounded her, an arm on the table, one on the seat back, and leaned close. "What do you want, love? I'll give you anything."

She reached up to his jaw, the thick day-old scruff scraping her fingertips in a pleasurable way. "I want to give your home a chance. I would like to come back here, too, but it doesn't feel right anymore. The day we spent at your home, I don't know what it did, but it connected with me. That place is alive and beautiful and I want so badly to go back."

"I can arrange that."

"Did I tell you I love you?"

Syn leaned in slowly. "I can lie and say no so I can hear it from your lips over and over."

"You won't have to lie because I will never grow tired of saying it."

"Corner booth."

Briella jerked back before Syn could close the slight gap between them. She looked around, the strange voice in her head breaking the dull drone of conversations with its sharp tone.

Syn's demeanor changed in a blink, going from the laid-back man she could lose herself in for ages to the hawkish dragon on alert. "What is it?" he asked, his voice soft, but firm.

"Something's off." She leaned over the table to look past him. "I just heard—"

It took Briella a valuable moment for her mind to make sense of the blur that appeared at the end of the table. Syn shoved her back in the same second his head snapped to the side from the punch he took to the face. She gasped as he was pulled from the booth.

"I'm done with you."

Briella's eyes widened when she realized who spoke with such viciousness. Who laid another punch to Syn's face.

And Syn took the beating without attempting to defend himself.

She scrambled out of the booth and shoved her way between Syn and Mark as her former friend released another punch. His fist rushed straight at her head.

The pain never came, but the sharp clap of skin hitting skin brought her attention to where Syn had caught Mark's fist in his palm.

"You can hit me all you want. Harm a hair on her head and you're a dead man," Syn growled. *Growled.* With a jerk, he tossed Mark's hand aside.

"What the hell is wrong with you?" Briella hissed at Mark.

The last thing she expected was a snide grin that made her former friend look maniacal. "Getting my girl back."

"Oh shit."

Briella hardly had a chance to respond to Syn's cuss when she realized the room had frozen in time. No one moved, stuck in impossible positions with the help of magic.

Mark laughed and raised his fist again.

Syn snarled, smoke and all. He gripped Briella's forearm at the same time he grabbed Mark's shoulder and threw him to the ground.

"Run!"

Briella bolted from the intimate dining room and stumbled to a halt.

Syn appeared in front of her, forcing her back until she bumped into a wall.

"Well, well, well. Look here."

Briella peered out from behind Syn's arm to stare at the man who spoke. The tall, lithe man had a series of black tattoos on the side of his neck that stretched up his face to disappear into his black hair. Eyes like onyx stirred with shattered silver, cold, evil. He and a half dozen other men similarly adorned with facial tattoos spread out around the main dining room. The diners and servers looked like they'd been captured in a still frame from a movie. Candles flickered and music continued to play through the speakers, but not a single person moved. The utter stillness chilled her to her soul.

"Two for the price of one. Darieth will be pleased."

One man lifted his hand. Gray smoke swirled around his fingers. Another man held an eerily familiar blue orb in his palm.

The apparent leader of the pack pinched a large shrimp from a plate as he slowly walked past a table, coming closer. Briella could barely breathe, fear choking her and making her heart pound crazily.

"Syn?"

"Don't. Move. Not unless I tell you."

"Hmm. Heard she was something to look at. No exaggeration there. We'll definitely enjoy the view. Question is"—the man cocked his head to the side, those icy black eyes narrowing as his lips curled into a menacing grin for Syn—"will we make you watch what happens before we force her to watch you die?"

Briella gripped his waist, her fingers biting hard into the steely plates of his scales. He hadn't puffed up in size as she recalled from the voodoo shop, but his dragon was certainly preparing for a faceoff beneath the cover of this clothing. She dared to glance away from the tattooed men to see the tips of Syn's dark talons stretching from his curled fingers.

"These are Baroqueth, aren't they?"

"Yes."

Syn's confirmation was of no help in calming her rising anxiety.

"Who has the dragonstone?" the leader asked. He tore the meat of the shrimp from the tail and chewed, flicking the tail onto a nearby table. "Someone opened it earlier."

Briella swallowed hard. *"Oh no. Syn, I'm sorry—"*

"Don't start apologizing. They were already onto us."

The leader paused a few tables away and cocked his head. "So, is this the game we're going to play?" He snickered, a sound as cold as his dark eyes. "For a dragon, you're pathetic. Look at you. Back against the wall like a coward."

A flash of light shot through the dining room. Briella stifled a shriek as a table exploded into splinters. The three businessmen and one woman seated there, stuck in their helpless frozen states, flew back over the floor in different directions. Blood oozed from their wounds, but they did not move.

Syn stiffened against her.

"Oops," the leader said with a snide grin. "Looks like you have a decision to make, dragon. A few, actually."

The bastard crouched next to the closest fallen man, tilted his head and shrugged.

"This guy's going to die in a few minutes. Give me your stone and I'll save the lot of these worthless creatures."

"Syn?"

"It's a trick, Briella. No matter what, death will come. Either to them or to us. And I won't let death come to you."

She could feel the torment in his mind, the swirling storm of fury and hatred battering against the pliant walls of their connection.

"Where's the stone, dragon?"

"Not here," Syn said. His voice was barely recognizable through the fierce growl.

The leader nodded thoughtfully.

In a blink, he reached down and snapped the injured man's neck.

CHAPTER 25

Briella screamed and shrank behind Syn, her fingers gripping his shirt.

"Not a good answer."

Syn watched all of the Baroqueth in the room with a keen eye. He sensed another somewhere, but couldn't pin the location. The very idea that the woman from the voodoo shop was hovering somewhere close by, concealed in her misted form, left him seething in his scales and hyper wary.

He could not leave Briella unprotected, which meant these innocent people would die.

The Baroqueth laughed and swept his arms out. "I have an entire restaurant at my disposal. What will it do to you, Syn Terravon, to watch us kill every single person here because you won't give up your stone? How bad will it rip your insides and twist your valiant mind not to protect these worthless humans?" The beast leaned forward at the waist, arching his dark brows over equally dark eyes that swam with malice. "How about your lifemate? Think about the trauma she's about to witness. The carnage."

He had to get Briella out of the restaurant and to safety, but the only direction he could go was up, through the roof—and risk exposing his dragon to a city that wasn't under the Baroqueth's frozen spell.

If that's what it took, then he would do it.

Briella's safety came first. The only protection he could offer was that of his scales and his size as a dragon.

"All you have to do is give us your stone."

Syn ground his teeth. "You really need a better line because we don't willingly give up our stones. You know that."

The Baroqueth lowered his arms and hooked his thumbs casually in the belt loops of his jeans.

A twisted arc of blue and gray magic exploded across the ceiling of the restaurant like a vicious storm preparing to unleash havoc.

Syn's stomach knotted. He'd damn well just lost the opportunity to escape skyward.

Bolts of electricity sizzled in the blue-gray cloud.

"One more chance." The Baroqueth straightened up. "Oh, wait."

A spear of light whipped along the wall. Syn spun, unleashing his dragon as he cocooned Briella in his arms, absorbing the powerful hit meant for his lifemate. The dark magic spread over his scales as he twisted away from its iron-like grip.

The magic sky rumbled.

"Syn!"

Fear shook her telepathic voice. The dragon within him swelled, prepared to protect and attack.

"Whatever you do, love, don't fight me."

Syn crushed Briella against his chest and lunged toward the smaller room they'd just left. The potent scent of electricity and humid energy filled the restaurant as the Baroqueth unleashed their deadly magic, aimed at the invisible target on his back.

Brick exploded in front of them, a dusty plume erupting from a strike.

Syn ducked, covering Briella's smaller frame as he ran toward the line of windows at the front of the room. He dodged strike after strike, refusing to let the monstrous guilt unleash his dragon as innocent restaurant patrons and servers were maimed because of him. Because of Briella.

Because of greed.

"Protect your head, Briella, and hold on."

Syn launched them off the ground a split second before a ball of magic slammed down where he had been, creating a crater in the floor. He used the closest table as leverage and lunged toward the windows, twisting in midair, curling around Briella as they crashed through the plate glass.

The entire line of windows exploded in a wave of magic, showering the sidewalk and street with shards of glass.

Screams echoed through the evening.

Sirens wailed.

Syn hit the ground, back first. He absorbed the impact with a grunt, reined in his dragon until his scales disappeared, and unfolded from around Briella in one fluid moment. He kept his arm around her back, hand hooked under her arm, and dragged her to her feet before she had time to fully recover.

Pedestrians parted to let them through.

Syn didn't get far before Gabe and Tajan dropped down in front of him.

Without a word, Tajan grabbed Briella, unleashed his dragon, and rocketed toward the sky.

"Syn!"

"You're safe with him. I won't be far behind."

He shut off the telepathic connection, unable to stand the terror in her voice, unable to wash away the fear in her expression before Tajan disappeared from view.

Gabe grabbed his arm and pulled him into a small space, off the sidewalk. "We need to go. There's no way we can fight them without more humans dying. They've got the advantage."

"Cade?" Syn asked.

"Regroup at Taryn's house."

"Where's Taj taking Briella?"

"Hollow. It's the safest place for her."

Syn bristled as Baroqueth energy grew dense in the air. "Let's go."

They peered around the corner of the building. The street crawled with slayers on the hunt, their dark eyes glinting in the night and magic sparking along their fingers without regard to the humans who watched in shock. So many innocents.

"Up?" Gabe asked quietly.

"No." He did a quick survey and motioned down the street. "Run that way. Take the alley across the way and try to zigzag. The longer we can keep to the ground, the better. We go up, we'll have to come down again, and it'll draw them straight to Taryn's."

"Well"—Gabe jutted his chin toward the approaching wall of sorcerers—"let's move."

Syn and Gabe shot from their hiding spot and bolted down the street.

A loud *boom* shook the ground.

Chunks of shattered pavement rained down, pelting their heads and backs.

Syn weaved back and forth, dodging strikes. Pedestrians jumped aside, shrieked and shouted as they passed. Two men tried to stop them until they caught sight of the fire that erupted in Syn's gaze and the smoke that came from his mouth and nose.

Syn and Gabe cut down the alley.

Baroqueth magic crashed through the corner of the building, leaving a gaping hole in the masonry.

"Sure you don't wanna fly?" Gabe growled.

Syn glanced skyward. "Let's go up."

They used their talons to scale the side of one building to the rooftop, their bodies swelling as they transformed.

Gabe launched first, his dragon filling out and his wings lifting him up. Syn followed a heartbeat later.

The air caught beneath his wings. Stormy blue bolts flew around them. Gabe spiraled, avoiding the hits.

Syn kept on Gabe's tail until a bolt cut painfully through his wing. He tilted as the membranes failed to catch air and give him lift. The burn of the hit coasted up through his wing and down his body.

Another bolt tore through a membrane in his other wing.

A shocking vision of the last battle with the Baroqueth flashed through his mind. His wings tattered, unable to lift and carry his dragon's weight. The reality of dying. The explosions and screams and roars that filled the air with battle's lament.

Only now, he had Briella to live for. To fight for.

There was no way he could recover his flight pattern. He pulled in the dragon slowly as he descended in a chaotic spiral. The ground came up fast and he braced for impact. Even with scales, he'd still suffer pain and possibly more damage to his body.

Searing heat and the force of the universe slammed into his chest. Fire spurted from his mouth as the crush of his chest squeezed the air from his lungs. The hit drove him tumbling backward, off his original course, head over feet.

A roar erupted somewhere from the night.

Fire cut through the darkness. Several bursts of flame.

Syn tried to suck in a breath. He tried to get out of the uncontrolled flip. He tried to see the damage that last bolt caused him, but the pain that ripped and tore and shredded through his body and his bones was too great.

He slammed into an unyielding object, back and head cracking stone and brick.

His vision faded until blackness shoved him into unconsciousness.

CHAPTER 26

Briella couldn't shake the fear that plagued her and controlled her nerves. She trembled, a very uncharacteristic response for her, to the point her legs barely held her steady once the dragon lowered her to the ground. His wing flicked out, catching her beneath her arms before she stumbled to her knees. She grappled for strength, for breath, for control over the burn in her eyes and the tightness in her throat as she watched the night sky over the French Quarter light up with streaks of red and blue and purple.

A strangled sound escaped her lips.

The dragon nudged her side with his wide muzzle, urging her toward the harness he dropped in front of her.

"I can't go. Not without Syn," she said, shaking her head.

The dragon snorted, smoke pluming around her. He gave her a firmer nudge, clearly insisting she put the harness on him, and only his wing beneath her arms kept her on her feet.

She turned to him, lips pressed tight, and stared into the fiery orb that glowed more red than orange. This dragon, Tajan, had ripped her from her feet, from Syn, and dragged her into the sky wrapped in his talons.

There was no way to communicate with him in this form. She had tried, but the only link she had was with Syn, and he'd shut her out as soon as she was airborne.

The dragon opened his mouth, then snapped his teeth together. He nudged again, motioned with his head to the sky, and waited with impatience scoring his eye.

"We need to wait for Syn. For the others. What if something happens? What if—"

Briella's body jerked at the waist.

Her feet left the ground. A scream ripped through her throat as she dangled precariously several feet in the air.

The dragon thrashed in an orb of smoky purple. Fire reflected off the orb, cresting over his encased form.

The invisible grip released her and she plummeted to the ground, landing sprawled facedown. She coughed, choked on a breath that stuck in her throat, her lungs refusing to open for air.

"Your precious dragon will be dead by the end of this battle."

Briella managed to lift her head from the patchy grass and dirt.

The woman from the voodoo shop crouched before her, even more beautiful and ethereal than she remembered. Her eyes seemed to drink in the black of night as she stared at Briella. No smile. No satisfaction. Her expression was impossible to read.

And in that instant when they regarded each other, a flash of foresight shook through Briella's mind. A vision so clear yet so impossible it sent her scrambling to her knees as air finally filled her lungs.

The woman's eyes widened and her lips parted.

"You have the Sight," she whispered.

Briella stifled a gasp. Slowly, she started to get to her feet. The woman followed her up, like a mirror image of her every move. She cocked her head, dark eyes narrowing and red-painted lips tilted down.

The dragon imprisoned in the orb roared, the sound reverberating through the ground and shivering through Briella's soles despite being muffled by magic.

"What did you see?" the woman asked, her voice soft.

Cautious.

Briella remained silent. If by the love of the gods what she saw was true—and never in her life had her visions proven otherwise—there would be no possibility of destroying this woman.

An eerie chill slithered through her bones.

The woman shot out one hand. A rope of smoke left her palm and snatched Briella around the chest. It lifted her to her toes and drew her close to the woman. So close, Briella could smell the patchouli and jasmine from her skin and another strange, exotic scent from her hair.

She didn't fight the bindings. There was no point. No point in fighting. No point in angering the woman.

"Tell me, Keeper. What did you see?"

"How do you know I saw anything? What makes you believe I have visions?" Focusing on the woman helped keep her mind off the deadly fireworks over the Quarter and the thrashing dragon fighting encasement.

"I felt it. The energy of the vision."

Briella shook her head. "I don't understand."

"Nor do you have to. I want to know what it is you saw."

"And I want for you and your people to leave the dragons and my people alone."

Briella's defiance intensified with each second that passed.

Shadows burst from the trees that lined the patch of land, diverting Briella's attention from the woman to two Baroqueth running toward them.

"We must go. Now," one urged.

"What of the dragons?" the woman asked, her voice musical in a terrifying way. Her eyes never left Briella's.

"We've lost track of three. One is down, but we can't locate him. The others have killed many of our own."

Briella's stomach dropped. One dragon was down, and she still couldn't feel Syn in her mind. Raw fear unlike any she'd known slid down her spine.

"We can't risk losing any more." The Baroqueth looked at Briella, his vague panic slipping behind a cold mask. "Why are you toying with the Keeper? And the dragon?"

"That is not your concern."

"Your father—"

The woman hissed, her eyes flashing with bolts of ice blue. Her magic dropped Briella to the ground and she spun on the two Baroqueth. Briella watched with a mixture of curiosity, horror, and desperation as the men recoiled and shuffled back a few steps.

"Gather my men and retreat—"

Fire lit the grassy field. Briella scrambled back as a thick plume of roaring hot flames swept over the Baroqueth before curling over on itself to threaten the woman.

Unafraid, the woman shot Briella a dark glance before vaporizing into black mist and disappearing into the swells of smoke rising from the dragonfire.

Tajan whipped his head toward Briella as the blast of his flaming breath tapered off, growled, and twisted to show the side of his huge form. He lowered to the ground.

Briella didn't hesitate this time, but there was no time to secure the harness. She climbed up onto his back, fitted herself between a set of spines that weren't nearly as long or pointed at Syn's, and gave his scales a hard pat.

"Ready," she called.

Tajan sat back on his haunches, spread his wings, and launched straight up into the sky. Briella held on for dear life.

They climbed above the clouds until she could no longer see the blazing lights of New Orleans. They soared fast, the wind merciless against her poorly clothed body, her skirts plastered against his scales. The air chilled her, but not nearly as much as the thought of Syn in pain.

What if the Baroqueth had him? What if one of the other dragons was caught and taken by the sorcerers?

Who was that woman? Why did she have blue sparks in her eyes? Syn told her the Baroqueth had silver flecks, not lightning bolts of blue. She was a leader of some standing if the men cowered in her presence.

And she got away.

Briella's hands were clenched stiffly around Tajan's spike, her arms frozen and her teeth chattering by the time they broke through the portal to The Hollow. Saturated with worry, her heart sick with fear, she kept her head pressed against the warm, hard scales of the dragon beneath her until he coasted to a smooth landing. She fumbled her grip free with numb fingers. Though Tajan tried to lean to the side to ease her move to the ground, she managed to fall the last few feet to the thick grass.

If only she had a jacket.

If only she had Syn's arms around her.

She didn't try to stand. Instead, she wrapped her arms around her knees and rocked in her misery, uninterested in Tajan's transformation from dragon to man.

He crouched in front of her, his long black hair cutting over a sharp, rugged face. Eyes so deep a blue they seemed as black as his hair watched her. Everything about him screamed dark, brooding, and dangerous.

Predator.

"Here." His voice was a deep, husky baritone, one that matched his looks. He swung a jacket around her shoulders and drew it closed at her neck. "Next time, don't fight."

The edge of disgruntled frustration in his voice brought her shoulders straight. "Excuse me?"

Tajan arched an angled brow. "Don't fight. The last thing you want to do when those slayers come around is play stubborn. The only reason I landed was to get you on my back. Far more comfortable for you than being clutched in my talons."

Briella stared, aghast, as Tajan pushed up to his feet. The man was towering and muscled and everything she would hate to meet on a bad day.

Such as today.

He held out his hand to help her up.

She stared at it, wanting to snap at the man for being an ass. "Do you have a lifemate?"

"Whether I do or I don't remains to be seen. I'm aware of the pull, but your safety comes before all else. You could've well made any sacrifice Syn may have made worthless."

Briella snorted, getting to her feet without his help. "What's your name?"

"Tajan."

"Not a social butterfly, are you?" Briella glanced past the man's shoulder. They had landed in the field close to her parent's cottage.

Tajan dropped his hand. "No. I'm not."

"Do you know what's happened to Syn?"

"He was hit."

Briella snapped her attention back to Tajan. "How can you be sure?"

"Belle!"

Her father sprang from the front stoop and sprinted toward her. Tajan separated himself from her, arms crossed over his chest.

"Thank the gods! You're safe!" Her father crushed her in his embrace. At last, Briella sank into familiar arms, her muscles and bones practically dissolving with relief and worry. Over her head, her father said, "Taj, thank you. Thank you."

"Get inside your home and stay there until we return," Tajan said. He twisted and leaped toward the sky, his dragon unleashed and pulling him away from the ground between one breath and the next.

Briella didn't say a word until the dragon disappeared and her father guided her trembling body toward the house.

"He's a jerk," she muttered.

Her father closed the door behind them and shook his head. "Taj is far from a jerk, Belle. He's not very social, so he comes off like one."

"Seems very jerky to me." She shed the jacket Tajan had gently wrapped around her and draped it over the back of a chair. "When did you get here? Where's Mom?"

"She's changing. Not long ago."

"Have you received any news on Syn? He cut off our telepathic link. Tajan said he was hit." Her voice cracked on the last word. A fresh wave of sickening anxiety washed over her. Her father's brows furrowed and he shook his head. "Has he ever done that with you? Cut you off?"

"Yes. It's not uncommon for them to separate themselves when there is danger. It's to preserve our energy and allow them to concentrate on the fight." Her father kissed the top of her head. "Stay strong, Belle. Syn won't let them get him easily."

As the events of the past hour crashed over her and started to sink in, Briella's knees buckled. Her father caught her and helped her to the sofa, where she settled limply into the soft cushions.

The last image of her dragon had been a blur as Tajan ripped her away from him and took to the sky. Syn's expression had been stone cold.

"He has to be okay, right?" Briella looked up into her father's eyes. "I mean, he's a dragon."

"If they don't return in an hour, I'll use the stone to try and contact him."

An hour.

Her entire future and the future of her heart rested on an invisible clock that ticked closer and closer to the final minute.

One hour.

And she would know if her dreams would evolve or shatter.

CHAPTER 27

"Hey, dude. You good?"

"Back away from him!"

Syn groaned. Every damn inch of him hurt. Pain such as what he'd last felt when he was nearly killed by Baroqueth over thirty years ago.

For a long moment, he didn't move, mentally noting the damage he'd sustained. He was precariously slouched against a solid wall, arm draped over something, head in a plant. Branches prodded at the side of his face, still half-protected by his scales. Both arms burned mercilessly, signaling the residual effects of his wings being torn. Every inhale sent a wave of dull pain through his chest. A few of his ribs ground together.

Had he retracted his scales that much to open himself to the severe consequences of a Baroqueth hit?

Foolish. Novice move, Syn.

Damn. He'd have to deal with this mess until he got back to The Hollow, where his body could heal quickly.

"Dude, I heard a thud and came outside. I didn't do that to him," the unfamiliar voice said defensively.

A strong hand clamped down on Syn's shoulder. "Hey, brother. Gotta get you out of here."

Taryn.

"Looks like his face is bleeding. I'll go call 9-1-1."

"No," Taryn snapped. "He's fine."

"After that light show in the sky? Maybe he was hit with—"

"I'm fine."

Syn retracted his scales and opened his eyes. He pinpointed a young man, beer bottle in hand, cigarette in the other, shifting from foot to foot. The bystander pushed his glasses onto the bridge of his nose with his shoulder.

With a deep breath that stung like bullets, Syn climbed to his feet with Taryn's help. Dear gods, the pain.

"Come on," Taryn said quietly. "Cops are prowling the streets. If we want to get out of here, we'll need to do it soon."

Syn nodded once. "Briella?"

"Taj got her out safely."

"Good." Relief flooded him as he looked toward the sky. "It's quiet."

"Think your eardrums were shot out." Taryn snickered. "Can you walk?"

Syn took a step. Yeah, pain from head to toe. Between the magic bolt that shocked through his body and the impact of his fall, he was thankful he *could* walk so soon.

"Let's go."

"Um, hey, man. What about my wall?" the stranger asked.

Syn and Taryn exchanged a confused look. Syn's eyes cut to the concrete wall. Cracks webbed the surface, clearly splaying outward from a point of impact. Chunks off the top were missing or littered the ground as pulverized rubble.

Taryn snorted, pulled out his wallet, and dug out a bunch of hundreds. He took the man's hand and slapped the money into his palm. "Here, *dude*. Should be plenty enough to cover the damages and buy you a year's worth of beer."

Taryn returned to Syn's side. "Guy sees a near apocalypse over his house and a damn dragon in his backyard and he's concerned about his wall."

"I might actually laugh if it didn't hurt," Syn grumbled, pressing his arm to splint his chest.

"Cade's at the house. Emery and the others should be heading to The Hollow, now that the Baroqueth have retreated and I've found you." Taryn threw out an arm to stop Syn's forward march as they came to the sidewalk. Two police cruisers rushed by, lights flashing and sirens blaring. "We're going to have to blend in."

"Been doing that all night."

Taryn snorted. "Bro, you're horrible at making jokes."

"Never said I was good at it." Syn grimaced as he rolled out his shoulders. "Gods."

"Wings got clipped, I saw. Cade'll bring you back to The Hollow."

"Gio and Saralyn are there, I presume."

"Of course. Zareh decided to join the fun and lend a bit of backspace for the ride home. Gio took your stone, too."

Syn shot Taryn a narrow-eyed look. "Zareh? What about Kaylae?"

There was no way Zareh would leave his lifemate alone. Not with their new baby on the way.

"I don't know the details. Haven't even seen him. Just heard from Cade that Zareh came to take your Keeper. I was lending a hand setting this city on fire."

"Well, it's good to know you failed in your mission to burn the city down. I actually like this place."

Taryn punched him playfully in the shoulder. Syn snarled.

"Ha! I knew you'd come around."

By the time they reached Taryn's house—avoiding the chaos of first responders, large groups of people huddled together on the sidewalks and in the streets, and the very pronounced inclusion of dragons in all conversations—Syn was in agony. Aside from reaching Briella and reassuring himself she was safe with her parents, he wanted nothing more than for his body to heal the way it was supposed to: over the course of a few hours versus a few weeks.

Cade greeted them at the door, his eyes narrowed on Syn. "How're you feeling?"

"Like I fell from the sky and hit a concrete wall." Syn tilted his head one way, then the other, and listened to his neck crack. "Damn. I'm a mess."

"You okay to ride?"

"If it gets me back home, and to Briella I'll deal with the discomfort. Let me grab a few things from her room. I'm sure she'll want clothes."

Cade followed him up the stairs to Briella's room. "What can I help with?"

Syn motioned to the closet. "She keeps shirts and pants in there. I'll get the other items."

A few minutes later, Syn had gathered Briella's more private essentials from her drawers and stuffed them in one of her bags. When he returned from the bathroom with her toiletries, he found Cade standing in front of the painting of the Baroqueth woman, a peculiar expression darkening his face. His eyes flickered with fire.

"Who...is this?" Cade asked.

"Briella wanted to share it with you, but things went a bit off-schedule tonight." Syn dropped the toiletries into the bag and joined Cade. "This is the woman who attacked Briella at the voodoo shop last week. She was able to paint her, giving us the first visual evidence of one of our enemies."

Cade's head tilted slowly, his lips stretching thin beneath his deep red beard and mustache. His eyes took on a strange glow that left Syn curious.

"Everything okay?"

Cade cleared his throat, turning with a stiff jerk to face Syn. He held up the armful of clothing. "Will there be room in that bag?"

"Yeah."

Tension had settled in the big man's shoulders and his expression as he put the clothes in the bag. Fastening it shut, Cade slung the bag over his shoulder.

"Let's get out while we can," Cade said, casting the painting one last glance.

Had Syn not been fiercely aching and needing to see Briella, he would have insisted Cade explain his reaction to the painting.

He never thought he'd see the Firestorm leader unnerved by anyone, let alone a two-dimensional image of a woman.

Briella paced the living room for an hour, pausing only to go to the window and scour the night sky for any sign of the dragons. Her fingers ached from twisting them together. Her stomach rolled uneasily to the point she couldn't even look at the cup of tea her mother had made for her without suffering a strong urge to vomit.

She had tried several times to mentally connect with Syn, but their bond remained silent. Her father must have known what she was trying to do, because he explained there was too much distance between them to use telepathy.

She was at the breaking point, not knowing the fate of the dragons. Of Syn.

Her father returned to the living room, dragonstone box in hand. Briella stopped pacing and looked at the box. For the last hour, she'd wanted to open that box and talk to Syn.

Now?

She moistened her lips. Her mouth went dry. She lifted her gaze to her father's when he held the box out to her.

Answers sat within that box, and she wasn't sure she was prepared to face the haunting truth of what might have become of Syn.

"All you have to do is open the box and speak to the stone. He will hear you. It's a catalyst, of sorts. Since you're lifemates, you need not bleed into the stone first. The essence of my blood in connection with you and the stone is enough to connect you to Syn."

"Will he be able to speak to me?"

Her father nodded once. "Yes." His eyes dimmed. "If he hears you."

Briella forced back the lump in her throat. "You mean, if he's still alive."

"Here, Belle." He stretched the box toward her again.

Briella's arms felt leaden when she reached for it. Her fingertips tingled with energy from the dragonstone magic.

The truth lies here.

"Dad, I don't know…" She cleared her throat, but the lump swelled and tears finally slipped over her eyelids. "I don't know if I can."

"I understand, sweetheart." He produced the small key for the lock. "Take your time, but never lose hope.

Your mother and I held onto that hope for over thirty years. We were blessed by the gods for never relinquishing that hope." He kissed her forehead. "I'll let you be, but we'll be in the kitchen if you need us."

"Thanks."

Briella sat down on the sofa, box in hand, heart thumping hard and her head dizzy. She rubbed the delicate key with her thumb, hoping to somehow get an inkling as to what had happened to Syn without facing the merciless truth. He'd been hit, Tajan said. Down. How bad down was in dragon and Baroqueth terms, she wasn't sure, but in human terms, the prospect was usually pretty grave.

"You can handle this. You're strong," she whispered.

Her inner voice laughed mockingly at her pep talk. She was strong. She was independent. But the moment Syn stormed into her life, all of her personal strength seemed to have abandoned her. *He* was her strength. *He* was her encouragement. He was her *life*.

Without him, she feared she'd be nothing more than a shell of a human being, going through the motions of living without passion or hope.

"I hate men," she said on a half-sob. With a fierce swipe of her hand to dry her face of tears, she jammed the key into the keyhole.

The front door flew open.

Taryn lunged at her, his eyes wild, his hair matching, and urgency in the way his hands grabbed her arms and yanked her to her feet. She grappled for the box, catching it against her belly before it slipped from her fingers.

"Come on. Now," Taryn breathed.

"What—"

"Now."

The man practically dragged her from the cottage and up the hill to the landing field. He shifted into his dragon, caught Briella around her midsection with one of his enormous talons, and launched them into the air.

Briella fought to keep her anxiety from pushing her into a full-blown panic attack. She clutched the dragonstone box tight for grounding. What would they step into? Or fly into?

What had happened to Syn?

Taryn soared to the top of a mountain she instantly recognized. He circled the mountain peak to the landing shelf, where he set her on her feet and transformed back to his human form.

Taryn snatched her arm again and pulled her into Syn's mountain home. The maze to reach the main living quarters was dark and steep, lit only by a torch Taryn ignited for her benefit.

"How is he?" Briella finally asked when they slowed in front of a door.

"Here." Taryn used his extended talon to unlock the door. He stepped aside and urged her forward. She stumbled into what was as close to a foyer as possible in a mountain. "Go."

"But—"

Taryn closed the door, leaving her to stare at the thick wood and iron in confusion.

Until her lifemate connection with Syn flickered to life, a brilliant golden warmth inside her head.

"Syn," she gasped, spinning away from the door. She hurried through the halls, taking only moments to glance in each room. "Syn!"

When all the main living spaces came up empty, she almost ran to his room.

For a heartbeat, the shock of seeing him lying in bed paralyzed her.

"Syn!"

He turned his head toward her as she sprinted across the room, dropping the box along the way. She jumped onto him, wrapping her legs around his waist, her arms around his neck, and crushing a kiss to his mouth as tears flowed down her cheeks. Her fingers fisted against his scalp as she clung to him, each hard kiss desperate and relieved and overwhelmed at the same time.

Until he groaned and stiffened.

She pulled back. "Why didn't you tell me you were okay? Why didn't you come straight to me?" She poked him hard in the shoulder. "They said you were hit. You were down. I've been so scared—"

"Hey, love. Easy." Syn reached up and tucked her hair behind her ear before wiping her tears with his thumb. His face grew taut when he leaned his head back against the pillow. "I *was* hit. Tore my wings. Took a bad crash and broke some ribs. The trip here did a number on my strength."

Briella stared at him through her tears. "Oh no! I've hurt you more."

Syn stopped her from climbing off, pulling her back down on top of him. "No. This is what I want. What I need. Knowing you're safe. You're here. Sweet, sweet Briella. You are the only thing that matters to me."

"How bad off are you? Should I ask Taryn to get you spring water? Is there something else I can do?"

"Love, they're bones. They'll heal up in a few hours. Until then, the only thing I want to do is hold you."

"Syn." She lay her cheek on his shoulder and chewed her bottom lip, trying to control the rush of tears and the press of sobs as she inhaled his scent, absorbed the heat from his body, and melted into his arms. "I don't know what I'd do without you. Don't you ever scare me like that again. And why didn't you try to connect with me once you arrived?"

"I just got here. Taryn must have retrieved you while Cade helped me get into bed." Syn growled with a sharp intake a breath. Briella squeezed her eyes and cringed at the sound of his ribs grinding. She tried to gingerly move off him again, knowing her weight must be causing him pain, but his arm tightened around her. "No, love. You're perfect where you are. I don't want you to go anywhere."

"Only a dragon would cast off broken bones like a paper cut."

Syn chuckled, though his amusement was short-lived. He combed his fingers into her hair and sighed. "I love you, Briella. You are my world."

Briella looked into his heavily-hooded eyes and saw the pain etched in his rugged features. She glimpsed the raw red slashes over his arms through the tears in his sleeves. What else had he endured?

Later, there would be time to ask. Right now, she was grateful to have Syn back. Alive.

She kissed the rough scruff on his chin, loving the feel of the scratchy day-old hair against her lips.

"I love you, dragon. Not knowing what happened to you almost killed me. Having you here has made me whole again. I can't be without you, Syn. I just can't, so don't ever make me suffer that pain."

"The last thing I ever want you to suffer is pain on my behalf." His eyes closed. "I'll make it up to you as soon as I heal. Trust me, there will be no pain in that."

She smiled as she tucked her head under his chin and closed her eyes. "I'm holding you to that."

CHAPTER 28

Men scattered as she stormed down the obsidian hallway. A dim blue glow lit the way ahead, while several lines of energy provided light along the walls.

For the first time, she had failed.

She couldn't understand why she was okay with that.

The Keeper girl had a vision. The residual shock of energy as that vision passed through the Keeper and linked with her stirred unease within her body. She couldn't explain it, didn't understand it, but it had happened.

The Keeper had seen something. And that something had a direct correlation with *her*.

The set of Baroqueth guards standing before the double doors bowed their respect. She ignored them, too consumed by her thoughts and the evidence of what she'd encountered to notice, and pushed her way into her father's chambers.

Darieth Constantine sat in his gothic throne, a gilded chair with obsidian trim and black upholstery.

Not a real throne, but the grandeur of the chair made his position clear. So did the tattoos that decorated his head where it was shaved on the sides. Those tattoos marked his neck, his shoulders, his arms. The power in those designs put fear in all Baroqueth.

Except her.

"Malla, my dear." Darieth stood, one single fluid motion that blended with the faint misting of his figure. He met her in the center of his chamber, took her shoulders in a gentle hold, and kissed the top of her head. She kept her back straight, never once showing him submission. "I understand our attack did not go as planned."

"I told you it was a bad idea to attack in the center of the city. A mess was left in our wake, one that exposed us." Malla cut her arm to the side. The chamber doors slammed shut with her small pulse of magic. "You should not have sent those extra men. We lost over half our men tonight. The one thing going for us is that the dragons do not know our numbers. Numbers that have been practically depleted.

"Your breeding program, Father, has failed after the first two waves of births. The strength of your men has become diluted and miniscule at best. After losing ten men before tonight in the last two standoffs with Zareh and Alazar, we might well have to forgo future attacks until our strength increases."

Darieth's eyes darkened to cold black orbs that chilled her skin. His growing anger was evident in the flicker of energy coasting across his chest. His mouth set in a firm line.

"You failed me this evening, daughter."

Malla scowled. "I failed you only because you failed to listen to my advice... *Father*." Her hands fisted by her sides. "Nerrick? You sent that idiot to lead the attack in the restaurant? He went ahead of me. I didn't have a chance to get there, to get Syn Terravon, before they escaped. That soldier of yours is a risk you can't take right now. I don't want him on any of my assignments in the future."

Darieth's nostrils flared briefly. Silver poured through the tattoos on his face and neck before disappearing. "You *had* his lifemate. How did she escape? And the other dragon?"

Malla stood her ground. "I was distracted by the chaos raining down on the French Quarter."

Her father tilted his head in a motion that warned of his impending rage. The silver in his eyes glowed. "Since when do we care what happens to mortals? Kill the lot of them, if you must, but I want those dragons and their mates. I don't care what it takes, Malla. If we don't syphon more of their power, our entire race will die. We must strike while we're still strong."

Darieth spun away, his black robe curling around him. Malla stared at his back, the long black ponytail tied at the point above where his hair was shaved. Her nails bit into her palms. Her father loved his hair. Right now, she'd love to cut it all off.

He paused in front of his throne and cast her a half-glance over his shoulder. "Malla, you are my daughter and the strongest in our fleet beneath me. Do not fail me again. I would hate to force you into the breeding program."

Malla clenched her teeth to keep from saying something she'd regret. It wasn't the first time he'd threatened to throw her into a cell with a dozen other women, waiting to be used by every Baroqueth until she bore a child. The only difference between her and the other women was that they happily agreed to be part of the program.

It would be the greatest punishment for her.

Her father dismissed her when he looked away and refused to sit. She swallowed a growl, spun on her heel and stalked from the room.

Her father's men averted their heads as she passed. She didn't stop until she reached her quarters and secured the doors with locks and spells. She'd have to come up with a new plan. She doubted the dragons would stay in New Orleans long. Not with the attention this evening brought to both dragons and sorcerers. A few of the Baroqueth had stayed behind to perform damage control on the humans. She had received a report from one she stationed in Georgia to oversee Zareh and his lifemate that the couple had taken a hasty leave, despite the woman being near to term with their first child.

As she fell into her plush chaise lounge and pinched her forehead, she couldn't shake the unease caused by the woman tonight.

Syn's lifemate had a vision. A vision Malla wanted to know.

A vision, she feared, showed the end of the Baroqueth.

The end of herself.

Epilogue

Two Weeks Later

"Well, I think that's about it." Briella brushed her palms on her jeans and looked over the bags of her belongings. The guest room she had been using was barren once more.

Syn wrapped his arms around her waist from behind and layered kisses along her neck. She giggled.

"Stop that, you insatiable beast. Taryn's waiting for us."

"He won't mind waiting a little longer," Syn murmured against her shoulder. His teeth scraped her skin and she shuddered in delight. "Mmm, a little more of that and I might have my way with you."

Briella twisted around to face Syn. "Dragon, you *always* have your way with me."

Syn chuckled, straightening up. "I do. But so do you."

"I'm not arguing that."

He pinched her hip. "You have no argument against it." He placed one more kiss on her forehead before releasing her to pick up the bags. "Are you certain this is what you want?"

"To live with you in The Hollow?" Briella snorted. "I think that's a dream come true."

Syn nodded once. "And you're certain you don't want me to go in with Taryn on the house?"

The events from the battle between dragons and Baroqueth remained vivid in her memory. That night had been one of the best in her life, and one of the worst. She knew moving full time to The Hollow was not a guarantee of safety, but they were far safer in Syn's world, where his powers were strongest.

She loved New Orleans and all the promise it held. She loved the opportunities she'd been given and the friends she'd made. Friends with whom she promised she'd keep in touch. She had fabricated a story about returning to Upstate New York to spend time with an ill family member and wasn't sure whether she'd return to New Orleans. Mr. Harper was understanding, but impressed upon her his desire to host more showings of her work, to which she happily agreed.

Somehow, she'd make it work. Syn promised her the chance to see her dreams come to full fruition.

With a sigh, she shook her head. "No. After the other week, it seems Taryn is anxious to sell. And I think it's best if we stay away from here for a while. That all of the dragons have returned to The Hollow speaks volumes of the dangers here."

"We'll still come back and visit." Syn caressed the side of her face with his knuckles. "Taryn isn't going to put the house up for another month or so. If you change your mind, all you have to do is say it. He's sitting on the house just to make sure you don't regret your decision."

Briella smiled. "He's such a great guy."

"Hey, now."

She nudged his arm and they laughed. "But you're the greatest."

Syn winked and led her from the room.

Taryn was in the living room, the last box of her paintings wrapped up in a custom dragon-sized sling he had a friend design to transport her pieces and equipment to The Hollow. He flashed them a smile as they descended the stairs.

"And here I thought I'd have time for a beer and a sandwich."

"We know how to behave," Syn told him, taking Briella's hand as she stepped off the last stair. His chivalric manners never ceased to amaze her. As if he didn't own her heart in its entirety—after fearing she lost him, she insisted on bleeding into his jewel and sealing their lifemate bond—somehow he managed to find a new little piece to take as his. "Probably should get going. Dawn's quickly approaching."

Taryn's attention turned to Briella. "Are you sure you're okay with this?"

Briella looked around the house. So much had happened here in such a short time. Her entire life changed when she walked through the front door. Myths became reality. Goals turned onto new paths.

And love. Sweet, powerful love found her at last.

She would always love this house for all it gifted her, but now, as she took it in one last time, she knew it wasn't *home*.

Home was The Hollow. Home was in a mountain.

Home was with Syn.

She nodded. "Yes. I'm sure."

Taryn grinned. "You're always welcome to come here and hang out. My house will always be open to you, until I sell it."

"Of…"

The living room disappeared, taking Syn and Taryn with it. For a split moment, she stood on the front stoop, staring at the door, her skin tingling and her heart racing. A mixture of anxiety and delight twisted together in a strangling rope of emotions.

The one-line thought that ran through her head shocked her more than the vision itself.

"Sweet?"

Syn's concerned voice sounded far away.

Briella blinked.

She stood beside Syn, both he and Taryn watching her in confusion. She waved their concern away, but couldn't shake the words that echoed in her mind. The voice of a woman, not herself.

"Are you okay?"

"Yeah. I am. Just a vision."

Taryn snickered. "Your visions aren't 'just' visions." He hoisted the sling with her paintings and secured it over his shoulder. "Let me get this in the truck."

"You said Taryn's Keeper died, right?"

Syn arched a brow. *"Yes. Why?"* His eyes narrowed. *"Your vision was about Taryn? His Keeper?"*

"I don't know."

The doorbell rang.

Briella's shoulders stiffened. Taryn paused in the act of reaching for the doorknob. He glanced at Syn, then his gaze lingered on Briella.

"I think we're about to find out," Briella said.

"Expecting someone?" Taryn asked them. They both shook their heads. "Maybe one of your friends?"

"They think I've already left. Unless Emma is hoping to see you."

She knew that wasn't the case. Whoever stood on the other side of the door was a stranger, but someone who knew Taryn.

Knew he was a dragon.

Taryn hesitated before he pulled the door open. Syn angled his body in front of Briella, prepared to protect her if danger presented itself.

A tall, slender woman looked up at Taryn from brown eyes painted with makeup. Her lips parted on a gasp and her cheeks took on a light rose. She looked to be the same age as Briella's mother, but time had not been as kind to her.

"Taryn," she said, hands clutching her purse. "I've been searching all over for you."

Taryn's head cock and his brow quirked. Briella glanced up at Syn, noticing the way both men had gone rigid.

"You know her?" she asked her lifemate.

"Yes and no. She's not someone we cared to associate with."

"Why?" She didn't miss his use of the past tense.

"She's what you'd call a gold-digger. A selfish creature who wanted to mate a dragon for what he could give her, not who he was."

"What are you doing on my doorstep? Certainly up to no good," Taryn said, his voice chilling. The good-natured man Briella knew was gone. "How did you find me?"

"The news." The woman shrugged. "Not many things can breathe fire from the air. I need to talk to you."

"I'm about to leave, so it'll have to wait."

Syn took Briella's hand and led her to Taryn. The woman gave Syn a smile, then dropped her gaze to Briella. Her smile vanished. Briella lifted her chin at the woman's reaction.

"I don't think it can. Corvin told me if anything happened to him, I needed to find you," the woman said.

Taryn's expression turned stone cold. "Corvin died over thirty years ago. Why are you looking for me now?"

"Who's—"

"Corvin was his Keeper. Killed before he could escape The Hollow."

Ohhh. Somehow, she knew this wasn't going to be good.

"I tried to find you, but I couldn't. I couldn't get in touch with anyone until I saw the news report a couple weeks ago. I came straight to New Orleans."

"Well, you're here and you can leave. If you'll excuse us." Taryn began to sidle past the woman. She threw up a hand and grabbed his arm.

"You're not going to want to leave until you hear me out."

"Why?"

"Because." The woman pulled a photograph from her purse and held it up. Briella leaned forward enough to catch a glimpse of the young woman in the photograph. Her eyes widened. "Corvin would have wanted you to know I carried his child."

"Holy shit."

Briella might be new to the Firestorm way of life, but she heard the shock in Syn's cuss as strongly as she felt it in her chest.

Judging by the look on Taryn's face, he was far from pleased. "Ridiculous. He'd never lay with you."

The woman shrugged, a smug grin on her mouth. "He did. The night before he died. And I conceived. His *daughter*, might I add, in case you couldn't tell by the photo. You know what that means, right?"

"Nothing, because you had a way of laying with more men than most could keep track of," Taryn snapped. He yanked his arm from her hand and stormed down the stairs toward his truck. The woman turned to Syn and held the photo out for him. He took it reluctantly.

"Let him know that my daughter is ready to meet him at his earliest convenience. She's going to need his protection, after all," the woman said. She took her leave, barely glancing at Taryn before disappearing through the gate.

Briella's fingers tightened on Syn's. "This isn't good, is it?"

Syn took a deep breath and let it out slowly. "The one thing we can't ignore is the pull to our lifemates. If what she says is true, then there's a chance her daughter might be Taryn's lifemate, which ultimately means that conniving piece of shit might finally get what she's wanted all this time."

His lips thinned in an unhappy line. "Her claws sunk into Taryn, with easy access to his hoard. And if it turns out her daughter really is Taryn's lifemate… If she's anything like her mother, he'd be better off never meeting her."

THE END

Watch for *Dance of the Dragon, The Firestorm Chronicles*, coming Spring 2019!

About Kira Nyte

Born and raised a Jersey girl with easy access to NYC, Kira was never short on ideas for stories. She started writing at the tender age of 11, and her passion for creating worlds exploded from that point on. Romance came later, but since then, all of her heroes and heroines find their happily ever after, even if it takes a good fight, or ten, to get there.

Kira resides in Central Florida with her husband, four children, two bunnies, two hermit crabs, and a parakeet. She works part-time as a nurse when she's not writing or traveling between sports, other activities, or her characters' worlds.

Kira loves to hear from readers!
kiranyteauthor@gmail.com

67435260R00211

Made in the USA
Columbia, SC
26 July 2019